How could this man kiss her that way?

How could he make her lose all sense of the world around her, and then simply let her go and step back with nothing more than curt, chiding words? Ellen had overlooked it once, back in the forest, but this time he'd pay for his knavery.

"You underestimate me, Master Brand. You think I'm powerless to punish you for your offenses."

He seemed to wince, but his voice was strong as he answered, "Milady, 'twas an error, a grievous one. I ask your forgiveness."

She'd not expected that. When he'd kissed her in the forest he'd not appeared in the least sorry, nor had he apologized. "I could forgive once..."

He nodded firmly. "But twice is unpardonable. My only defense is that the first kiss was too pleasurable to leave it at one."

Dear Reader,

Ana Seymour's new medieval novel, *Lord of Lyonsbridge*, marks her *twelfth* Harlequin Historical title! Critics have described her books as "superb," "heartwarming" and "wonderful," and *Lord of Lyonsbridge* follows suit. It's the charming tale of a spoiled Norman heiress who is sent to her father's new estate, Lyonsbridge, to set up household. There she falls under the spell of the sinfully handsome Saxon horse master, Connor Brand, and sets tongues wagging!

And if you enjoy Western romances, we have two very different selections for you. The first, *Heart of the Lawman* by Linda Castle, proves that love can heal even the deepest wounds when a widow falls for—and forgives—the man who mistakenly put her in jail. And don't miss *Plum Creek Bride* by Lynna Banning. Here, a German nanny travels to Oregon to care for a baby girl, and arrives to find a grieving single father whom she teaches to love again.

Finally, we have *The Captive Bride* by Susan Spencer Paul, who also writes mainstream historicals as Mary Spencer. This medieval novel features Senet Gaillard, the tortured brother from *The Bride Thief,* who'll stop at nothing to reclaim his father's estate—even marriage!

Whatever your tastes in reading, you'll be sure to find a romantic journey back to the past between the covers of a Harlequin Historicals® novel.

Sincerely,

Tracy Farrell
Senior Editor

Please address questions and book requests to:
Harlequin Reader Service
U.S.: 3010 Walden Ave., P.O. Box 1325, Buffalo, NY 14269
Canadian: P.O. Box 609, Fort Erie, Ont. L2A 5X3

Ana Seymour

Lord of Lyonsbridge

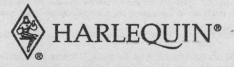

HARLEQUIN®

TORONTO • NEW YORK • LONDON
AMSTERDAM • PARIS • SYDNEY • HAMBURG
STOCKHOLM • ATHENS • TOKYO • MILAN • MADRID
PRAGUE • WARSAW • BUDAPEST • AUCKLAND

ISBN 0-373-29072-1

LORD OF LYONSBRIDGE

Copyright © 1999 by Mary Bracho

Visit us at www.romance.net

Printed in U.S.A.

Books by Ana Seymour

Harlequin Historicals

The Bandit's Bride #116
Angel of the Lake #173
Brides for Sale #238
Moonrise #290
Frontier Bride #318
Gabriel's Lady #337
Lucky Bride #350
Outlaw Wife #377
Jeb Hunter's Bride #412
A Family for Carter Jones #433
Father for Keeps #458
Lord of Lyonsbridge #472

ANA SEYMOUR

has been a fan of English history since her childhood, when she devoured the historical epics of Thomas Costain, Rafael Sabatini and Anya Seton and spent late nights up watching the swashbuckling movies of Errol Flynn and Tyrone Power. She spent a number of years working in the field of journalism, but she never forgot the magic of those tales. Now she is happy to be weaving some of that magic herself through Harlequin Historicals. Ana loves to hear from her readers at P.O. Box 47888, Minneapolis, MN 55447.

The Lyonsbridge Brands were named in honor of my
Brand descendant cousins:
Kathy Brodniak, Beverly Killiam,
and Brand and John Frentz,
who have all said such nice things about my books!

Chapter One

England, 1130

It was a rare day. Around the stable yard a crystalline lace of hoarfrost outlined the trees and fences in white. Connor's breath showed in puffy clouds as he struggled against the big man in his grasp.

"I trow, you've put on another stone since last sennight, Martin," he gasped.

Father Martin, friar of St. John's, shoved his shoulder against the slighter man, sending them both tumbling to the frozen ground. "'Tis you who've grown weak, big brother. Best you lay aside your lute and spend more time with the quarter staff."

Connor gave the priest a great heave to roll his considerable bulk off to one side, then sat up. "Not too weak to snatch you up and set you right-side down on your bald pate, Martin, if I were a mind."

Father Martin grinned. "Try it," he challenged.

Connor returned his baby brother's smile. "I've too much respect for the holy church."

The priest snorted. "Now there's a tale. When was

the last time I saw you at vespers, brother? Or in confession?''

Connor stood easily, offered his hand and pulled his brother upright. ''I've a reason for avoiding the confessional.''

''As your spiritual advisor, my son, I'd like to hear it.'' Father Martin's words were solemn, but there was a twinkle in his bright blue eyes.

''You're my brother by blood, Martin, not my father. No church vows can change that.''

''Well, I'll hear the reason, for all that. Why've you been neglecting the sacraments?''

Connor brushed at the frost that clung to his leather tunic. ''By the saints, Martin. If I gave a true confession, I'd have to sully the reputation of half the maids in Lyonsbridge. Is not chivalry a virtue in the church's eyes?''

Connor thought he detected a slight blush on his brother's round face. Not for the first time, he wondered what it would be like if he, Connor, had been the third Brand son, destined to give his life to the church, instead of the firstborn. He gave a little shudder. Of course, if the gossips were correct, the vows of celibacy sat lightly on some members of the holy orders. But Connor suspected that his brother, for all his jovial nature, took his vocation seriously.

As if affirming Connor's thoughts, Father Martin frowned. ''You should be shriven, Connor. The account of your sins would never leave the confessional.''

Connor shook his head and began walking toward the stable. It was past feeding time. '''Tis safer if the account of my sins never leaves my lips, Martin. Do you have time to help with the animals?"

Father Martin matched his brother's long strides, undeterred by his clerical robe. "Aye. Brother Augustine will be giving compline this night."

"Mayhap we should resume our wrestling match, then. Let me seek revenge."

The priest laughed. "Give it up, brother. 'Tis small wonder I can best you if the only wrestling you're doing these days is with the fairer sex."

Connor studied his brother. His cheeks were ruddy from the cold, making his eyes look bluer. The hair that was left around his tonsured skull was blond, identical to Connor's own. Before Martin had taken his vows, the brothers had sometimes been thought twins, though they were four years apart in age. Handsome and strapping, the three Brand sons had begun turning female heads when they were still youths. Their adventures had provoked outrage and awe in nearly equal measure. "Do you not miss it, brother?" Connor asked softly.

Father Martin hesitated a moment, then shook his head. "I'll leave the maids to you, Connor, and I'll add you into my prayers each night, since you seem determined to risk your immortal soul."

They'd reached the door of the massive Lyonsbridge stable. When the Brands of Lyonsbridge had held dominion over the entire fiefdom, it was widely known that there were no finer horses in all of England. Connor's father had had requests for Lyonsbridge bloodstock from as far away as Spain, a land that boasted proud stock of its own.

"If the Lord finds objection in the pleasuring of a

man and a maid, then he's a cruel lord indeed," Connor objected. "For he's left us Saxons with little enough joy in our lives."

His brother grew solemn. It was true that life had not been easy for the Saxons these past few years. With the Norman king, Henry, firmly established on the throne, the fighting was ending. But the hardships continued.

"Aye. Times have been hard, and I believe if the man and maid are both willing, the Lord might be willing to overlook a tryst or two outside of the marriage bed."

Connor clapped his brother on the shoulder. "Lucky thing for me. But might he not then also overlook one or two outside of your holy vows? Leofric the miller has two daughters that are among the tastiest morsels I've set eyes upon. I had a deal of a time choosing the elder. The younger is still ripe for plucking, but I have scruples about two sisters—"

Father Martin interrupted him with an upheld hand. "I'll be on my knees until midnight if you continue, brother. I'm asking you humbly to turn your conversation to more noble paths."

Connor grimaced. "They've made a holy man of you at last, I'm afraid," he said. "Can I not interest you in at least hearing about the maid's virtues?"

"'Tis not of her virtues that you want to speak, brother, so leave it be. Did you not tell me that you've work to do aplenty?"

Connor pushed back the sleeves of his surcoat. "Aye. They're due on the morrow—our new masters."

"Lord Wakelin himself?"

"Nay, it appears the new Lord of Lyonsbridge is too delicate to face the people whose land he's usurped. He's sending a nephew and, I hear, his daughter."

"The lady Ellen?" Father Martin asked in surprise.

"Aye."

"Well, now." The priest looked over at his brother, who had begun to curry a huge black charger named Thunder, one of the stable's finest. "Are you not curious to see her?"

Connor shrugged. "I doubt I shall. I hear that Norman maidens bathe in milk, sleep in silk and never let the light of day fall on their lily skin." He gave the big horse a slap on its polished rump and gestured to his brother. "Are you going to help me or not? That holy life of leisure is padding you with lard."

Father Martin picked up a second brush and moved toward Connor, but stayed with the prior topic. "'Tis said the King of France himself wanted her. They sing of her beauty."

"Let them sing. I'll take a robust, blooming English lass any day."

"Aye, I wager you would," Father Martin said with a twisted grin. "But even I find myself curious about whether the lady Ellen does justice to the ballads they sing of her."

Connor laughed and gave the priest a gentle shove. "Curious, eh? Ah, brother, mayhap all hope is not lost for you yet."

"I knew England would be primitive, but I didn't realize it would also be colder than the devil's cellar," Ellen of Wakelin said with a shiver.

Sebastian Phippen grimaced at his cousin and hastily made the sign of the cross on his chest. "'Tis no wonder your father has exiled you, Ellen, with the tongue you wield."

Ellen sat straighter in her silver-tooled saddle, stretching her weary back. "It's not exile. Father asked me to come to Lyonsbridge because it wants proper Norman management. He said he'd neglected it for too long."

"Which is why he asked me to serve as castellan in his stead," Sebastian replied smoothly. "I hadn't expected he'd want me to bring you along." At Ellen's scowl, he added hastily, "Though 'tis always a pleasure to be in your company, fair cousin."

"Don't think I look any more kindly on the task, Sebastian. The sooner we can put some proper order into these estates and return to Normandy, the better."

Ellen looked out over the bright green countryside. Here and there it sparkled with frost in the waning sunlight. It *was* pretty, and she'd probably be enjoying the ride if she hadn't lost all feeling in her fingers quite some time ago. She hadn't complained, since it had been at her insistence that they had continued riding, even though it meant they might not reach the castle until dark.

"We should have found lodging," Sebastian grumbled, lifting his own hands one at a time to blow on his fingers. He turned around to address one of the six Wakelin men-at-arms who were accompanying them. "How much farther?"

The man rode toward them, peering ahead and paying little attention as he crowded their big horses on the highway. "Have a care, man," Sebastian shouted. His horse pranced nervously, but Ellen kept her mount perfectly controlled.

"These infernal hillocks all look the same," the guardsman said. "But I think we're almost there."

"I hope you're right. We're coming hard on twilight." Sebastian shot a look of disapproval at his cousin, then asked the guard, "Are there brigands abroad at night?"

"Not these past five years. Before that, of course, the fighting was fierce. Lyonsbridge was one of the last territories to give over to Norman rule."

"Which is precisely why King Henry awarded the grant to Lord Wakelin," Sebastian told the man with a smug smile. "He knew that he was a warrior who could control the people with a firm hand."

The guardsman shrugged. "As I say, milord, there've been no problems these years past. Lyonsbridge has been peaceful."

Sebastian spurred his horse to move ahead of the soldier. "I intend to be sure it stays that way," he said.

Ellen gave the soldier a smile and watched as it elicited the typical male expression of bedazzlement. At past twenty years, she was old to be still a maid, but her conquests numbered more than the old Conquerer himself. Her father had had offers for her hand from the four corners of Europe, though she'd not yet found the man she considered worthy. Her father had indulged her finicky nature, since, as she was his only child, he was, in truth, loath to give her away.

Lord Wakelin probably would not have suffered her traveling as far from him as England if it hadn't been for the minor skirmish she'd recently caused between two princes from rival principalities. They'd fought a joust for her favors, even though she hadn't the slightest intention of granting them to either young man. One of the princes had been gravely wounded.

The last piece of the sun disappeared behind a copse of trees, and immediately the cold bit harder. Ellen shivered again and tucked her hands up underneath her arms. She had no worry about letting loose the reins. She could trust Jocelyn to keep to the road without guidance.

"I think I see it ahead," Sebastian said, pointing.

Ellen caught her breath. They'd rounded a bend in the road, bringing into view a small castle, the stone washed in scarlet from the fading sun.

The structure was dominated by two imposing towers, a square one to the left and an octagonal one on the right. The dark towers and the jagged outline of the battlements against the pink sunset made an extraordinary sight.

"That's Lyonsbridge Castle?" she asked in awe.

Sebastian also appeared impressed, but as usual, chose to make his comment with a negative slant. "'Tis not as large as they'd told of it," he said.

"'Tis nigh as large as Wakelin," she argued. "And twice as lovely." She spurred her horse into a full gallop, leaving her cousin behind her in a cloud of dust.

"Ellen!" he shouted after her. "Come back here! 'Tis not seemly—" He broke off as Ellen and her big mare continued up the road, out of earshot.

"Shall we go after her, milord?" the guardsman asked from behind him.

Sebastian shook his head. "Nay. We'll catch up soon enough."

"Pardon, milord, but will the vassals know who she is if she arrives in such fashion?" the man persisted.

"If they don't," Sebastian answered with a cold smile, "you can be sure the lady Ellen will make them aware of it in short order."

Connor and Father Martin emerged from the stable arm in arm. Though the friar managed frequent visits with his brother at their childhood home, there was always a flicker of sadness at the moment of parting. They couldn't entirely escape the memories of the carefree days when neither the inexorable encroachment of the Normans nor Martin's inevitable fate with the church had dimmed their youthful enthusiasm for life. Much had changed.

"When will I see you again?" Connor asked, taking his hand from his brother's shoulder.

Father Martin straightened, once again becoming friar of St. John's, forbidden by holy decree from unnecessary fleshly contact with a living soul. "Mayhap soon if your Norman visitors send for me to say a Mass for them."

Connor frowned. "Will you tell them who you are?"

"I'm Father Martin, their friar. That's all they have to know."

Connor's chiseled features hardened. "You won't

mention that their Norman compatriots killed your father and brother and as well as killed your mother?''

His brother sighed. "'Tis past, Connor. And you swore an oath to keep it that way.''

"There's no need to remind me of an oath taken at our mother's deathbed, Martin,'' Connor said stiffly.

"Aye, I know, it's just—'' He held up a hand to shade his eyes from the glare of the setting sun. "*Jesu,* who is that?''

Connor followed the direction of his brother's gaze down the road, and his expression grew thunderous. "Whoever it is must be a bloody fool to ride like that over slippery ground.''

"It's a woman,'' Father Martin said, his voice awed.

Connor had already seen for himself that the approaching rider was indeed a woman. Though mounted sideways in a woman's saddle, with her skirts billowing around her, she rode like a man, straight and sure—and fast. "She's a bloody fool, for all that,'' he said under his breath.

The woman was approaching so quickly that it was difficult to get a clear view of her, but her garments were obviously rich and her horse looked to be magnificently bred. By the time the horse and rider pulled to a stop directly in front of them, both the brothers had surmised the identity of the new arrival.

"It appears your curiosity is about to be satisfied, brother,'' Connor said in an undertone.

"She comes alone? Where's her entourage?''

"From the pace she sets, they're undoubtedly left behind at the coast,'' Connor replied with a grin as he stepped forward, ready to lift a hand to stop the big horse, if necessary.

But the mount came to a perfect halt not two yards in front of him, and the lady perched on top appeared unruffled by her breakneck ride. She scarcely looked at Connor, focusing her attention instead on his brother.

"Be you the friar of Lyonsbridge?" she asked without preamble.

Father Martin shot a glance at Connor before he answered calmly, "I am Father Martin, my daughter, priest of St. John's and administering friar to this estate."

She extended an arm in Connor's direction and said to Father Martin, "You may direct this man to help me down and see to my horse."

Her attention to his brother gave Connor time to study her. He'd been unwilling to admit to Martin that he shared his curiosity about the Norman maid, but the tales of her beauty and spirit had piqued his interest as well. As with most tales oft told, he'd discounted their validity, but looking up at the young Norman woman as she sat haloed in the sunset, he had to admit that this time there had been no embellishment. Lady Ellen Wakelin was all they told of her, and more.

Father Martin spoke with a slight smile. "You may feel free to address the man yourself, milady, since he is your new master of horse."

She glanced down at Connor, and this time appeared to take in all aspects of his appearance. Unaccountably, for the first time in years, Connor missed the grander clothes he was wont to wear when his family had been masters at Lyonsbridge. The humble fustian fabric of his undertunic and surcoat indicated peasant garb.

His chin went up a notch. "Milady," he said, without being addressed. "Welcome to Lyonsbridge."

Ellen's eyes widened and she hesitated a moment, but then seemed to recover herself, placed one foot in his cupped hand and put her arm on his shoulder to dismount.

As she stepped nimbly to the ground, she made no reply to his welcome, but turned once again to the priest. "We're not expected until the morrow, Father. Sir William will need to be informed of our arrival."

William Booth had been serving as bailiff since the awarding of Lyonsbridge to Lord Wakelin the previous year. Booth had recently been knighted by the king for bringing order to what had been considered an unruly part of the country. No one questioned what his efforts had cost the people he had subdued.

Father Martin looked at Connor, waiting to see if his normally outspoken brother would protest the slight by the Norman beauty. But Connor merely took hold of her horse's reins and stepped back, watching her with an amused smile on his face.

"Certainly," the priest answered. "But, my child, where are the others in your party?"

"Lagging behind, as usual," she said breezily. "My cousin is not known for his horsemanship."

"Perhaps your cousin has more sense than to ride a tired mount at full gallop on a frozen path," Connor said.

Father Martin and Ellen both turned their heads toward him. The priest's expression was a combination of amusement and reprimand, but there was instant outrage on Ellen's pretty features.

"How dare you?" she gasped.

Connor shrugged. "As the good friar has told you, milady, I'm horse master here. 'Tis my business to see that the mounts are not ill used."

As if to reinforce his words, he put a hand on her horse's muzzle. Instantly, it dropped its head and stood stock-still. Ellen looked surprised, but her voice was still angry as she snapped, "I've ridden Jocelyn these past five years, and I know a deal more about her abilities than some bondsman."

Connor's temper would have risen at the slur if he hadn't been so fascinated by the way her anger heightened the winter red of her cheeks. By the rood, he'd never seen such a beauty. And her hair! Unlike the gentle Saxon maidens of Lyonsbridge, she wore no wimple over the thick black tresses. They hung in unruly waves, held in place only by a simple circlet of hammered gold.

Connor tried to keep his gaze casual as he said, "I owe no bond to your family, milady. I work as a freeman."

"Then you'd best have a mind to your position, horse master, for you stay here at my sufferance."

Connor kept his expression impassive. He had no intention of letting Lady Ellen or any of the other Normans know of his family's former status at Lyonsbridge. At his father's death, the estate had been taken over by the Conquerer's son, William. It had passed through a number of hands before the younger William's successor, King Henry, had bestowed Lyonsbridge on Ellen's father. "I'll try to remember that, milady," Connor said after a moment.

Ellen nodded and turned back to Father Martin, who was watching the exchange with interest. "Will you escort me inside, Father?" she asked.

Father Martin looked over at Connor, who spoke in a voice thick with irony. "By all means, *Father*," he said. "Escort the lady into the castle. We'd not have our Norman visitor take a chill in the cool English air, now would we?"

Father Martin shook his head at his brother's dangerously impudent tone, but Ellen appeared to pay no attention and was already walking briskly toward the castle gates. He leaned toward Connor and whispered, "Mind your tongue, brother. Never forget that it's a Norman world now." Then he bustled off to catch up with the estate's new mistress.

Chapter Two

Unlike the highly fortified castles in some parts of Europe, Lyonsbridge had no moat, no defenses. In addition to the stables, a number of other outbuildings were outside the low walls that surrounded the castle bailey. A small bridge crossed a token trench to the big wooden gates. As they approached, Ellen observed, "He's a strange manner of man, the horse master."

Father Martin looked at her sharply.

Ellen bit her tongue, realizing that after the way she'd dismissed the stableman, her sudden observation about him seemed odd.

"I believe you'll find that Connor is a valuable servant, milady," the priest replied after a moment. "You would do well to take advantage of his experience here."

"Experience with the horses?"

Once again Father Martin seemed to hesitate. "With everything—the animals, the people, the estate itself."

"He's been here long, then?"

"All his life."

Ellen looked back down the gently sloping hill that led to the stables, but the tall blond man was nowhere in sight. "All his life, yet he's not a bondsman?" she asked.

"Nay, milady. You'd not likely see Connor Brand in bond to any man."

"He does seem to have an obdurate nature."

Father Martin smiled, but all he said was, "Mayhap."

"Well, he'd best not show it with my cousin. Sebastian does not have the easiest of tempers."

"I shall pass your warning on to Connor."

Two yeomen had swung open the gates to admit them into the castle yard. One of the men carried a torch, as it was fast growing dark. Ellen nodded at him, then swept past to get her first look at the home she'd be inhabiting for the next several months.

Though the stone building had made an imposing sight from the road, she quickly realized that her fears about coming to this uncivilized part of the world were likely to be realized. She sighed. "Is this the central courtyard?" she asked the friar.

"This is the only courtyard," he replied.

There was scarcely room to walk, so filled was the space with all manner of clutter. Logs for the fireplace lay in a haphazard pile, half blocking the small stairway at the far end of the bailey. A heap of what looked to be rusty armor lay scattered around to the left of the front gates, and to the right was a ramshackle wooden hut that reeked of stale urine.

Ellen wrinkled her nose as they passed it. "Who has been keeping house for Sir William?" she asked.

Father Martin kicked at a pile of bones being scavenged by two of the castle hounds. "He has no wife, milady."

Ellen watched as the two dogs scampered off into the dusk. "That's well evident," she said softly.

"Here's Sir William now," Father Martin said, pointing to a low arched entryway on their left.

The man who appeared there was stocky and short of stature, not as tall as Ellen herself. Almost at once she sensed a belligerence in his nature that she didn't like. But her father had spoken highly of his bailiff, and she knew Lord Wakelin was exceedingly grateful for the way Sir William had been able to put some structure into the estate with very little help from Normandy.

She'd be wrong to judge his efficiency by the appearance of the castle, particularly if he'd had no woman to help. Indeed, the neglect of this aspect of the estate justified her father's wisdom in sending her here. Ellen felt a sudden sense of mission, which warmed her voice as she greeted the man approaching her.

"Well met, Sir William," she said in response to his murmured welcome and bowed head. "My father sends his greetings."

"Would that he could have accompanied you, milady. I'm anxious to have him see how his holdings are prospering."

As he raised his face to look at her, his black eyes darted around, reminding Ellen suddenly of a rat. The back of his head was shaved in Norman fashion and his black beard was sleeked with some kind of grease, adding to the effect. It made Ellen want to giggle, but she stifled the impulse and kept her voice gracious. "I'll see your efforts in his stead, Sir William, and make faithful report of your good work."

"Thank you, milady." His eyes shifted from her to the gates behind her, then to Father Martin, then back to her. "I'd understood that your father was sending his nephew to review his English estate."

"Sir Sebastian is directly behind me," Ellen explained. "I found myself with a spurt of energy and rode ahead, to the disapproval of your master of horse."

Sir William scowled, and the ratlike expression that had amused her suddenly looked more sinister. "He's a troublemaker, that one. Begging your pardon, since he be blood, Father," he said to the friar, "but Lyonsbridge would be better off without the likes of Connor Brand."

Ellen looked at Father Martin, questioning. "Connor is my brother," he explained.

"Your brother!" She couldn't decide why it was such a surprise to learn that the forceful man she'd met at the stables was brother to the friar. Now that she knew, she could see the resemblance immediately. They had the same handsome features, the same smile. The priest appeared to be bulkier under his robes, whereas the horse master had, she recalled with an uncharacteristic blush, been of a decidedly muscular build.

"Perhaps I should have mentioned it right away," Father Martin said apologetically.

"Brother or no, he's been a thorn in my tabard ever since I came to Lyonsbridge," Sir William grumbled.

When Father Martin made no response to the

charge, Ellen asked, "Then why haven't you dismissed the man?"

Sir William shrugged and waved his hand vaguely. "He's good with the horses," he said. He made a nervous shuffle with his feet. "Enough of the stable. Let me show you inside the castle."

Ellen put her hand on the arm Sir William offered her and let him lead her across the courtyard toward the stairway, but she remained puzzled about his answer. It seemed odd that the bailiff would keep a servant whom he professed to detest, no matter how good the man was with the livestock. In fact, there was something odd about Connor Brand himself. A strange manner of man, she had told the priest. Indeed. And perhaps the strangest thing of all was that she, mistress of the entire estate and acclaimed by the most noble men in Christendom, couldn't seem to banish the stable master from her thoughts.

The previous day's frost had disappeared overnight, leaving a mist that hung heavy and thick near the ground. It was not a good morning for a ride, but after breaking her fast with bread and strong ale, Ellen found herself wandering toward the stables. It made sense, she assured herself, to check on Jocelyn's welfare after the grueling trip.

She was within yards of the stable and had just about decided that Jocelyn would prove to be her only mission after all, when suddenly the tall figure of the horse master emerged through the fog. Her heartbeat jumped.

Once again, he did not wait to be addressed first.

"Good morrow, milady. You're up and about early. The very sparrows still sleep, I trow."

She put aside her annoyance at his boldness. Perhaps manners were not as formal in England. "You were here before me, Master Brand."

"Ah, but I'm a poor laborer whose lot it is to work early and long. You're a noblewoman, made to while away the hours in play and pleasure."

The proper response to such an inappropriate comment would have been to ignore him, but the amused scorn in his tone made Ellen bristle and answer, "I've come to England to oversee a household, one that appears to be in sore need of management, I might add. I've not come to play."

Connor took a step closer to her, then paused. His blue eyes boldly ran the length of her, taking on a sparkle as he smiled and said, "I'll admit I don't picture you quietly weaving tapestries the day through."

She was standing uphill from him, which made their faces level, less than a yard distant. He gazed at her frankly, without apology. For a moment, she stared back. Then she realized that her face had grown warm and the breath had halted in her throat. She backed up a step. "I'd thank you not to picture me in any way whatsoever," she said. Her tone was not as imperious as she'd hoped.

Connor smiled more broadly. "Norman rule has robbed Saxons of many things, milady, but not of their thoughts, nor yet of their fantasies."

In Normandy a servant could have been beaten for such insolence, but instead of the reprimand that had leaped to her lips, she found herself arguing with him.

"Norman rule has brought the Saxons much more than it has taken."

Connor's eyebrow raised. "So says the Norman lady?"

"Aye," Ellen answered firmly. "So says the Norman lady."

"Perhaps one of these days you'll enlighten me about these wonders our conquerers have brought us, milady, but at the moment, I must take leave to go muck my Norman master's stables."

This man was like no servant she had ever encountered, and, for the life of her, she couldn't understand why she continued to stand there like a tongue-tied maid and let him speak to her in such a fashion. It had something to do with the fact that her heart had not slowed from the time he'd first startled her, coming out of the fog.

One thing was certain. If she was going to put some good Norman order into this place, she'd have to start by regaining control of herself. "You forget yourself, Master Brand," she said, and this time she was pleased to note that her tone was properly haughty. "If my cousin were to hear you speak the way you have to me just now, he'd turn you over to the king for sedition."

Connor turned his back on her and walked down to the stable, collecting a pitchfork that was leaning against the building. Over his shoulder he said, "You misjudge me, milady. I'm a man of peace."

"I think not. You and your brother appear to be cut of wholly different cloth."

Connor turned back to her in surprise. "Martin told you, then?"

"Father Martin? Aye."

"We're not so different. Our destiny has given us two different paths, but we walk toward the same end."

Ellen shook her head in confusion and finally gave voice to the thought that had been circling in her head since meeting him the previous day. "You don't talk like any stable master I've ever heard."

Connor dug the end of the fork into the ground, threw back his head and laughed.

There was, indeed, an *independence* about this servant that totally discomfited her. "I'm serious," she insisted, her voice raising a notch. "Who are you? Father Martin said you've lived here all your life."

"That I have, milady. Who am I? Why, I'm your stable boy, your horse trainer, your livestock manager." He left the fork standing by itself in the dirt and took a long step to bring himself once again close to where she was standing. Very softly he said, "I'm your faithful servant, milady."

His voice rumbled deep into her midsection.

She stood there facing him, eye-to-eye, as blood pounded behind her ears. She swallowed once, then again, before making a reply that came out as not much more than a whisper. "Aye, Saxon, you are my servant. See that you act like it."

Then, abandoning her intention to visit her horse, she turned abruptly and made her way up the hill toward the castle as quickly as dignity would allow.

"What worm is gnawing at your innards today, Connor?" Father Martin asked, irritated at being snapped at by his brother for the third time since he'd arrived at midmorning.

Connor set down the wooden bucket he'd been carrying and boosted himself up on the fence next to the friar. "Forgive me, Martin. 'Tis the infernal mist, no doubt. It leads to melancholy."

"You used to love foggy days."

Connor looked around. It was midday, yet they could barely see as far as the castle. He sighed. "Mayhap. I used to love a lot of things in the old life."

"You *are* melancholy, brother mine. 'Tis unlike you. My guess is that it has something to do with the arrival of the Normans yestreen. Mayhap in particular the arrival of a certain *female* Norman."

Connor squinted toward the castle as if expecting to see her coming toward him, as he had that morning. He'd given no sign, but her visit had hit him with visceral impact. It was not that he'd been long deprived of the company of women. There were always plenty of obliging maidens in the village to see to his needs and amusement. But he couldn't remember ever having the sight of a female affect him so absolutely. He'd felt it the previous day, the first time he'd set eyes on her. This morning, seeing her emerging from the mist like some kind of regal faerie queen had quite simply robbed him of his senses.

It had robbed him of his reason, too. He'd spoken brashly, without a thought for the consequences, which was a luxury he no longer allowed himself. He had too many responsibilities to be so foolhardy. It couldn't happen again.

"The lass has me muddled," he admitted to his brother.

Father Martin looked surprised at the admission and a little worried. "Connor, you know you would never be able—" He broke off and laid his hand on his brother's shoulder. "She's a *Norman*, brother."

"I know. Don't mistake me, Martin. I'm not likely to forget my—" he looked around at the stable yard "—my *place* at Lyonsbridge. 'Tis clear enough at which end of the salt I sit."

Father Martin looked relieved. "I suspect you'll grow used to seeing her around in time. It appears she's something of a horsewoman."

Connor jumped to the ground and gave his brother a grin. "Aye, there's no law against *looking* at a pretty maid, is there?"

Father Martin rolled his eyes. "Not in your world, at least."

His brother laughed. "Ah, Martin, the Lord won't punish you for a glance or two. When you're at Mass with her today, give it a try and tell me if you don't think her eyes are golden."

With more difficulty than his brother, Father Martin slid to the ground, shaking his head. He turned with a rueful smile. "I've already looked, brother, and, yes, a truer gold I've never seen."

The lady Ellen didn't come to the stables the next two days. Her mount—Jocelyn, she'd called it—grew restive in its stall, and Connor walked it around the stable yard. She was a fine animal, and he'd have enjoyed riding her, but decided it would be prudent to await the mistress's orders on the matter, particularly after his outburst the other morning.

He still berated himself for losing his usual control in such a fashion. At his father's deathbed, he'd promised to look after the people of Lyonsbridge, and at his mother's, he'd promised to keep peace in the land. He could do neither task if he made the new masters so angry that they ran him off the place.

Since something about the beautiful new mistress of Lyonsbridge seemed to spark the defiant streak he'd worked so hard to tame, he knew he'd do well to stay out of the lady's way. He should be glad she hadn't come again to the stables. Still, he found himself glancing toward the castle several times a day, hoping to see her heading toward him.

This morning it was not the lady Ellen scurrying down the hill, but John the cooper's son. Connor was repairing a shoe on one of the Norman horses. He paused in his work to greet the boy with a smile.

"Whoa, lad, slow down. What's your hurry on such a beautiful morn?"

John skidded to a stop near Connor and took a gasping breath. "Good morrow, Master Connor."

Connor marveled at the boy's unfailing courtesy, even though he was obviously agitated. "Good morrow, John. Now tell me what's troubling you."

The words tumbled out as the boy shifted from one foot to the other. "I'm sorry to bother you, Master Connor. I haven't forgotten your words in the village—that we have to give the new masters a chance. Everyone's trying, truly they are. But you know that me mum's doing poorly. She's hardly been able to eat these past four days, and Sarah must stay there to mind her, but Sir William's men have ordered all tenants to the castle. No exception, they say, by order of the new mistress.''

Connor sighed and carefully lifted the horse's hoof out of his lap. The animal didn't move. ''Did you explain to Sir William's men about your mother? Surely they know she has the wasting sickness?''

''No exceptions, they said.'' The boy gave a vigorous shake of his head, jiggling his cropped blond hair like a shaft of wheat. ''They don't care, these Normans.''

''Why are they commanding everyone to the castle?'' Connor asked, laying aside his chisel.

John shrugged. '''Tis daft, if you ask me. They say the lady Ellen has ordered a scouring from floor to ceiling, every room.''

Connor couldn't argue with the fact that a ''scouring'' was sorely needed. There had been times when he'd winced at the forlorn state of Lyonsbridge Castle, thinking that his mother would be lying restless in her tomb. He glanced over at the stables, where even the hay was stacked in neat bundles. Though its occupants were animals, he'd daresay his domain was a sight tidier than the great hall of the castle.

''The cleaning's not a bad idea, lad,'' Connor told the boy. ''But they've help aplenty to carry it out. They shouldn't need your mother, nor your sister.''

''They've already taken Sarah. One of the soldiers dragged her off.''

''Dragged her off?'' At this, Connor stood, overturning the stool behind him. Sarah Cooper was barely thirteen years, a slight, pretty girl and much too fragile to defend herself against a randy Norman soldier.

"That's why I came to you, Master Connor. I couldn't stop them. There was too many of them."

Connor's heart went out to the lad. Only a year older than his sister, young John had tried to be the man of the cooper's household since his father had been killed by the Normans five years earlier. Connor put a hand on his shoulder.

"You did right, John. It would have been foolish to defy an entire band of guards. It was good that you came to me."

"They wouldn't hurt Sarah, would they?" he asked. His voice broke, making him sound younger than his years.

"Nay, they wouldn't dare hurt her if 'tis the lady Ellen's orders they're following." Connor had no idea if his optimistic words were true, but the boy looked relieved. "Come, we'll go find her and straighten this out."

"Will you talk to the lady Ellen directly?" John asked.

Connor began to lead the horse into the stable. At the boy's words, he felt a tingle of awareness along his limbs. The image of Lady Ellen Wakelin's golden eyes danced in his head.

"Aye, lad. I'll talk to the lady Ellen directly."

Chapter Three

Ellen tucked the long sleeves of her silk bliaut into the wristlets of her undergown. For a moment she wished she could strip off the elaborate finery and don a simple, coarse linen garment such as the one worn by the peasant girl working alongside her. The trailing dress and the heavy silver corselet that she wore atop it were not at all practical for hard labor. But donning rude clothing would not help her cause of showing these Saxons something of the civilized world beyond Lyonsbridge. By the time her father visited in the spring, she wanted the estate to be as smoothly run, the table to be as richly victualed, and the people to be as properly mannered as any back in Normandy. As the lady of the household, she would set the example.

"Will the table need polishing, too, milady?" the girl with her asked. They'd been rubbing oil into the two heavy wooden dining chairs that were reserved for the master and mistress of the household. Their carved backs had been thick with grime, but Ellen had to admit that the workmanship was as fine as any Norman craft.

"We'll oil only the legs. The top must be scrubbed with sand." Ellen stopped rubbing for a moment to look at her helper. "'Tis Sarah, is it not?"

"Aye, milady, Sarah."

The slender blond girl's eyes flickered briefly to Ellen's face, then skittered away as if afraid that her mistress might cuff her at any moment. Ellen took pains to make her tone friendly. "You're from the village, Sarah?"

"Aye, milady."

They worked in silence for several minutes, before once again Ellen tried to engage the girl in conversation. "What family have you in the village, Sarah?"

The girl's pale face flared with color. "She's not been able to eat in days, milady. She'd be of little use here. She can hardly stand, much less work—" She broke off and looked up at Ellen, her eyes brimming.

Ellen frowned. "What are you talking about, girl?"

The girl's tears spilled over. "Me mum. Sir William's men said we were all to come here, no exception. But me mum's got the wasting disease, and she's took bad in this cold. Please don't punish her, milady."

Ellen straightened up from the chair she was working on and looked at the weeping girl in horror. "No one is going to punish your mother, child. *Mon dieu,* what a notion."

"Begging your pardon, milady. I meant no impertinence, but Sir William said that 'twas by your or-

ders. He said she'd be whipped if she didn't come to
work today.''

Ellen felt a shiver of alarm. Surely there had been
some kind of misunderstanding. In their zeal to please
the new mistress, the guards may have been overly
enthusiastic about rounding up the workers she'd requested. But whipping a sick old woman? She gave
an uneasy laugh. ''You must have misheard Sir William's men, Sarah. There could have been no such
talk of whipping.''

Sarah looked away. ''Not his men, milady. 'Twas
Sir William himself who said it. Verily, I heard him
meself.''

The girl appeared sharp-witted. Ellen could not
completely discount her tale, but neither could she
champion the word of a serf over that of the bailiff.
The matter required further investigation.

''Who is caring for your mother now, Sarah?'' she
asked.

''She's alone, milady. I'd not leave her, but the
men forced me to come.''

''Then go to her. You're finished here for the day,
and you're not to come back while she still needs you.
If anyone bids you come, you tell them to speak with
me.''

The girl's tears had stopped, and she gave Ellen a
piteously grateful smile.

''Run along,'' Ellen told her. ''I'll visit you on the
morrow to see how your mother fares.''

''Oh, *milady*,'' Sarah gasped. She grasped Ellen's
hand with both of hers and made a quick curtsy, then
turned and ran lightly across the dining room.

Ellen gazed after her, lost in thought. Her first impression of Sir William had not been favorable, and so far he'd done nothing to change that opinion. She considered him pompous and obsequious, but her cousin had appeared to be pleased with the accounting he'd given of the estate's affairs. Still, if he was bullying her people, she wanted to know about it. Proper management of an estate was one thing, abuse was another.

She hadn't seen the two people enter from the small door behind her and gave a start when one of them spoke.

"May we have permission to speak with your ladyship?"

It was the horse master, accompanied by a boy. Though his manner of address was more respectful than it had been the other day at the stables, he spoke forcefully, indicating that the request for permission was a meaningless formality. Nevertheless, after the news she had just heard from Sarah about ill treatment in the village, she was inclined to be tolerant.

"Good morrow, Master Brand." It was easier speaking to him here in the castle than it had been at the stables. She felt more in control, though she couldn't decide if it was because she was in her own home or because the gloom of the dining hall dimmed the intense blue of his eyes. She turned toward the boy with him and asked, "Is this lad your apprentice?"

Connor shook his head. "This is John Cooper. He's asked my help in a certain matter about his family. Tell milady, John."

The boy was looking at Ellen as if she were the

Holy Virgin come to earth. He opened his mouth, but
no speech emerged.

Ellen looked from John to Connor. "What matter?" she asked.

"It seems your men have taken the lad's sister.
He's worried about her, with good cause."

The tall Saxon had advanced toward her until he
stood just on the other side of the chair she'd been
polishing. That close, she could feel it again—the dis-
concerting force of the man. Since the age of twelve
she'd had men fawning over her, petitioning for her
hand, buzzing about her like bees at a flower. Yet this
horse master, this *servant* who continued to treat her
as if he had more important things to think about,
made her knees grow weak like the most inexperi-
enced of maids.

The boy with him finally found his voice. "Her
name's Sarah, milady. And she's a good girl."

"If your men have done the girl harm, there will
be the devil to pay," Connor added.

The square set of his jaw as he warned her did not
detract from his attractiveness. Ellen felt infuriating
flutters in her midsection. Sweet saints above, perhaps
the man had cast an enchantment on her in the way
he appeared to with his animals. She bit the tip of her
tongue until the pain cleared the fog from her brain
and she could manage a proper response. She could
relieve the boy of his worry in short order, but first
she felt as if she should make an effort to remind the
stableman of his position in her household. "What
affair is this of yours, horse master?" she asked
coldly.

"Old John the Cooper is dead these past five years.

Folks hereabouts are protective of his widow and children.''

She hesitated. Put like that, Master Brand's interest didn't seem so out of place, though she shouldn't allow the master of her stables to be meddling in affairs between the castle guards and the villagers. She would no doubt do well to order Master Brand back to his horses, but she had the feeling he would not go easily. Finally she gave up trying to determine the propriety of his inquiry and said, "The girl was with me much of the morning. I've sent her home to take care of her mother."

Young John's chest sagged with relief. "Thank you, milady," he said.

"'Tis fortunate that she's safe and sound," Connor said. "The surest way to trouble in the village is harassment of the womenfolk. I don't know how you do things back in Normandy, but the men here won't stand for it."

He was lecturing her again. Ellen's temper boiled over. She curled her fingers tightly over the carved back of the chair. "Master Brand, I believe we've had this conversation before. You're a servant here. I'll thank you to keep your advice on running Lyonsbridge to yourself. In fact, I'll thank you to keep your opinions in general to yourself. Speak when spoken to, as befits your station."

Connor did not seem the least bit impressed with her outburst. "You'll find I can be of use to you, milady. If the boy had alarmed the other men in the village instead of coming to me, you wouldn't have progressed well today in your cleaning. There are some who would rather strike out first and talk later.

Even Sir William has taken advantage of my arbitration a time or two.''

"Sir William had little help when he first arrived, but now that my cousin and I are here with more of my father's men—''

Connor interrupted her. "All the more reason to be careful. In general, the Saxons of Lyonsbridge are a peaceable sort, but the more soldiers about, the more chance for problems.''

Ellen tried to remember if any of her father's retainers had ever spoken to him with such boldness, but she was sure Lord Wakelin would not put up with such behavior. "Keeping the peace at Lyonsbridge is Sir William's concern, horse master, not yours. I think it would be best if you kept to your own dominion, which is the stable.''

Connor cocked his head as if considering further comment, but finally only nodded. A half smile played about his lips, which sparked Ellen's temper once again.

"Where are your quarters in the castle?'' she asked, seized with the sudden impulse to demote him to sleep in the rushes with the scrub boys.

"I don't sleep in the castle. My home is the stables.''

Ellen's eyes widened. "You *sleep* there?'' In Normandy not even the lowliest stable boys slept with the animals.

His smile broadened. "Aye. Feel free to pay me a visit, milady.''

They'd both forgotten about the presence of the boy waiting behind Connor. He cleared his throat softly and Connor turned to him. "Run along, lad. Go to your mother and sister."

John looked up at Ellen, uncertain. She nodded to him, and he turned and scampered away.

"It was my place to dismiss the lad, not yours," Ellen pointed out.

"Aye. And that you just did, did you not?" Connor answered pleasantly.

The man was infuriating. There was no other word for it. She drew herself up and straightened her shoulders. "You're dismissed, too, Master Brand. See that you have my horse saddled and ready for me tomorrow noon."

"I'm at your service as always, milady," he answered with a small bow, never taking his eyes from her face.

When he made no move, Ellen threw the rag she'd been clutching on the table and turned to leave. She could feel his gaze burning her back all the way across the hall.

Connor had a feeling that in spite of the lady Ellen's imperious manner, she was looking forward to their next encounter as much as he. They had nothing in common and, in fact, much opposed. But their proximity struck sparks more surely than a smithy's anvil. He'd wager a pretty penny that she felt it as strongly as he.

It was mad, of course. He hadn't needed Martin's reminder to tell him that any association, much less friendship, between a Norman noblewoman and a Saxon stable hand was absurd. But that didn't stop him from tossing on his bed well into the night think-

ing about her. By the next morning he was tempted
to leave one of the stable boys in charge and hie himself off to visit his brother at the abbey church. He
had a premonition—a "sight", his mother would
have called it—that further meetings with Lady Ellen
were going to end in trouble for them both.

He was still considering the wisdom of such cow-
ardice when he saw her coming down the hill. She
was earlier than promised, leaving him no time to flee,
and he realized at once that he was glad.

He greeted her with a smile, but this time let her
speak first.

She looked uncertain as to how to address him.
Finally she said, "The sun has come out to warm us
at last, it appears."

"Aye. 'Tis a fine day for a ride, milady. But forgive me, I've not yet saddled your mount." She was
wearing a green frock that made her coloring more
striking than ever. Connor realized that he was staring
to the point of rudeness. He turned toward the door
of the stable. "I'll just be a minute. Your Jocelyn is
not a troublesome animal."

One delicate black eyebrow went up. "Strange,"
she said. "In Normandy the lads used to draw lots
not to have to care for her. They said she was naturally wild."

"All horses are naturally wild, as are all living
things, for that matter. But they'll respond to the right
hand. You seem to ride her with no difficulty."

"They said she was a one-woman mount. She re-
sponds to no other."

"Ah." Connor smiled. "I'll saddle her for you,
milady. Would you care to watch?"

She followed him into the shadowy recesses of the stable, a cavernous building with a double row of stalls on each side of a center aisle. "You've many horses, Master Brand," she observed.

Connor slowed his pace so that he would not be walking in front of her. "No, milady, *you* have many horses. These animals belong to the Lord of Lyonsbridge. It's always been so." Connor kept his voice carefully even. He was not going to repeat his mistake of the previous day and rail on about Norman masters.

"Fine animals," she said as they walked along the center stalls. "They're thicker than ours."

"Aye, and stronger." He smiled at her. "I will refrain from saying that the animals mirror the Saxons themselves in comparison to the weaker Norman counterparts, because I'm determined not to anger milady today."

She was standing in a shaft of sunlight that filtered in from a loft window on the far wall. In her leather riding gown she looked unattainably regal, but when she returned his smile, he felt it like a swift kick to his gullet. "Then I shall determine not to *get* angry," she said. "And you may boast about your Saxons' strength, if it pleases you. I made ample witness of it yesterday when we were cleaning the castle."

"Hard work makes a man, we say."

"Aye." She appeared to be taking in his own strong arms and chest when she mused, almost to herself, "You, for example, would make two of my cousin."

Connor had seen Sebastian Phippen touring the estate with Sir William. The Frenchman was tall, but reed slender, and his face looked white and pinched

compared to the ruddy, broad faces of the Lyonsbridge residents. Connor did not, however, think it
prudent to make such a comment about the new castellan, so he turned and continued on toward Jocelyn's stall.

He stopped a couple of yards away and pointed to
the animal. "Do you see the tenseness? She carries
her head high, her tail tucked in. She waits to see
who approaches. So talk to her and let her know.
Softly."

Ellen watched in wonder as he murmured gently to
the animal and placed a hand on her neck. Her head
lowered at once. "Watch how she licks her lips,"
Connor said. "That means she's ready to cooperate."

He hoisted her expensive saddle to the horse's back
and tightened the cinches. The sleek animal didn't so
much as lift a hoof in protest.

"Mayhap she's not as wild as I'd been told, horse
master," Ellen observed. "Mayhap my trainers back
home were just telling tales."

"Mayhap," Connor said simply, then finished his
task and stepped backward to lead the horse out of
her stall.

"Can you give me directions to the cooper's
house?" Ellen asked.

"Aye, but…" He paused. "Milady, forgive me,
but is it the custom in Normandy for maids to go
about the countryside alone?"

Ellen laughed. "Nay. But I'm accustomed to doing
as I please."

Connor smiled. "Now that I believe, but I'd urge
caution upon you. If you don't think of yourself, think

of the public weal. If aught happened to you, I trow your father would turn this land into a battleground.''

Her expression sobered, and she didn't answer for a moment. Finally she said with a little pout, "'Tis vexing to be a woman."

They'd walked out of the stable and both blinked at the sunlight. "Begging milady's pardon," Connor said, "but 'tis not vexing to the rest of us."

His sweeping glance over the length of her left no doubt as to the meaning of his comment. It was bolder than should have been allowed, but Ellen did not seem upset. In fact, her cheekbones tinged a sudden pink.

"Sir William says that order has been brought to Lyonsbridge," Ellen said, ignoring Connor's remark.

Connor stiffened. "There's a kind of order, aye. But that doesn't mean you should be tempting the devil by giving him opportunity for mischief."

"In Normandy they do say that the devil walks about here in England," she said with an impish grin.

"You shouldn't be tempting the devil nor anyone else," Connor admonished, remaining serious. "If you've no escort today, I'll take you to the cooper's myself."

He hadn't intended to say any such thing, and the sudden light in her eyes at his offer set off danger signals deep in his head. As he'd told his brother, the lady Ellen had him muddled. The last thing he needed was more time in her company. But, he told himself as he quickly saddled Thunder, it would be worse if she ran into trouble her first week at Lyonsbridge. If she was so foolish as to travel abroad without a protector, he'd have to see to it that nothing untoward occurred.

It was his duty, he continued to assure himself as they set off together on the road to the village. When he had seen her safely back to the castle, he'd ride to find Martin and insist that the friar call on Lady Ellen and her cousin to explain that she needed to have an escort at all times.

He would ride with her just this once, admiring how well she sat her horse, how straight were the shapely lines of her back. He would ride with her just this one day....

Ellen couldn't remember when she'd been so utterly conscious of another person. When he moved, making the leather of his saddle creak, her ears perked as if he had shouted. When he looked at her, his bronzed skin crinkling at the corners of his eyes as he squinted from the sun, the glance felt like a touch of his hand.

It was a glorious day, mild and sunny, yet she couldn't relax and enjoy her communion with her horse and the road as she was wont. Instead she sat stiffly, waiting for him to speak, wondering if she should say something first.

As the silence stretched past the point of comfort, in the same instant they both spoke at once.

"Milady—"

"Master Brand—"

Then they laughed together and each sat a little looser in the saddle. "The lady speaks first," Connor said.

"I was just going to ask you about the family— the Coopers. You said the father is dead?"

"Aye. Killed in one of the last skirmishes before the peace."

"He was killed by Normans, then?"

"Aye, leaving two children and a widow with child—children, as it turned out, for she gave birth to twins."

Ellen was silent for a long moment, then said quietly, "Twins! She was left with four little ones, then, and the people here have long memories."

"You can't ask people to forget their loved ones, milady, their husbands and brothers and fathers."

His face had hardened, and Ellen was suddenly sorry she had brought up the topic of the cooper. "Of course not," she agreed quickly. "But I daresay there are wives and mothers aplenty mourning their menfolk back in Normandy. That's why we must all be glad the peace is finally here and endeavor to keep it."

"Amen to that," he answered, and fell silent. But a pall had been cast over the bright day.

Chapter Four

The village that had grown up around Lyonsbridge Castle was still crude, especially by Norman standards. For someone who had spent much of the previous two years at the court of King Louis in Paris, the primitive conditions of England were barely tolerable. In dismay she looked up and down the dirt path that ran past the rough homes.

"The Coopers live at the far end of town, near the abbey," Connor said, slowing his horse. He appeared to notice her reaction. "In spite of your faith in the benefits of the Norman occupation, up to now the war has brought little but hardship to these people."

Ellen remained silent and let Jocelyn lag behind as the horse master's mount picked its way along the street. Strangely, though it was midday, there was no one about. Just ahead, a shutter banged, and she thought she saw a head duck inside.

"Where is everyone?" she asked finally.

Connor smiled. "At their windows, I suspect. Watching us through whatever crack they may find."

"But why don't they meet us openly? I'd greet them if they'd show themselves."

"I'm afraid the people of Lyonsbridge have learned that it's safer to stay out of the way of their Norman masters."

Ellen remembered the girl Sarah's words of yesterday about the threat to whip her mother. It was time to get to the bottom of this. "Why are they afraid of us?" she asked directly.

Connor pulled his mount to a halt and looked at her, surprised. "You yourself said you could not blame them for keeping the memories of husbands and sons killed."

"But the conflict is now well past." There was a rustling behind the straw door of the house where they'd stopped. Ellen looked toward it expectantly, but no one emerged.

"'Tis but a different kind of conflict, milady. Is the ant not afraid of the boot even though it is left to scurry about at will?"

Once again it occurred to Ellen that the man talked more like a courtier than a peasant. Her curiosity about him grew with each encounter.

"I'd not like to think that my people live in fear of being crushed like ants. 'Tis a situation we must mend."

Connor seemed about to offer a comment, but after a long moment, he shook his head and silently signaled to his horse to resume walking. "We're almost there, milady. I daresay the Coopers will be fair astonished to have you on their doorstep."

Ellen allowed her horse to follow. "I told Sarah yesterday that I'd be visiting."

Though Ellen's mother had been dead these past ten years, she vividly remembered having to accompany her on visits to the tenants on her father's estates in Normandy. It was one of the distasteful obligations of nobility, she'd decided early on as she'd stared uncomfortably at the dirty peasant children and tried to keep her fine embroidered skirts from being soiled in their huts.

Connor stopped in front of a small cottage. Attached to one end was a pen that held a fat sow and what seemed like dozens of squealing piglets. Ellen watched the squirming creatures with a smile.

"John was too young to take over his father's trade," Connor said, nodding his head toward the animals. "The family has bartered piglets for their needs."

"'Twas fortunate they were left with such a fine breeder."

He smiled slightly. "The Normans did not leave old John Cooper's family with a roof over their heads, much less livestock. The house and the pig were gifts from the village so the family could survive."

Ellen turned her head to look back at the street they'd just traveled. "It doesn't seem that these people would have anything extra to spare."

"We take care of our own," Connor said briefly. "We're not totally helpless in defeat." He dismounted and tied his horse's reins to the top rail of the pigpen.

Without waiting for his assistance, Ellen jumped to the ground, then followed his example in tying up her mount. He turned toward her, surprised. "I'm not totally helpless either, horse master," she said smugly.

She wasn't sure exactly why, but she wanted to impress him. Unlike any other servant she'd ever known, he made her feel as if he was not only her equal, but her superior. Older, wiser and more worthy.

Well, older he may be, and wise with horses, mayhap. After all, it was his position in life. But it was an absurd notion that a Saxon servant, even a freeholding one, could think of himself as equal to a Wakelin.

He glanced briefly at the knot she'd tied, then nodded, his face impassive, and gestured toward the house. "We'd best knock, milady. I daresay they'll be bashful enough about opening to us."

Ellen thought back to her mother's obligatory tenant visits. If memory served, when Ellen and her mother had arrived, the families were always awaiting them outside their doors, bowing and scraping. "Then please announce me, Master Brand," she said.

Connor took two long steps to the thatched door and knocked, rattling the flimsy structure. After a moment, it opened and John Cooper peered shyly out, his eyes wide.

"Lady Ellen has come to see to the welfare of your mother," Connor told the boy.

"Sarah said she was to come, but I misbelieved her."

"Well, she's here, so let us in, lad," Connor said with a smile. "Your mother is abed?"

John nodded. "Sarah's with her." He pulled the door wide to allow them to enter.

Ellen resisted the impulse to sweep up her skirts so they'd not be soiled as she moved into the house, but to her amazement, the interior of the home appeared to be immaculate. The dirt floor was raked and free of debris. The wooden table in the center of the room was spotless. Against the far wall a cupboard held neatly stacked dishes. The odor of rich pork stew wafted from a pot that bubbled over the fireplace. The girl Sarah sat in a small chair next to a cot in the corner of the room. She stood up quickly and made a little curtsy.

Ellen smiled at her, then shifted her gaze to the bed, where a thin, gray-haired woman was struggling to sit up. "Please be at rest, Mistress Cooper," Ellen said quickly. "I've not come to put you to exertion."

The woman continued her efforts for another moment, then evidently realized that her frail body would not respond. She collapsed back against the straw mattress. "I'm sorry, milady," she said faintly.

For the first time in many months, Ellen had a wave of longing for her mother. She'd had it often in the years after her death, but the past couple of years at court had been so full and exciting that the pain of her absence had subsided. Her mother would have known what to do for the cooper's widow. She would have had herbs for her body, and words for her spirit with exactly the right combination of encouragement and incitement.

Ellen sighed and walked across the room toward the woman. "I've come to see how you're faring, Mistress Cooper, not to disturb your rest."

"May God bless you for such kindness, milady. My daughter said you treated her gently yesternoon," the woman said, her watery smile echoing the one Sarah herself had given Ellen yesterday as she'd clutched her hand in gratitude.

"You have two fine children," Ellen said.

"Thank you, milady. But my blessings are great. I have four."

At the direction of the woman's fond gaze, Ellen turned and for the first time noticed two smaller children, scarcely five years of age, standing stiffly in the dark corner opposite, still as statues, their hands tightly joined. They had identical dresses and cropped blond hair, and Ellen couldn't tell if they were lads or girls.

She moved toward them. Neither one moved. "What are your names?" Ellen asked.

"They're Abel and Karyn," John supplied, still standing near the door. "They were the names my father had picked before he—" he broke off, then started in again. "Abel if it be male and Karyn for a lass. As it turned out, there was one of each."

"Good morrow, Abel and Karyn," Ellen greeted them with a smile. The two smaller children remained frozen.

"Born a month after their father's death," Connor added, which dimmed Ellen's smile.

"As I say, milady, I've been greatly blessed," the woman behind her said, but as she ended the sentence, she broke into a paroxysm of coughing.

Ellen turned back to her in alarm. The coughs seemed to rattle every part of the woman's fragile body. Sarah stopped staring at Ellen and dropped to her mother's side, reaching for a rag that lay behind her and bringing it up to her mother's mouth so she could cough into it.

"What has been done for her?" Ellen asked.

"'Tis the cold weather, milady," Sarah said, looking up apologetically. "If the day is fine, we'll take her into the sun later and she'll be some better."

"She should have a tonic for that cough."

"Aye, milady," Sarah agreed, but offered nothing further. Her mother's body continued to be wracked with silent spasms.

"I suspect the family has not wanted to ask about medicine because they have not the coin to purchase any," Connor explained.

"'Tis worse these three days past," John said. "I would've told you if it kept up another day or two, Master Brand."

Connor nodded, evidently finding nothing rare in the fact that a stable master would be the one the boy would come to in distress. The man had an air of self-confidence and authority that went beyond his post, Ellen thought once again.

"She must have medicine. I'll ask Sir William to see to it." She walked to the bed and, after a moment's hesitation, reached over to put her hand on the widow's shoulder. The woman's lips had turned white and tears leaked from each closed eye, but the spell appeared to be passing.

Sarah looked up from her kneeling position, the same grateful smile on her face. "Thank you, milady."

John looked doubtful. "Sir William will like not being bothered with such a matter, milady."

"Sir William will like what I tell him to like," Ellen said. There were several long moments of silence as the widow's coughs continued to subside, turning into relaxed, deep breaths.

"You've calmed her, milady," Sarah said, awe in her voice.

Rather self-consciously, Ellen withdrew her hand from the woman's shoulder. She looked around the cottage, suddenly feeling out of place. "I believe she wore herself to sleep with her coughing, child."

Sarah shook her head. "Nay, often when she starts in like that it lasts nigh on forever. 'Twas you who calmed her."

"The girl's right." Connor had walked over to crouch beside the twins and put his arms around them. "I've seen the spells last an hour or more with nothing to stop them."

"Look, she's sleeping," John added, his tone as awed as his sister. It was true. The widow's breast rose and fell in the even breathing of slumber.

Ellen gave a small, uncomfortable laugh. "Then mayhap we should leave her to rest."

Connor stood, lifting a twin in each arm. The two children had not made a sound since she and Connor had entered the cottage, but secure in the horse master's long arms, they each ventured a smile. There was an unfamiliar melting sensation inside Ellen's chest. She walked over to the trio and asked softly, "Which one is Karyn and which is Abel? Will you tell me your names now?"

The child in Connor's right arm ducked his head and said in an almost inaudible voice, "Abel." Then he unfurled a tiny arm from where it was clasped against Connor's side and pointed around the horse master's broad chest to his sister. "Karyn," he said.

The little girl would not look at Ellen. "Mayhap Karyn will tell me her name herself," she suggested.

"Karyn will hear you, milady, but she doesn't speak," Connor told her.

"She was struck dumb," John explained. "But my brother talks for both of them."

The girl lay her head on Connor's shoulder and at last looked up at Ellen. Her eyes were light crystal blue, her features tiny and perfect. Ellen was smitten. Without thinking, she reached for her, but Karyn clung to Connor's shoulder. "What do you mean, struck dumb?" Ellen asked, dropping her arms and stepping back.

She'd addressed the question to John, but the boy merely exchanged an uncomfortable glance with Sarah and remained silent.

"Me mum says 'twas a sign from God, to make her special like," Sarah said. She made the sign of the cross and her brother did likewise.

Ellen looked back at the child. With her blond curls wreathing her face, she looked like one of the cherubs painted on the ceilings of the grand churches back home. "Mayhap your mother is right," she said.

Connor gave each of the children a final squeeze and set them down. "Are you ready to go, milady?" he asked.

Ellen nodded. She was feeling shaky inside, as if she'd not had food in overlong, though she'd eaten well that morning. She turned to Sarah. "I promise that you'll have a tonic for your mother by this afternoon. I'll come again in two days to see that it's having some effect."

All the children, even the twins, bobbed their thanks, and Ellen turned to leave, with Connor following behind. When she emerged into the fresh air, it felt as if she'd been inside for a long time, though the total stay in the cottage had surely been only minutes.

This time she let Connor help her mount. Neither spoke as they made their way back through the village and out onto the road. Finally Ellen said, "They are a special family, are they not?"

"Aye. You saw her in a weakened state, but Agnes Cooper has single-handedly raised extraordinary children."

They rode abreast. His big horse swayed easily next to hers. "A remarkable woman, I trow," Ellen agreed. "But she's had some help, it appears. The boy seems to look to you for guidance."

"John's a good lad," was all he said in answer.

After several more moments of silence she asked, "Do you take such an interest in all the villagers, horse master?"

He looked at her with that amused smile she was beginning to recognize. "Surely 'tis not against Norman law for neighbors to help one another?"

"Of course not." It was infuriating how he managed to skirt her question, how he refused to satisfy her curiosity about him, which seemed to burn brighter the more time she spent with him. She would have to be more direct than her gentility would normally allow. "I find myself pondering the nature of your relationship to these village folk. Does your family live here?"

"I have no family left, milady, other than my brother Martin, with whom you're already acquainted."

"But you grew up here?" she persisted.

"Hereabouts."

She gave it up. If this strange manner of servant didn't want to reveal more of his background, of what concern was it to her? But the frustration still stung. She spurred her horse into a gallop, expecting to leave him in her dust, but somehow his horse managed to move at the exact same instant as hers, keeping them abreast.

"Do you favor a race, Master Brand?" she called to him.

He grinned back at her. "I'm escorting you, milady. I go where you go. I'll not leave your side."

"We'll see about that," she shouted with a laugh, flicking the reins against Jocelyn's neck. She knew it was all the urging her mount needed to stretch out into a pace that was difficult for most others to maintain.

His horse didn't miss a stride. Side by side the two animals raced up the road, scattering dirt and pebbles in their wake like a minor dust storm. It seemed they'd scarcely begun when suddenly Lyonsbridge Castle loomed into view over a small hill. Ellen reined in and Connor's horse slowed in tandem.

"We're here already." Her tone was disappointed.

"Aye, milady. 'Tis a short journey at such speed."

Ellen wrinkled her nose. "I wasn't trying to win," she said.

There was that mocking smile again. It quirked the corners of his mouth in a most annoying fashion. "I wasn't," she repeated. "And, anyway, 'tis easier with a regular saddle."

Connor raised his eyebrows. "Surely milady doesn't ride astride?" he asked.

She shrugged. "I did in Normandy when my father and my chaperons weren't around to see."

"I imagine your mother cautioned you against such unladylike behavior."

"My mother died when I was but ten years of age," she said, then immediately regretted the confidence. The man had told her nothing of himself, but now had her trusting him with this most sensitive detail of her life's history.

A shadow crossed his face. "I'm sorry. I venture to say that she'd be proud to see the lovely lady her daughter has become."

It was another of his totally inappropriate comments, but in spite of herself, Ellen felt a flush of pleasure.

They were almost to the stables. Connor moved his horse ahead and pulled it up neatly next to the fence. By the time Ellen reached his side, he'd dismounted and was ready to help her down, in spite of the fact that she'd dismounted without assistance back in the village.

"I'd not have you break your neck within sight of your father's castle, milady," he explained, holding up his arms, but his smile was no longer mocking. His blue eyes looking up at her seemed younger. The guarded look was gone, as was the insolence. For a moment she wished that she and this horse master were simply a man and a maid like any other, free to ride the countryside and laugh and tease.

Shaking the notion from her head, she slid into his arms. He smelled not of horse, but of fresh straw and something more tangy, perhaps mint. His hands clasped her waist firmly and he set her on the ground, rather than letting her drop. They lingered there for just an instant, then he stepped back and, for the first time in their acquaintance, made a slight bow. It was almost as if he, too, felt the need to remind them both of their respective positions.

"Thank you for the escort, Master Brand," she said after a moment. "Next time mayhap I'll ask to use one of your saddles and we'll have a true race."

But as soon as he stepped away from her, his face had changed back to its old expression, and it appeared his thoughts were once again on his villager friends. "If you do send the tonic to the widow Cooper, it will be a gesture looked on kindly by the rest of the populace," he said.

Ellen felt a touch of pique at the abrupt distance in his tone. She realized that she'd wanted him to banter with her. She suspected that Connor Brand, in spite of his servant garb, could offer gallantries that would rival any of the courtiers in Europe.

"The tonic," he prodded gently when she didn't reply.

"I don't need to be reminded of my duties by my horse master," she said finally. "'Twas I who chose to go into the village today. I promised the widow her tonic, and she shall have it forthwith."

The intensity of his eyes dimmed as he gave another light bow. "By your ladyship's leave," he said, reaching around her to grasp Jocelyn's reins. "I'll see that your mount is well combed down this morning after her run."

Leaving her standing where he himself had placed her in the dirt of the yard, he led her horse away without looking back. She stood watching until the man and animal disappeared into the cavernous stable.

All the way back up the hill to the castle, she worked to soothe her rising temper. He'd done nothing untoward. He'd even bowed this time, as befitted his station. But she knew as certainly as she knew her own age, that there was nothing subservient about Master Brand and never would be.

And perhaps the most annoying thing of all was the knowledge that, contrary to Master Brand's assertion, her mother would *not* have been proud of her at all this day. For after the exhilaration of their ride together, until Master Brand reminded her, all thought of the widow Cooper's tonic had gone totally out of Ellen's head.

Connor knocked with his fist on the huge slab of wood that guarded the Abbey of St. John. The gesture made scarcely a sound. He pulled his knife from his belt, intending to use the hilt to announce his arrival with more authority, but before he could do so, the big door creaked open. A tall monk, thin even in his robes, smiled at him and said, "Welcome, Connor."

Brother Augustine was older than Connor by a score of years and had always seemed to him to be among the wiser of the brothers who spent their tedious days and nights in holy contemplation. If Connor were ever in need of a spiritual counselor, he might choose Brother Augustine.

But it was not a spiritual matter that had brought him to the abbey this day. "Good day, Brother. You are well, I trust?"

"By God's grace," the monk answered, making the cross.

"Have you seen my bro—ah, Father Martin?"

The monk nodded briskly, causing the sunshine to gleam across his totally bald head. "Your brother is at the church. In the sacristy, I believe. The new masters have decided to refurbish the chapel up at the castle, and he's trying to decide what needs to be taken there."

Connor thanked the monk and made his way across the abbey courtyard to the stone church at the opposite end from the gate. He found his brother as the monk had predicted, seated on the stone floor of the sacristy, sorting through a box of silver vessels used to administer the sacraments.

"So now the Normans want to take over God's possessions, as well as ours," Connor observed as he walked over to him.

"Everything is God's possession," his brother argued quietly, "be it housed in His holy place or in a humble hut."

"Or in a Norman castle," Connor added dryly.

"Aye."

"Are you going there today?"

"As soon as I finish here. You may help me transport some of this, if you will."

Connor wrinkled his face in a scowl. "'Twould sit ill. These things belong in the church."

"They'll be in a holy chapel."

"But no longer accessible to the people, only to those the Normans choose to invite."

Father Martin sighed and struggled a bit to boost himself to his feet. "Leave it be, Connor. 'Tis not something you'll miss, after all. You won't be taking sacraments at either place.''

Connor bent to help his brother lift the heavy box back into a chest. ''Nevertheless, I'd as soon not be a party to the looting of God's church, if you can find other assistance. But I've come to ask a favor of you.''

Father Martin lifted his eyebrows, aware, as was his brother, that Connor Brand asked favors of no man.

Connor hesitated. *Next time,* she'd said. She'd promised that the next time they rode together, it would be a contest. Indeed. He was afraid the true contest would not be between their two mounts, but between his own reason and his unruly impulses. When she'd dropped into his arms at the end of their ride, it had been all he could do to keep from clasping her closer. The urge had been that strong, against all good sense. The lass had bewitched him, and he simply couldn't afford to succumb to the spell.

''What would you have of me?'' Father Martin asked as the silence stretched out.

'''Tis not for me, really,'' Connor said, looking away from his brother. '''Tis for the safety of the lady herself.''

Father Martin's eyes gleamed. ''I assume you're speaking of the lady Ellen?''

''Aye. You must tell her and her cousin that she needs an escort if she's to travel around the countryside.''

''Are you hoping for the post?''

''Lord, no. I'm hoping to avoid having to leave my

own duties to nursemaid her, as I was forced to to-day.''

''Ah.'' Father Martin slowly unrolled the sleeves of his robe, watching his brother out of the corner of his eye. ''Did you find the duty onerous, then?''

Connor's face reddened. ''You may well guess that I did not, brother. But you yourself warned me about the dangers of such proximity.''

The amusement faded from the priest's eyes. ''Aye, brother, I did. I *do*. And I shall speak to the lady myself today.''

Connor nodded, his face stiff. ''You'll not tell her that 'twas I who sent you?''

His brother's voice became gentle. ''Nay, brother. I'll not tell her.''

''I'm in your debt, Martin,'' Connor said. He cleared his throat awkwardly, then turned toward the door saying, ''I'd best get back.''

Father Martin's eyes were troubled as he stood watching his brother until his tall form had disappeared through the door back to the courtyard.

Chapter Five

Father Martin's words had not had the desired effect. Two days following their ride to the village, Lady Ellen appeared once again at the stables, alone.

Connor had two of the village boys helping him to repair a stretch of rotten fencing in back of the stable. Both the boys stopped work to stare at Ellen as she approached, and Connor found himself hard-pressed not to follow their example.

"Master Brand," she called. "I've come for our race."

The lads looked up at Connor in wonder. He tried to keep his reply casual, belying the sudden acceleration of his pulses. "Good morrow, milady."

Heedless of the mud, she made her way around the corner of the stable toward where they were working. "Are you up to the challenge, horse master?" she asked with a smile and a defiant tilt of her head.

Connor took in a deep breath. "I'm in the middle of fence mending today, milady. I thought you were going to find another escort for your travels abroad."

She stopped a couple of yards from him. "I was

well satisfied with my escort of the other day. I'd
engage his services again.''

''Jem and me'll be fine by ourselves, Master Connor,'' said one of the lads. ''''Tis an easy enough task
for two.'' As if to prove his words, he single-handedly
hoisted in place the final railing.

Ellen clapped her hands. ''There, you see? Your
crew no longer needs you. You're dismissed. And it's
a fine day for a ride.''

In this, at least, he had to agree with her. He'd not
ridden in two days, separated by two nights of restless
tossing in his bed. It would be good to feel Thunder
underneath him and go hurtling across a green ex-
panse of lush English countryside.

He met her eyes. They shone with challenge.
''Very well, milady,'' he said. ''We'll have our
race.''

And he'd not be responsible for the consequences.

They'd agreed to visit the cooper's family first, and
during this visit Ellen felt much more at ease, though
perhaps it was simply the contrast between the
friendly warmth of the cottage and the icy tension of
the ride there. She'd seen yet another side of the horse
master. He was neither the audacious servant nor the
charmer she'd seen in glimpses. Instead, he appeared
to be almost angry, holding himself in readiness
against some unknown foe.

But as soon as they entered Agnes Cooper's home,
his demeanor changed. The twins came running to
them, and he scooped them up in a double embrace.
Sarah's pale face flushed at his greeting and John's
brightened with a big smile.

To Ellen's surprise, the widow was sitting up in a rocker by the fireplace. "You are better today, mistress?" she asked her.

"Aye, milady. No doubt thanks to the physic you sent." She struggled to stand up, but Ellen motioned for her to remain where she was.

"I'm so pleased to hear it," she said.

"Sir William himself brought it, milady," John added. "Everyone in the village is talking about it."

Ellen was gratified, though a little surprised to hear that the bailiff had been so diligent in personally carrying out her instructions. "We shall see you continue to get it until you're on your feet again," she told the woman.

She hadn't noticed that one of the twins had crawled out of Connor's arms and crept up beside her. The child was carefully tracing the gold-embroidered pattern on Ellen's overskirt with a single tiny finger.

"Karyn, leave the lady's dress," Sarah admonished.

The girl looked straight up, her blue eyes meeting Ellen's with a tentative smile. Ellen felt that same warm rush again. "It's fine," she said. She crouched down and spread her skirt out in front of her. "You see?" she said to the child. "It's a dragon, but it's not a fierce one like the creatures at the ends of the earth. Mine's a friendly one, don't you think?"

The girl bobbed her head, her eyes still fixed on Ellen's face.

"You can trace its tail, if you like." She grasped the girl's hand so the two could feel the pattern together. Karyn turned her attention to the skirt and carefully followed each bump of the beast's tail, then she looked up again at Ellen, her smile brilliant.

Ellen had a strong urge to hug her, but she wasn't sure how the embrace would be received, so she merely said, "I'll bring you a dragon of your own one of these days." When the girl's eyes registered some alarm, she added, "A wooden one, not a real one, *cherie.* Another friendly one, like the one on my skirt."

Once again the girl looked up, and this time her eyes held something akin to adoration.

"She says thank you, mum," said her twin brother, who still stood clasped in the kneeling Connor's arms.

Karyn nodded a silent agreement.

It was heartbreaking to think that such a perfect little creature could not speak for herself. Ellen wondered what could have caused the affliction. She'd been "struck dumb," they'd said. Had she once spoken, then? Of course, Ellen knew that such things occurred, and that sometimes it was best not to inquire too deeply into the why of it, lest it be a witch's spell. She couldn't imagine that even a witch could be so evil as to wish harm on a sweet little child such as Karyn Cooper.

"You are good to us, milady," the widow said. "As soon as I feel better, I'll be bringing up a pork cake for your table."

Ellen blinked. She couldn't ever remember a tenant in Normandy offering food for the master's table. The idea seemed almost absurd. It was obvious that this peasant family had so little, while her father's household wanted for nothing. She didn't know how to reply.

Connor saved her from doing so. "Widow Cooper's pork cake is famous in the shire," he said, smiling first at the older woman, then at Ellen. "'Twill be a rare treat for you."

The widow seemed pleased with the praise, but looked noticeably more tired than when they'd entered the cottage. "I should get me mum back into bed," Sarah murmured, her eyes downcast.

Ellen straightened up quickly. "Of course you should, child. I didn't come to tire her further. We'll take our leave, Master Brand."

She looked at Connor, who gave little Abel a final squeeze and stood. She'd almost forgotten about him for several moments as she spoke with the tenant family, but now, looking at how his tall form dwarfed the shadowy cottage, she felt a stir of excitement. They'd yet to have their promised race.

After John and Sarah refused their offer to help get the widow back into bed, they said their goodbyes and left. Once again, Ellen was struck with a sense of freedom as she emerged from the gloomy cottage into the sun. What would it be like to live with five people in such a tiny place? she wondered for the first time in her life. But her thoughts did not linger long with the question.

As on their first visit, there had been no one to greet them when they'd ridden through town, but on the return trip, Ellen could spot a villager here and there, usually behind their cottages tending gardens. None were near enough to hail, so they rode through without stopping. If any of them thought it unusual to see the lady of the land riding astride a big horse, her skirts bunched up about her, at least none was rude enough to stare.

"I have to give you the right of it, milady," Connor told her as they left the village. "You ride that saddle almost as well as a man, in spite of the difference in raiments."

Ellen's eyes flashed gold. "*Almost* as well, Master Brand? Now there's a challenge if I've ever heard one."

"I didn't mean it so," he replied with an easy smile. But he didn't withdraw his words.

"I can see I'll have to convince you with deed rather than word."

"You'd fancied a race, as I understood it."

"Aye, but since I know not the countryside, you'll have to set the course, which gives you the advantage."

He drew up his horse and stood in the stirrups to survey the landscape. The road from the village back to Lyonsbridge was gently hilly, but to the west lay a stretch of meadow that was mostly flat and even. He pointed in that direction. "We can cross Anders' Lea for nigh on five miles without an obstacle. 'Twould seem fair enough to you?"

It was the charming Connor she was glimpsing today, but as he indicated their route, his expression challenged. There was something between them, she and this horse master. It wanted resolution. She needed to defeat him at his own game and put this to rest once and for all.

"Aye," she said, gathering Jocelyn's reins firmly in hand. "Give the word."

"Nay, 'tis always the privilege of the fairest lady

to start the race.'' His eyes lingered on her face as he spoke.

Ellen tamped down the knot that rose in her throat. It was past time to put this foolishness over a servant behind her. She'd show up the man at his own mastery, then she'd go back to concentrating on putting her father's castle to rights, which was, after all, the reason she was here.

''Then let it begin,'' she said with a toss of her head.

Before the last word even left her lips, both horses had sprung into action, moving smoothly, side by side, the sleek bay mare and the heavier black stallion, hooves reverberating hollowly on the grassy terrain.

They rode in silence for several minutes, riders as well as horses lost in the sheer enjoyment of speed and freedom. Ellen clutched Jocelyn's back between her legs, ignoring the indecorous bit of hose showing at her ankles, and laughed with delight. They neared a middle section of the meadow where the grass grew higher, but Jocelyn was undaunted by the weeds whipping around her legs. Connor's horse slowed slightly, and she pulled ahead.

''I'll see you at the finish, horse master,'' she shouted back at him, her smile taunting.

He appeared totally relaxed in his saddle and returned her smile with a small wave of his hand.

The course was longer than she'd anticipated, and she could tell that Jocelyn was tiring, but the noble animal kept running at full speed. She'd not stop until Ellen bade her, even if she exhausted herself.

Less than a quarter mile distant, Ellen could see

that the meadow ended abruptly at a grove of mature oak trees. She smiled to herself as she realized that the victory she'd sought was at hand. "Just a little more, girl," she whispered under her breath.

Suddenly Connor's horse flashed by, nearly twice the speed of hers, knocking away her breath like a blow to the stomach. She almost lost her grasp on the reins, but Jocelyn stayed on course and did not slow her pace. Nevertheless, when they reached the trees, Connor was already there and dismounted, his face annoyingly impassive, standing ready to catch her mount's reins.

As Jocelyn obligingly pulled up, her flanks heaving, Ellen sat in her saddle, stunned.

"'Twas a good race, milady," Connor said after a moment. "You led me a chase."

"You were well behind," Ellen said in disbelief.

"Nay. I was but pacing."

She shook her head. "'Twas not a distance to be paced. Jocelyn rode full out the entire way."

"That was your mistake. A slower middle makes for a lightning-fast ending."

His tone was not mocking, which helped her pride. Grudgingly, she said, "'Twas lightning fast, in truth. I've never seen such speed."

Connor allowed himself a small smile. "Thunder's a good mount."

"I'd like to ride him sometime."

Connor nodded. "I'd not trust him with many, but your ladyship rides well."

She sensed that the compliment was genuine, and one that he gave rarely. It pleased her immensely.

He walked a couple steps, leading both horses into

the shade of the oak grove. "Would my lady dismount a few moments so they can rest?" he asked.

"Aye." She swung her leg over her mount's back in a most unladylike fashion and twisted around to slide to the ground. Connor watched her, an odd expression on his face.

"You move like a nimble young lad," he said after a moment.

Ellen laughed. "My chaperon would be wailing to hear you say that."

"Your chaperon?"

"I left her in Normandy," she explained. "Against my father's wishes. I'm a grown woman now, not a girl to have every move studied by a dour old nursemaid."

Connor was the one studying her now, she realized, and he did not have the look of a nursemaid. After a moment his scrutiny grew uncomfortable. "'Tis not polite to stare, horse master. Do they not teach that in England?"

He grinned, not insulted. "I beg your pardon, milady. My sainted mother tried to teach me manners, but she also taught me to appreciate the beauty of all living things."

His gesture encompassed the stately trees around them, but both knew that it had not been the trees he'd been admiring. "She sounds like a wonderful woman," Ellen said, wondering if at last she would find out something about the background of this extraordinary man. "Does she live in the village?"

"Nay, milady. If 'tis true that God is just, she lives with the angels."

"I'm sorry, Master Brand. What about your father?"

Connor grinned. "Ah now, the case is not so clear with my father. God might have had to sprinkle a bit of mercy in with the justice in order to lift Geoffrey Brand to the holy choir. But I like to think of them as being together."

"As I'm sure they are," Ellen said, making a hasty sign of the cross. "They have your brother to pray for their souls."

"Aye."

He turned away from her, evidently dismissing the topic of his family. Ellen watched as he neatly tied the reins of both horses to a low branch. He was wearing a leather doublet today that emphasized the broad stretch of his back. With his wide shoulders and blond hair, he had the look of the fearsome Viking raiders of old that they sung of in the ballads.

He pulled a flask from a pouch at the front of his saddle and turned back to her, offering it. "Art thirsty?" he asked, then stopped as both realized the impropriety of his informal address. "Would you have some wine, milady?" he amended.

She nodded without mentioning the oversight and reached for the flask. Their fingers met alongside the smooth leather, his warm, hers cold. He held on for an extra moment before relinquishing the flask.

Ellen's throat had gone dry, but not from the ride. She pulled out the stopper and took a long pull of the sweet berry wine. Then another.

Connor chuckled. "Milady can drink as well as ride," he observed.

She looked for signs of his earlier mocking smile,

but there was no trace of it. "I was my father's only child. He taught me as both daughter and son," she told him, handing him back the flask.

"Did you leave any?" he joked, taking a short drink, then offering it to her again.

She refused it with a shake of her head, wandering instead into the grove, where the grass gave way to moss, soft and spongy under her slippers. He followed behind her.

"They say some of these trees are a hundred years old," he said. "They were here before the first Norman ever laid eyes on this land."

Ellen looked over her shoulder and gave him a saucy smile. "Are you trying to claim these trees as Saxon, Master Brand?"

He smiled back a bit sheepishly. "I remember coming here when I was a child. The spot has not changed since then, though most other things have."

"'Twould be a dull world without change, horse master."

"Mayhap."

They'd reached a small clearing, where the trees formed such a perfect circle it appeared that they had been placed there by design. "This is where the faeries dance," Connor told her.

She stopped and gave a small twirl. "'Tis an enchanted place, then?"

He'd stopped behind her and was watching her again with that intense expression. "So say the old wives of the village."

"I can almost feel it." She spun again, and nearly lost her balance. She reached her hand out to steady herself against the trunk of a tree, but instead found

Connor's broad chest as he stepped near to keep her from falling.

"I'm not as graceful as the faeries, I fear," she gasped, laughing up into his face.

His smile had disappeared.

"But thou art twice as lovely, Ellen of Wakelin," he said, his voice suddenly grown hoarse.

Her laughter died as his arms went around her, pulling her against him. His face loomed over her in the shadows, then blurred as he lowered his mouth to hers and kissed her, softly at first, then with mounting passion.

She felt the flow of it through every limb, like hot honey, melting and sweet. Her mouth opened naturally under his and their tongues swirled together, sending a shaft of feeling plunging through her midsection. Her head fell back, and he moved his kisses from her mouth to the soft white skin of her neck.

She'd never so much as imagined such sensations.

Then it was over, with the suddenness of a dousing in an icy pond.

He stepped back, his expression angry, and swore softly under his breath.

Ellen's mind was ajumble. She was bewildered and hurt by the abrupt shift in him, but even more, she was afraid at how powerless she'd been those few moments in his arms. She'd been courted by many men and had *allowed* a fortunate few the favor of a kiss. But she'd never *been* kissed, not like this. And by a mere *servant*. Was this what it felt like to be a wanton? she wondered.

"I'd not meant to let that happen," Connor said

finally. "We'd best get back, and mayhap next time you'll bring an escort from the castle as I told you."

His expression was returning to normal, probably faster than her own, and it infuriated her even more to think that he could dismiss what had just happened so easily.

"I could have you whipped for what you just did, horse master," she snapped.

He grinned. "I think not. I suspect you'd go to great lengths to ensure that your cousin doesn't learn that you took advantage of your lack of chaperonage and challenged one of his servants to a race alone across the countryside."

"I'd engaged for a race, not a kiss." The more she thought about the encounter, the angrier she became. Connor continued to smile, the mocking one again.

"Mayhap 'twas the faeries," he said nonchalantly, glancing around the clearing. "We'll pretend we weren't responsible and take care not to let it happen again."

"You can be sure of that, horse master. You'll not lay hands on me again, or I swear my cousin and everyone else in the castle will hear of it. 'Twill not be my reputation that will suffer. You'll be banished from this shire, if not worse."

As angry as she was, even saying the words left her with a feeling of loss. Somehow Connor Brand and Lyonsbridge seemed inextricably linked. She couldn't imagine the place without him.

He stood only a couple of feet from her. She could still feel the power of those arms. Her lips still burned. *Sweet St. Ellen,* she prayed silently, *purge these sensations from me. Obliterate the memory.*

She spun around on her heel and started walking, then realized she had no idea which direction to go in the thick grove.

From behind her, his hand gently grasped her shoulder and turned her toward the right. "This way, milady," he said softly.

She pulled away from his touch and marched briskly in the direction he had indicated, her eyes fixed ahead. She'd not look at him again, this audacious servant. She'd never again make the mistake of looking into those devastating blue eyes.

All the way back to the castle she kept silent, and kept her pledge. She allowed him to assist her off the horse, but did not look at his face. She offered no thanks for the day's excursion, and made sure not to let his hand brush her as he reached for Jocelyn's reins.

Climbing up to the castle without looking back, she repeated it to herself as in a litany. This madness was over.

Chapter Six

Sebastian Phippen scowled across the table at his bailiff. "Lord Wakelin may be satisfied with the current revenues, but I believe there are more to be had."

Sir William shook his head. "We've near bled the village these two years past, gathering monies for the crusades. And now with Lady Ellen wanting all these changes at the castle, the expenses here have gone up rather than down."

Slamming his hand on the thick ledger in front of him, Sebastian replied, "Female fripperies. She's having furniture shipped from Normandy and has engaged for a tapestry to be sewn depicting a view of the castle from the coast road. I've sent for her to discuss the matter."

Sir William's eyes darted from side to side. "Begging your lordship's pardon, but I trow she has the right. 'Tis not true that Lord Wakelin has declared his daughter heir to Lyonsbridge?"

"I'm not a lord, man. Not as yet," Sebastian replied smoothly with an oily smile. "Naturally, 'tis my *cousin's* interests I'm protecting by these measures.

Since she's a woman, she can't be expected to understand the importance of such matters.''

They were seated in Sebastian's antechamber, a small, cold room on the third floor of the castle, much less luxurious than the rooms surrounding the master's chambers, which had been occupied by Lady Ellen herself.

The door creaked open and Ellen entered, a petulant expression on her face. ''I've come because I deemed it unseemly that the servants should see my displeasure, Sebastian,'' she said icily. ''But I'll have you know that I'm not to be *summoned* by you in such fashion ever again. You are not my father, nor even my guardian here. I'm fully of age.''

''Forgive me, Cousin,'' Sebastian said, rising to his feet with obvious reluctance, his pinched face growing a shade more sallow. ''We've matters to discuss in private, and I thought 'twould be easier here than in the more open spaces of your chambers or the great hall.''

''What matters?'' Ellen asked, unmollified. She'd had the headache and had been in a temper for two days, ever since her ride with Connor Brand, and her cousin's imperious summons that morning had helped neither her mood nor the throbbing of her temples.

Sir William had risen from his chair as well and held it for her to sit. There were only two chairs in the room, so he remained standing as Sebastian resumed his seat and spoke evenly. ''As you know, 'twas *I* whom your father appointed to look over the monies at Lyonsbridge, and I'm trying to go over the accounts with Sir William. It appears that there are still economies to be made.''

She frowned and squinted. Her cousin sat framed in bright sunlight coming through the leaded glass of the room's only window, and looking directly at him made her eyes hurt. "Economies such as what?" she asked.

Sebastian flipped open the leather book under his hand and looked at it idly. "I'd thought to sell off most of the horses, for one thing. 'Tis your father's intention that his soldiers will come with their own mounts. We have no need of so many of these thick English stock."

"They're good horses," Ellen argued.

"For plowing, mayhap," Sebastian said with a scornful twist of his thin lips.

"Nay, I've seen them run."

Sebastian peered at his cousin through narrowed eyes. "I had report that two days ago you left the castle once again without escort, Cousin. I'd hate to have to report such behavior to your father."

Ellen sat up in her chair, bristling with anger. "You forget yourself, Cousin, and this is the last time I'll warn you. You may be in charge of the *numbers*—" She broke off and waved her hand dismissively at the accounting book. "But you're *not* in charge of me. I hold my behavior responsible to my father and none other."

"'Tis your safety that concerns me, Cousin. Nothing more. You'll recall that Father Martin himself warned us that it was foolhardy for you to—"

Ellen stood. Her head would not continue to tolerate the audience, in part because she knew there was justice behind her cousin's admonishment. If Sebastian knew what had actually transpired when she had left the castle alone, he'd most assuredly be contacting her father, no matter how she might argue against it.

"Mind your ledgers, Cousin, and leave my behavior to me. I have no intention of putting myself at risk. In fact, I've taken on one of the village girls as my attendant, and if I have occasion to leave the castle, she'll be at my side."

From the corner of her eye, she saw Sir William nodding approval. "The cooper's Sarah. A comely lass, milady," he said.

Something in the way he licked his lips and bobbed his beard as he spoke made Ellen uncomfortable with his remark, but she brushed away the feeling. Sir William was a minor annoyance. It was Sebastian who was grating on her nerves today.

"I'm not feeling well," she told him. "If you have something to discuss with me further, you may do so after the midday meal. In *my* chambers," she added firmly.

Sebastian did not rise, but sat watching her, tapping the tips of his fingers together. "Very well, Cousin," he said softly.

She nodded and began to leave, unaware of the malice that lit his black eyes as soon as her back was turned.

Ellen found she was enjoying the companionship of her new attendant more than she ever had the various maids and chaperons her father had assigned back in Normandy. These had always seemed either too old and tedious to be of any fun or too much in awe of her position to dare demonstrate a spark of life.

Sarah, on the other hand, once she got over her initial shyness, was warm and friendly, and flatteringly eager to hear Ellen's tales of her romantic conquests at the various courts of Europe.

"I expect I'll never so much as see a man from outside Lyonsbridge," the girl sighed as the two finished folding and putting away a box full of linens they'd set out for airing.

Ellen clapped her hands, gleeful as a child. "Sarah, I'll take you back to Normandy with me when I finish here. Then you'll see all manner of gentleman. Mayhap even catch the eye of one of the lower ranks."

Sarah looked wistful for a moment, then shook her head. "'Tis kind of you, mistress, but I couldn't leave me mum. She needs me, at least till the twins are bigger."

Neither one uttered the unspoken thought that it was possible the twins would be needing Sarah if the widow Cooper succumbed to her disease.

"Are you sure she's well enough for you to be here with me?" Ellen asked.

"Aye. She's that happy for me, truly. And now that the weather's turned, she's much better."

"I'm glad, for my sake as well as yours. I appreciate your company, Sarah."

The girl beamed at her mistress's words. "I'd stay with you forever, milady, if I didn't have to think about me family first. I'm not sure me mum would have survived this winter freeze without the tonic you sent."

Ellen closed the big chest and wiped her hands on

her blue linen skirt. Little by little she'd taken to wearing her plainer clothes. It seemed silly to weigh herself down with impractical jewels and heavy gold baubles when the only people of her rank to impress were Sebastian and Sir William. In fact, she'd begun to like the more modest Saxon garb.

"We've gone through almost all the chests here," she said, looking around the linen room. "In truth, the old lords of this place had a wealth of beautiful things. I wonder what happened to the family?"

Sarah offered no suggestion.

Boosting herself to her feet, Ellen stretched the kink out of her back and asked, "Shall we begin the box room next or do you think we've done enough for one day?"

"Whatever milady says," Sarah answered, coming more easily to her feet.

Both started slightly at a knock on the door behind them. It was one of the castle pages, a stocky lad named Rolf, who looked first at Sarah, blushed, then addressed Ellen. "Milady, the horse master would beg an audience with you."

Ellen's mouth went dry. "Master Brand?" she asked.

"Aye, milady."

"What does he want?" It was a foolish question. Connor Brand would not be about to confide his business to a page.

"I know not, milady. He's awaiting you in the solar."

Ellen glanced at Sarah. One of the reasons she'd employed the girl was so that she'd not have to be alone—with Brand or any of the other men in the castle. But suddenly she was reluctant to include the girl in their meeting.

She fought a small battle with good sense, then said to her, "Sarah, you may be dismissed for today. We'll begin on the box room on the morrow."

Sarah did not appear to notice her mistress's hesitation. Instead she was busy watching the page out of the corner of her eyes. Her cheekbones were tinged with pink.

Ellen had an uncharacteristically romantic impulse. "Rolf, you may also be excused to escort Mistress Cooper back to the village," she said, and smiled to herself as both the young people's faces lit with pleasure.

The smile stayed with her halfway down the big stone stairs, but faded as she began to regret her decision to send Sarah away. She hadn't seen Connor since the day of their race, nearly a week before. She hadn't intended to see him again, certainly not alone. Yet he had "begged an audience" with her. Was that a ruse? Surely he wouldn't dare come into the castle right under her cousin's nose and take the kind of liberty he had back in the forest?

By the time she reached the wide double doors to the solar, the palms of her hands were clammy with cold sweat.

She should have refused to see him entirely. Or made him come back when she could see him in the company of her cousin. She should turn around and run as fast as possible back up the stairs and into the safety of her chambers.

Blessed Mary, she said to herself sternly. The man was her servant. They'd gotten carried away that day in the forest, but she'd made it quite clear that there would be no repetition of such an occurrence. It was absurd that the mistress of the entire household should be nervous about meeting with one of her servants. In spite of the fact that she'd lain abed these past seven nights with the memory of his lips on hers.

Connor paced from one end of the room to another, his long legs covering the distance in just four strides. He'd rather be chewing a barrel of nails than facing an audience with the lady of Lyonsbridge. At least the solar lacked the chill that much of the rest of the castle took on at this time of year. He remembered playing here as a child, moving along the stone floor with the progression of the sun as it streamed through the high windows.

He stopped walking and closed his eyes, bringing into his head a vision of the three of them, he, Geoff and Martin, turning their game into one of the inevitable wrestling matches, much to their lady mother's despair.

"You wanted to see me, Master Brand," said a voice from the door, breaking his reverie.

He opened his eyes and immediately met hers. A week of distance had not softened their impact. He felt it still in his gullet and then lower.

"Good day, milady," he managed to answer.

She held herself regally, once again the queen of faeries, rather than the wood sprite who had melted in his arms for one endless moment.

"State your business, horse master." There was not a flicker in her golden gaze.

So be it, he thought. 'Twould no doubt be easier for them both to pretend that their encounter in the forest had never happened. "They want to sell my horses," he said, his voice as direct as her own.

Her lips softened into the ghost of a smile. "To sell the Lord of Lyonsbridge's horses, you mean."

Connor let his shoulders relax imperceptibly. Somehow he had the feeling that, Norman or no, she would be his ally in this thing. "Aye. Your cousin wants to sell the Lyonsbridge horses. 'Tis a foolish notion."

One delicate black eyebrow rose as she pointed out, "My father gave over the management of the estate to Sebastian. I assume he has his reasons."

"I care not for his reasons. Lyonsbridge stock is the best in all England. Breed them, if you like. Trade or sell a few, but do not replace them with your scrawny Norman bloods."

His arguments had been more measured and reasoned when he'd rehearsed them back at the stable, but his tongue seemed to trip over itself in the most damnable fashion when he was with her. Though he'd sensed that she was sympathetic, perhaps it had been a mistake to come to her. He should have taken his case to Phippen himself.

She moved toward him from where she'd been standing near the door. He could hear each swish of her skirts, each soft fall of her slippers. She was dressed more simply than he'd seen her, in a plain, soft blue frock that molded to her breasts like a night rail.

"If I recall, my scrawny Norman mare almost defeated your Lyonsbridge stallion the other day." She clamped down on her tongue as she finished talking, as though regretting that she'd brought up the incident.

Connor had had no intention of mentioning it either, but it was obvious from the tension between them that it was on both their minds. He smiled. "*Almost,* milady, and due in large part to the rider's skill."

The compliment softened her expression further, and Connor began to feel on more familiar ground. She was, after all, a woman. He may have had little practice in dealing with Normans, but he'd had ample experience with females.

She moved to a curved bench beneath one of the windows and sat, not looking at him. "You may be surprised to learn, Master Brand, that I agree with you about the horses. 'Tis shortsighted of my cousin to get rid of them for quick coin when instead they could serve to improve my father's stock for future generations."

Connor stood looking down at her, since she'd not invited him to sit. "I applaud your wisdom, milady."

"Unfortunately, Sebastian's an ogre about the money," she said, still talking to empty space. "If we don't get it from the horses, he may try to take more from the people."

"There's no more to take. The entire shire is only now beginning to recover from the years of fighting. Just when things seem to be going better, Sir William raises the taxes."

Ellen nodded, lost in thought. "I don't know why men take such pleasure in accumulating more and more soldiers and arms and riding off on crusades to the other end of the earth."

"'Tis a holy call," Connor said. He believed in the cause, although, as he intended to honor the pledge he'd made to his mother, it was one he himself would never answer.

"I'd as lief believe in a less bloodthirsty God," she said. "The scriptures preach peace and forgiveness."

Connor remained silent. He had little experience with theology and none at all with *women* who argued theology, which was properly a man's realm. He must remember to ask his brother's opinion on the matter.

Ellen stood and, finally, looked at him directly. "Nonetheless, my cousin will have his revenues, squeezed as they may be. I shall try to work a compromise. We'll sell no more than one of every five horses, and of that one-fifth, we shall retain breeding rights for Lyonsbridge."

It was a good solution, and Connor regarded the lovely Norman with a respect that kept him from bristling as she abruptly indicated the audience was over and left the room.

Lady Ellen had a sharp head on her shoulders as well as a beautiful one, he realized, as the big doors shut behind her. The combination was doubly dangerous to his peace of mind. He sighed and started toward the rear entrance to the solar. Mayhap Martin would have advice for him on that subject as well.

In the end they made quite a show of it, a somber parade of sorts. Many of the villagers stopped their daily labors and came up to the castle, some carrying baskets of food to eat as they sat on the grass. The villagers watched as Connor, the stable boys and a number of helpers who had been recruited for the day, brought all four score of the Lyonsbridge horses out into the stable yard.

Those to be sold would be culled from the rest and taken to market at York the following day by several of Sebastian Phippen's men. Connor had pointedly not volunteered to make the trip with them, but he had agreed to give recommendations about which mounts should go.

John Cooper had been by his side all day, full of questions and avidly watching as Connor examined each mount as if he'd never seen it before, though he knew each one as well as the palm of his own hand. Everyone could tell that his decisions would be painful ones.

By midday, only six of the sixteen that were to be sold had been chosen.

Connor looked up from his work as a delegation appeared leaving the castle gates, led by Lady Ellen herself, followed by her cousin and Sir William. For once the sight of her did not cause his pulses to race. He'd hoped to be able to complete the selection process without interference from the Normans.

"Bring the next, John," he told the boy, turning away from the hill where the newcomers were approaching.

John obligingly led a cloudy roan up to the stool where Connor was perched. The animal was only a year old, but Connor had already decided that it would never show the distinction of several other horses foaled by the same mare. It would be a likely candidate for the trader's block.

It pranced restlessly in front of him. He stood, laid

a hand on the horse's withers and said something in a low voice. The prancing stopped.

"See what I was telling you?" Sir William said in a loud voice, still a little way up the hill. "I don't know how he does it. He has them tame as lambs, but they're monstrous beasts when my men try to ride them. I'd sell off the lot."

Connor continued his examination of the little roan, acting as if he didn't see the new arrivals.

"What say you, horse master?" Sebastian called to him. "Sir William claims you cast some sort of spell over these animals, else they'd be hopeless to train."

Reluctantly, Connor turned to face him. "These horses are bred for strength. They'll carry a man day and night for a sennight without faltering. You'll not find their like in all Christendom. As to spells, I know not of what Sir William speaks. I merely train them, in service of my liege lord."

Sebastian picked his way the last few feet down the hill, careful not to slip in the churned up mud of the yard. "They're not savage, then?" he asked, casting a doubtful glance at the roan's head.

"Nay."

Once they were on a level, Connor towered over the Norman, which allowed him to look over the man's head and meet Lady Ellen's eyes, which were dancing with mischief. "They only nip when they can tell that someone is afraid of them, Sebastian," she told him.

Phippen began to take a step back, but stopped when he saw Connor's amusement. He whirled around and snapped at his cousin, "Just because your father allowed you to be raised like a hoyden spending all day long on a horse, doesn't mean that we're all so inclined.''

There was no apology in Ellen's expression. ''Oh, pooh, Sebastian, don't be a donkey. The horses won't bite you.''

Sebastian turned his back on her, and Connor's amusement at the exchange between the two cousins died. The expression on Phippen's face was nothing short of malevolent. Connor wondered if Lady Ellen was aware of the extent of her cousin's enmity.

''Be sure you have chosen the required number by the end of the day,'' Sebastian told him. ''Else we'll sell whichever are handy. Beginning with that monster,'' he added, pointing over to where Thunder was quietly standing under a tree.

Connor's lips tightened. ''They'll be chosen by the end of the day.''

Sebastian nodded and turned back toward the castle, slithering in the thick mud. ''There's no need for us to stand here in the hot sun,'' he said, looking at Sir William. William's gaze was on Sarah Cooper, who stood quietly next to Ellen. The expression in his eyes made Connor uncomfortable, but Sarah seemed unaware of his scrutiny. Indeed, she had eyes only for a young castle page who stood conveniently nearby.

Sebastian cleared his throat and said more loudly, ''I'm going back.''

William tore his gaze from the girl and looked over at him. ''Aye, this seems to be progressing properly.''

Both men started walking up the hill. ''Are you coming, Cousin?'' Sebastian asked over his shoulder.

Ellen looked up at her cousin, then back at the yard full of horses and villagers. Finally her gaze went to

Sarah, who was still peering at Rolf out of the corner of her eyes. "Sarah and I will stay a spell," she said airily. "I'd like to bid farewell to the horses that are to go."

Sebastian gave a shrug of irritation. "As you will," he said, then continued trudging up the hill.

For a moment after they left, there was quiet among the crowd, and Connor did nothing to resume his work. Then he said, "Would you have us bring you out a litter to sit in, milady?"

She looked around at the groups of villagers arranged in festive groups up on the grassy hill. "Nay," she said after a moment. "I'll make do with the ground."

Connor smiled and gave her gown a pointed glance. It was one of her more elaborate ones, not like the simple cotton she'd worn the other day in the solar. He was quite sure she'd never before sat on the ground in such garb, especially not in mud such as covered the stable yard. He reached behind him and plucked up the stool he'd been using. "We'll compromise on a stool. I'd not have you soil your gown."

He planted it in the mud, making sure it was firmly set, then reached for her hand to hold it as she sank gracefully down on the little seat.

"Thank you," she said with a smile. It was not yet as sweet as the smile she'd given him the day of their race *before* he'd kissed her, but it was worlds from the imperious expression she'd adopted *after* he'd kissed her.

Connor had never had his talk with Martin about Ellen, after all. He'd decided that his problems with the Norman maid were beyond his brother's holy teachings. It was a dilemma he'd have to work out for himself.

"Did you want to review the animals yourself?" he asked her.

"Nay, horse master. I'm merely observing. Mayhap I'll catch you in one of these spells Sir William speaks of. Pretend that I'm not here."

Or pretend that the sky was green, for it would be about as easy a task.

"Aye, milady," he said.

Chapter Seven

Where had the indignation fled? Ellen asked herself as her eyes followed the horse master's every move. This servant had *kissed* her. The hands that were now running so smoothly and efficiently over each new horse had done the same to her. She should be repulsed and horrified, but she was nothing of the kind.

The hands were strong, but not coarse. His touch was firm, but not rough. The horses appeared content. If they'd been cats they'd be arching their bodies and purring with pleasure. She might be, too, with those hands on her, she thought, her face reddening at the idea.

He'd heeded her advice to ignore her. In fact, it seemed that he'd utterly forgotten about her presence.

"What are you looking for, horse master? How are you choosing which ones to sell?" Her voice sounded louder than she'd intended.

He shifted his gaze to her. "We'll sell a selection, old and young, but the weaker ones."

"Although I see you've chosen some of the larger animals."

"Some horses are weak in bone and muscle, some in spirit. As with people."

He went back to his work.

Ellen frowned. She'd grown used to young men fawning in her presence, waiting for the gift of a word or two from her. It was mildly annoying that this servant, who had dared to lay hands on her a mere week ago, now seemed totally uninterested.

"Will you finish choosing today?" she asked.

His glance flickered to her again, then back to the horse, and this time he answered without stopping his examination. "I have to. Your cousin's men are ready to leave for York tomorrow."

She made two or three more attempts to engage him in conversation, but he was obviously concentrating on the work at hand. When she wasn't watching him, Ellen studied the groups of peasant families, most of whom had finished their picnics. The children were tumbling up and down the hill, obviously delighted at the unofficial holiday. The wives had begun packing away the food, and some were beginning to return to the village, with fond glances back at the menfolk, who had joined the children in their tomfoolery. For a moment, Ellen envied them all their simple existence.

"Milady should have a care that her skin doesn't suffer from so much sun," Connor said suddenly, breaking into her thoughts.

She looked at him in surprise. She hadn't seen him so much as glance at her skin or any other part of her, but the remark proved that at least he was not totally unaware of her presence.

"My skin's well seasoned, Master Brand. I've

never been one for veils and unguents. But I thank you for your concern.''

He smiled at her. "'Tis my profession to be concerned about the welfare of the living things in my care.''

"I'm not one of your broodmares. Nor am I even remotely in your care.'' She looked to be sure that none of the stable boys was within hearing. "You forget yourself yet again, horse master.''

His grin was unapologetic and said better than words that he was thinking of the moment when he had "forgotten himself'' the last time.

Ellen jumped to her feet, toppling the stool behind her. "I'm going to look around,'' she said. "I've not had a thorough tour of this place.''

Behind her, Sarah was seated on the grass next to Rolf. She got reluctantly to her feet when Ellen rose, but Ellen called to her, "Stay there if you like, Sarah, or go on home. I've no more need of you today.''

She was rewarded with the girl's instant smile as she bobbed a curtsy and murmured, "Thank you, milady.''

"If you're wandering alone,'' Connor said, without raising his head from the horse's hoof he was examining, "do not go out of sight of the stable yard.''

Ellen wanted to ignore his comment, but since two of the stable boys had come up leading the next horse, she answered, "I want to look around the stables. I've never seen any so large. And I've brought a sweet cake for Jocelyn.''

At that Connor finally looked up at her. "She's a horse, not a babe,'' he said, but his tone was more amused than chiding.

Perhaps twenty horses remained in the yard, still to be examined. The rest had either been led into the pen of those to be sold, or placed back in their stalls in the stable. Ellen wandered through the herd, wondering idly which would be chosen to go. In truth, they all looked magnificent to her, strong in muscle as well as spirit. She was happy the decision was not hers, and she was even happier that after some argument, Sebastian had agreed to limit his sale to a fifth of the total.

It did feel good to enter the shadowy stable after sitting so long outside. Though it was a mild day, the sun had warmed her through her heavy clothes.

She strolled aimlessly up one aisle of stalls and down another. They smelled of fresh hay, and each was neatly raked. She'd never seen a stable quite like it back in Normandy. Of course, she'd never seen a stable master like Connor Brand either.

At the far end of the aisle on the left was a small spiral staircase leading to a second floor. She remembered that Connor had said that he *lived* here. The idea was so absurd, she hadn't known whether to believe him, but perhaps this led to his living quarters. With a sudden spurt of mischief, she looked around to see if anyone was watching, then lifted her skirts and darted up the stairs.

As her head ascended through the hole in the floorboard, her mouth dropped open. She'd been expecting something on the order of a hayloft. Instead, she entered a well-furnished room. Nay, *lavishly* furnished, she realized, as she reached the top of the stairs and stepped into the room. Where had a stable master obtained such things?

The room was dominated by a huge table of ornate dark oak, piled with manuscripts. Cupboards and shelves lining the walls contained more wooden-and leather-bound books, and what appeared to be silver and gold plate as fine as any she'd found inside the castle itself.

In a daze, she wandered across the room and through a doorway at the far side into what was obviously his bedchamber. The bed itself was huge, definitely no peasant's cot, and the wardrobe was painted with designs that could only have been done by a hired master.

On a small table by his bed was a candle and one of the manuscripts such as she'd seen in the outer room. It was in Latin, she saw at once, and appeared to be a book of law.

Standing next to the table was, of all things, a lute. Ellen went to it and picked it up, and began to pluck the strings. The pitch was perfect. She shook her head in amazement, then sank down on the soft mattress of the bed and began to pick out a tune.

Her music tutors back home had given her up as hopeless, but it was only because they'd insisted on making her play the dreary songs they considered proper. Finally one day she'd heard a gypsy play at a town fair, and ever since that time she had secretly played on her own, selecting the notes that struck her fancy, the wild sweet sounds that the gypsy had played that starry night.

She wasn't sure how long she'd been lost in her playing, but she almost dropped the instrument when Connor Brand's voice came suddenly from the doorway. "You're a woman of many talents, milady," he said softly.

She jumped up from his bed, still holding the lute, her cheeks burning. "You startled me, Master Brand."

"I wager that I did. I'm a sight startled myself to come upon a beautiful noblewoman ensconced in my bed."

Ellen laid the lute on the bed. "I beg your pardon. 'Twas rude of me to come up here without your knowledge."

He walked across the room toward her. "I forgive you. Besides," he added, reaching out to swipe a gentle finger along her left cheek, "the discomfiture becomes you. It adds an extra blush to the rose of your cheeks."

She couldn't back away from him, as the bed was behind her. All at once she realized how vulnerable she was. She'd dismissed her only attendant, and the rest of her cousin's party had gone back to the castle. She was alone with her stable master in his *bedchamber*.

Her chin went up. "Have you finished your day's work, then, horse master?" she asked, hoping her tone befitted the mistress of the castle.

He was smiling down at her, the skin around his blue eyes crinkled after the full day outdoors. Rays from the setting sun streamed through the small window and cast reddish highlights into his blond hair.

"A man might think he was having an apparition to suddenly see such a sight in his bedchamber," he murmured, ignoring both her question and her attempt to establish once again their proper roles. His thumb lingered at the base of her chin.

Ellen closed her eyes. Mayhap 'twas the velvet in his voice that charmed the horses.

"An apparition sent by the faeries of the enchanted wood," he continued with the same husky tone. She knew then that he was going to kiss her.

Connor didn't believe in the faeries, but he was beginning to become convinced that Ellen of Wakelin had bewitched him. When Sarah Cooper had told him that she'd never seen her mistress emerge from the stable, he'd been a little alarmed. The day's work was finished, except for taking the remaining horses to their stalls, so he'd entrusted that task to John Cooper and the stable lads and had set off in search of Ellen. The last place he'd expected to find her was on his bed.

But as he'd stood in the door watching her, her black hair streaming out wild around her like one of the gypsies in the song she played, he'd known that he was going to have to kiss her again. If it meant he'd end up hanged on a gibbet in the village square, so be it.

Her lips were warm as summer sunshine and as giving. His arms went around her waist and lifted her against him, slender and pliant. "Ahh, sweetheart," he said in a whisper. "You've put a spell on me."

She returned his kiss and sought more, opening her lips to his with a small groan of passion at the back of her throat.

He turned sideways and braced a knee on the bed so that their bodies could rock together, seeking a communion that was impossible with the layers of clothing they wore.

Her hands added pressure at the back of his waist, and his slid boldly up her bodice to seek the swelling of her breasts. "Thou art a rare beauty, Ellen," he said in a cracked voice.

The sun had faded, leaving the room in near darkness. Inches away from the comfort of his own soft mattress, his loins ached with wanting her. A pulse thrummed wildly in his throat. She looked up at him, her golden eyes hooded and reflecting his own need. With a deep, shuddering breath, he eased her down to the bed, and took a long, safe step back.

"'Tis more than unwise for you to be here, milady," he said, more harshly than he had intended.

Ellen shivered with sudden cold as he released her. It took her a long moment to bring the dim room back into focus, to sort out exactly what had happened, to *believe* that he had actually let her go. He'd not only let her go, he was scolding her once again, as though she were a naughty child.

She felt awkward and embarrassed, lying on his bed, looking up at him. She struggled against the soft mattress to push herself up. Had this been another one of his tests to prove to her that she shouldn't be alone outside the castle? She felt shaky inside and a little sick.

How could this man kiss her that way, make her lose all sense of the world around her, and then simply let her go and step back with nothing more than curt, chiding words? She'd overlooked it once, back in the forest, but this time he'd pay for his knavery.

She stood up from the bed, her face an icy mask.

"You underestimate me, Master Brand. You think I'm powerless to punish you for your offenses because I don't want to call them to the attention of my cousin."

He seemed to wince, but his voice was strong as he answered, "Milady, believe me, I was not thinking of your cousin or much of anything else a few minutes ago. 'Twas an error, a grievous one. I ask your forgiveness."

She'd not expected that. When he'd kissed her in the forest he'd not appeared in the least sorry, nor had he apologized. "I could forgive once...."

He nodded firmly. "But not twice, you say. And you'd be absolutely right. Twice is unpardonable." As in the forest, he seemed to be regaining his control much more quickly than she. In fact, he had the audacity to grin. "My only defense is that the first kiss was too pleasurable to leave it at one."

He continued grinning as she started to speak, gave a huff, tried again, and finally gave up. Just what *did* she intend to do about horse master Connor Brand? He was right, the first kiss *had* been too pleasurable to leave it at one. And just where did that put them? For if the first had been pleasurable, the second had been *miraculous*.

She rolled to her feet, ignoring his offered hand, then shoved past him and stalked quickly across both rooms to the top of the stairs.

"Milady," he called after her. "'Tis coming on dark. You need protection back to the castle. Wait for me to escort you."

"I find your suggestion absurd, horse master," she called, frustration punctuating her words, "since the only one I've needed protection from since I've come to Lyonsbridge is *you!*'' Then she raced down the winding stairs to the dark stable below.

It disheartened Connor more than he had suspected to see the sixteen horses led away by the Norman soldiers. He'd chosen well, and none of the sixteen were top-quality animals; nevertheless, they were, of a fashion, his children, the only ones he ever expected to have. He'd long ago decided that he wanted no part of bringing children of his own into this new Norman world.

Saturday supper with the cooper's family would brighten his spirits, he decided. John had offered the invitation after the horse examining the previous day. Connor strode down the road to the village on foot, since he considered himself too gloomy to inflict his mood even on Thunder. He tried to sing a little, a bawdy ditty that usually made him smile, but the notes came out sour.

It wasn't just the horses, he admitted to himself as he reached the copse of trees that marked the halfway point between the castle and the village. It was Ellen. Though he wasn't afraid she'd report his kisses to her cousin, he knew that his behavior had been beyond reckless.

He did not intend to sire his own children, but he'd promised his father that he would take responsibility for all their former tenants. He had a family to care for—the people of Lyonsbridge—and he had no business risking his position for a few stolen moments of selfish pleasure.

The Coopers greeted him gaily, without the slight

reserve they'd shown when he'd been accompanied by Lady Ellen. Both twins bounded into his arms and Sarah flashed him a saucy smile.

"Whoa, Abel," he said to the little boy, who'd almost knocked to the floor a sack he carried. "You'll have your Sunday dinner in the dirt."

He reached around the clinging child and offered the sack to the widow, who was now strong enough to be moving almost normally around her home. "What have you brought us, Connor?" she asked fondly.

She peered into the sack, then exclaimed and drew out a plump duck. The family did not lack for meat, thanks to their supply of pork, but the duck was a rare treat. Both the twins looked at the fowl with eyes wide.

"Where did you get it, Connor?" asked the boy.

Connor set him on the floor, then set Karyn beside him, more gently. Squatting to bring himself to their level, he said, "I was walking by Milton's Pond the other day and suddenly I heard a tremendous splashing. Next thing I knew that big duck took a running jump over the water and flew right into the sack that was hanging at my waist."

Abel looked uncertainly from Connor to his brother, John, who was smiling. "Verily?" he asked, a little wary.

Connor laughed and tousled the boy's hair. "Something like that, lad. But it's not likely that that old duck will be so cooperative as to pluck itself, too. Who do you think might be able to help your mum with that task?"

"May I, mum?" he asked her.

She nodded, and then, as Karyn tugged at Abel's sleeve, he asked, "Karyn, too?"

"After supper you and I and Karyn will do it together," Connor told the boy. "Sarah can supervise."

Sarah and her mother were beginning to put dishes on the table, but the older girl's expression indicated that she did not have the same enthusiasm for the job as her younger siblings.

"Or we can do it by ourselves," Connor amended.

"Sarah's got a sweetheart," John said with the teasing singsong of an older brother. He sang a few off-key bars of a light courting ballad, but broke off when Sarah made a face at him.

Connor was surprised. He'd seen Sarah with the page yesterday, a likely enough lad, he supposed. But courting? He'd held the girl when she was a babe, though she was now full thirteen years, age enough to be married. Suddenly he was hit by a wave of protectiveness, as if he were, indeed, the father he'd pictured himself on the road into the village.

He frowned. "'Tis Rolf, I warrant?" he asked.

Her blushes answered, making the nod of her head unnecessary.

"Mayhap Rolf would like to help us pluck the duckling?" he asked, realizing as the question left his mouth that the suggestion was preposterous. Connor himself had made enough Saturday-night courting forays into the village over the years to know that plucking ducks with the maid's family was not what was on a young swain's mind. At eight and twenty, Connor was but fifteen years older than Sarah herself. But he felt old.

The fare at the Coopers' was always delicious. Agnes had taught her daughter the skills she'd learned from *her* mother, who had been the best cook in several shires, often called up to the castle by Connor's grandmother for special feast days.

Connor and John made short work of an entire stack of barley cakes, while Sarah and the smaller children played idly with their suet pudding.

"I'd not thought to ever marry, Widow Cooper, but food like this is a powerful attraction," Connor joked, licking the last bits of grease off his fingers, while giving his hostess a quick wink. He turned to John. "Would you see your mum out of widow's weeds, lad?"

John chuckled. Agnes Cooper was in truth not much older than Connor, but her hard life and her disease had turned her into an old woman. Nevertheless, Connor's teasing had put color in her cheeks and a touch of youth to her expression. For a moment, the ghost of the village beauty of old smiled around the table at them all.

"Would you have more pudding, Connor?" she asked.

"Nay, I'll be as stout as Harry, the stone mason, if you keep feeding me thus, mistress."

The twins giggled, since Harry Mason was a favorite of theirs, but it was true that the jolly man was as wide as the brick walls he laid.

"Best enjoy it now, Connor," Agnes said, the mirth dying from her face. "This is the last of the currants and spices. There are no more to be had in town."

Connor frowned. "Has no one traveled to market?"

"No one has the coin to buy anything at market anymore."

John added, "Sir William's men have been on another round of tax collecting. They've taken nearly everything that's not been cemented down by Master Mason's trowel."

"What reason do they give this time?" Connor asked.

"Taxes for the king, they say," John answered bitterly, "but in truth most suspect that the taxes are to line Sebastian Phippen's purse."

"John," his mother admonished. "Have a care."

Connor looked from the widow to her son. "Your mother's right, John. Saxons can no longer afford to speak freely in this land. We must measure every word spoken, even within the family. One knows not who might be within earshot."

As if in confirmation of his remark, there was a sudden knocking on the door of the cottage.

Sarah jumped up. "'Tis Rolf," she said, her voice elevated.

But when she pulled open the wooden door, it was not her young page on the other side, but Sir William himself. His darting eyes appeared to take in every detail of her appearance, the black pupils lit with eagerness. It was several moments before he looked behind her to notice Connor's presence at the Coopers' table. He scowled at the horse master.

"What are you doing here, Brand?" he asked gruffly.

Connor stood slowly. "I was invited, Sir William," he said evenly. "What are you doing here?"

William looked down at his feet, suddenly ill at

ease. No one spoke as the family waited for his answer. Finally he looked up and said, "'Tis but a friendly call. I didn't know the family would have company."

Connor stepped out from behind the bench he'd been occupying. A friendly call? From the castle bailiff? Not likely. He looked from William to Sarah, and a shiver of disquiet ran down his back.

He walked over to the door, his tall frame towering over the short bailiff. "Widow Cooper is not yet recovered from her recent attack. She was about to retire," he told the man, careful to keep his voice calm. "Mayhap you'd care to state your business, Sir William."

Sir William licked his lips and once again looked over to Sarah, then back at Connor. "If the widow is feeling poorly, I'll call another evening," he said after a moment.

"As you wish," Connor told him.

The man backed out of the doorway, his eyes still darting furtively to Sarah, much like an animal keeping track of prey.

Connor reached around the girl to close the door behind him. "Has he bothered you, Sarah?" he asked her.

The girl's eyes were troubled. "I like him not. He looks like a rat," she said with a little shudder.

Connor did not press her further. "Best be sure you stay with Lady Ellen at all times when you're up at the castle. I'll speak to her about it, if you like."

"Oh, please do not, Master Brand," Sarah said quickly. "She might not let me come anymore, and then I'd not see—"

She broke off and Connor gave a sigh. "Tell your Rolf to watch out for you when you're at the castle and walking to and fro. We may need to design a plan to keep you out of William's way."

"But you'll not tell Lady Ellen?"

"Nay, I'll not tell her."

Sarah nodded, relieved, but Connor felt no such relief. The incident had given him a sense of foreboding. Sarah was a pretty young thing, and it wouldn't be the first time that a castle bailiff had decided to award himself with the maidenhood of one of his tenants.

Indeed, there were many things for Connor to be thinking about, he told himself sternly as he thanked the widow once again and made ready to leave. He had a large family to protect, and he'd best use his time to that end, rather than in senseless dreaming about the golden eyes of the castle's mistress.

Chapter Eight

It was unfair to Jocelyn, Ellen decided finally. She'd stayed away from the stables for nearly ten days, busying herself with all the changes she was making in the castle, which to her gratification was now beginning to look as tidy as any back home. But she missed her daily rides.

She'd almost convinced herself to hold out yet one more day. Then Sarah had asked to leave early in order to stop and pick up a knife she'd left for mending at the ironsmith's, and Ellen had decided that a brisk ride before twilight would be too enjoyable to pass up. With luck, she wouldn't even see the horse master. He'd probably finished his work for the day, and it was too early for the evening feeding.

Her eyes went to the narrow window toward the roof of the stable, which she now knew looked into Connor Brand's bedchamber. Mayhap he was there now, perusing those books of his. In the heat of their encounter, she hadn't been able to ask how it was that a humble horse keeper had more books than she'd seen together in one place other than the great abbeys.

Her father had taught her to read Latin and Greek and French, but it was a rarity, even in Normandy. Books were more precious than jewels. Yet her horse master had at least twenty of them, by her rough count.

She peered cautiously into the stable. It seemed to be empty, as she had hoped. With a smug little smile, she made her way down to Jocelyn's stall. She'd never attempted to saddle the horse herself, but she'd watched it done countless times. If the slight young boys who worked the yard could do it, she could.

It took a bit of struggle, but standing on a block of wood that she pushed over to the horse's side, she managed to flop the saddle in place and tighten the cinches. Jocelyn recognized her mistress's touch and stood peacefully throughout the process.

There was still no sign of Connor Brand or anyone else as she boosted herself onto Jocelyn's back and made her way outside, proud of her feat and looking forward to the ride.

She had perhaps three-quarters of an hour before twilight, she decided, steering her mount away from the road and up a grassy incline at the rear of the stables. She'd ride just a few minutes, see what was on the other side of the hill, then head back, unsaddle the horse, and no one would ever learn of her adventure.

Jocelyn seemed equally pleased to be out on the mild afternoon. There was a moist hint of spring in the air. Ellen took a great, cleansing breath and smiled.

Connor swore softly as he watched the solitary horse pick its way up the hill to the west of the stable yard. He'd been sitting in a window seat in his study. He'd designed it so that he could catch every possible ray of sun to read his manuscripts. They were his only remaining legacy from the old days. His parents had collected them from the far corners of Europe, and whereas he'd kept few other items from the family treasures, he'd been sure to keep every single one of the books.

Carefully he closed the illuminated tome, a particularly precious one written in a Germanic script he could only partially decipher. With occasional help from Martin, he'd been working on it for the past year. It was his escape from the world of Lyonsbridge, his one concession to his old life. In years past, he'd taken his escape in other ways with the obligingly friendly village girls, but these dalliances had become increasingly rare as he'd begun to feel more and more the weight of the responsibility his father had placed on his shoulders with his dying charge.

It was that responsibility that spurred him now, he told himself. Lady Ellen might be too spoiled or too foolish to recognize the danger, but Connor knew that his worry had not been idle. Most of the men of Lyonsbridge were good people, but there were still too many lawless elements in England for a beautiful woman to be safe wandering about the countryside alone.

He clattered down the stairs, threw a saddle on Thunder and headed out. She'd not have gone far.

Thunder seemed energized by the unexpected ride at this hour of the day. Connor felt his body awak-

ening to the horse's beat, his mind slowly leaving the
dusty depths of his books and bringing into focus
once again the image that had haunted it for too many
days and nights—the lady Ellen, laughing up at him,
lips full and red as berries, breasts thrust high.

He took in a deep breath of the mild February air.
It appeared they were about to be alone together once
again. He considered whether these continued trials
were some kind of penance sent to him for his dere-
liction in keeping the holy sacraments. "You said
you'd pray for me, Martin," he muttered under his
breath. "Mayhap now would be a good time."

He caught up with her easily, and she, of course,
knew that it would be he. In a way, she'd known he
would come, no matter how much she'd told herself
that she'd wanted to escape him.

She laughed back at him, challenging him to scold
her, but he didn't even make the attempt.

He pulled Thunder up beside her without speaking
and in silent accord, they let the two horses stretch
out into a race, their long legs burning the ground
underneath them, horses and riders exhilarated in the
dying afternoon sun.

The two mounts stayed neck and neck, neither trying to win, as if they knew that the race they ran had
nothing to do with speed.

Finally, the glowing orb of the sun sank behind a
low hill to the west, and Ellen pulled Jocelyn up.
Without Connor's bidding, Thunder stopped beside
the mare.

"'Tis a beautiful evening," Ellen said, a little
breathless from the ride.

"Aye." There was still none of the expected reprimand.

"I've not ridden her for too long," she said. "'Twas overdue."

"The mount's available anytime milady wishes," Connor said. He swung off his horse's back. "We'll walk them a spell to cool them down before we start back."

He reached up for her, but as soon as she jumped into his arms, he set her on the ground, avoiding any unnecessary contact of their bodies. Ellen tried to push away a feeling of disappointment.

He handed her Jocelyn's reins and began walking down the hill they'd just climbed, leading Thunder behind him. Ellen followed, her shoes slipping on the soft grass.

"Will we get back by dark?" she asked, finding the silence awkward.

He looked toward the west, at the darkening pink on the horizon. "Nay," he said.

"But you know well the route?"

"Aye."

She concentrated on making her way down the hill without stumbling. Connor did not look at her, but his expression did not appear hostile. Finally she asked flatly, "Are you angry with me, horse master?"

He stopped walking and gave her a long, steady look. "I've warned you about riding alone, milady, but I knew ten seconds after meeting you that you were a maid who does as she pleases."

"Are you saying that I am spoiled, then?"

His eyes studied her in the growing darkness. "Mayhap. Or call it stubborn, if you like."

She crinkled her forehead. "I'm not sure I do."

"'Twas not my intention to offend you."

His voice vibrated low with the husky resonance she'd heard before. He stood not inches from her. Each still held the reins of their horse, but the rest of the world had seemed to melt into some kind of vague background, leaving only the two of them, standing face-to-face, feeling it once again, this thing between them.

"What *was* your intention, horse master?" she asked, her own voice now gone hoarse, as well.

He dropped Thunder's reins and seized her. "This," he growled. Then he was kissing her, as he had before, but this time, in the darkness, Ellen felt the kiss like a quake through her entire body. Her feet left the ground and she was melted against him, merging with him, it seemed, as though their two beings were fusing into one.

"'Twas your intention, as well, was it not?" he murmured, still kissing her. "When you rode out today, you knew I'd come."

Of course, he was right. She *had* known.

Their horses moved away, forgotten, and somehow the two lovers tumbled to the ground, seeking more contact, deeper contact.

"I want thee, princess," Connor whispered to her. "'Tis a kind of madness you've set on me."

She couldn't answer. Her mind was too awash in new sensations as his hands made sensuous circles over her breasts and his lips nuzzled hers, then her chin, then the lobe of her ear.

An ache had begun in her loins, coming in waves with each movement of his fingers across her nipples.

She was filled with new and shocking longings. She wanted to be quit of her layers of clothing and feel his skin against her.

"Aye," she finally managed to whisper. "I want thee, too, horse master."

He stopped moving, but did not release her. Some of the desire had fled from his expression, replaced by sudden awareness and surprise.

Don't stop, don't stop, she repeated inside her head, but the words came out as a mere nod.

He appeared to be thinking, wrestling with himself. Finally he boosted himself to his feet and pulled her up beside him. She looked at him, her eyes hurt. Every portion of her body was clamoring a protest, but she was too proud to give it voice.

He spoke solemnly. "Aye, princess. I believe this thing is meant to be between us, though we've both fought against it. But I'll not take you here on the cold ground."

She shook her head in confusion, wishing he hadn't let her go. She'd wanted the delicious feelings to continue, but now there was only the cold air rushing over her, cooling her body and her brain.

In an instant he'd retrieved Thunder and mounted, then reached a hand down to her. She looked over to where Jocelyn stood nearby. "Nay," he told her. "You'll ride with me, in my arms. I'll not let you go this night."

So she let him pull her up in front of him and leaned back against him as they started back toward the castle, leading Jocelyn behind them. Her eyes closed and her mind drifted again to those few moments on the grass, as he whispered sweet things in her ear and moved his hand, slow and sure against the flat of her stomach. Once he lifted her hair and kissed the back of her neck and another time he stopped riding entirely to turn her in his arms for another long, drugging kiss. She hardly realized when they arrived once again at the stables.

Her eyes stayed closed as he tenderly lifted her down and held her locked between his own hard body and the side of his saddle, while he kissed her again, deep and hard.

"Just stay here a moment, sweetheart, while I stable the horses," he told her softly. "I'll be right back for you."

She almost collapsed when he withdrew his arms from around her, but a sudden gust of evening breeze cooled her face and her ardor. She opened her eyes. The breeze traveled along her arms and she shivered, awareness returning.

Connor may have decided to remove their lovemaking to a more private and comfortable spot in order to protect his own safety. A servant caught making love to the lady of the castle could easily be executed. However, she had the feeling that if his decision to return had been deliberate, it was not done out of fear, but rather to give her time to consider her actions. If she had a grain of sense, she'd flee back to the castle, as fast as she could, but her feet seemed rooted to the soft mud of the stable yard.

"Art certain, Ellen?" His low voice came from behind her, making her jump.

The sound of her name on his lips was sweeter than his earlier endearments. She turned and went into his arms. "Aye," she said in a throaty whisper, then offered her lips.

"I'll take thee upstairs," he said after claiming the kiss. "No one will disturb us, unless they'll miss you at the castle?"

She shook her head. "Sebastian knows not how I spend my days and cares less. He sups each night with his beloved ledger."

Connor nodded, evidently satisfied that their tryst could go undetected. He smiled at her, a smile so young and charming and heartbreaking that it made her gasp. "Shall I carry thee to my bower, princess?"

Tears sprung to her eyes. This was a moment she'd thought of for years, but never in a thousand lifetimes had she pictured it thus, in a stable yard with a common horseman. Yet her heart was soaring and her body thrummed with anticipation.

Tomorrow she'd deal with the consequences of this folly, but for tonight, she'd give herself up to this miracle, for miracle it was. That mysterious and miraculous force she'd heard sung in the ballads and had, indeed, sung of herself, had finally overtaken her. For the first time in her life, Ellen of Wakelin was in love.

She returned his smile. "I'd not tire you, horse master," she said, teasing, her breath high in her throat.

He grinned and scooped her up as if she were no more than a sack of feathers. "I want you to tire me, sweet maid. I promise I'll not beg for mercy."

He began walking toward the stable door, suddenly in a hurry. Ellen put her arms around his neck and clung to him. She could feel the pounding of his heart, even through the thick doublet he wore.

"Master Brand!" a voice cried from just down the road to the village.

Connor stopped briefly, then started walking again, faster. It took Ellen a moment to realize that the summons had been real, someone from the outside asking entry to this private world of theirs.

"It's someone calling you," she said, her voice small.

Connor swore, but finally stopped and set her down on the ground. He ran both hands back through his hair, frustration mirrored in his features.

He narrowed his eyes, looking up the road in the dusk. "It's all right," he said. "I think 'tis John Cooper."

Mayhap all was not lost. He could speak to the lad, then they could resume their plans, but somehow Ellen knew that the moment had been broken. Even if John's mission was something trivial, it would be hard to regain the feeling she and Connor had established back on the hill.

The two stood side by side, awaiting John's approach. The boy was running. As he neared they could see that his narrow chest heaved with exertion. Light from the rising moon glinted off streaks of tears on his cheeks.

"What is it, John?" Connor asked, with no sign of his anger at the interruption.

John stumbled the last few steps and nearly fell at their feet. Connor reached out to hold him steady. "Has something happened?" he asked grimly.

"Is it your mother?" Ellen added.

John shook his head and opened his mouth, but all that came out were several gulping sobs. Ellen moved next to him and put a hand on his bony back, which was shaking with tears or with fear. She looked at Connor, who shook his head helplessly.

After a moment, John's crying subsided enough for him to make himself understood, but the words that emerged were more alarming than his tears. "I've killed him," he said between gasps. "I've killed Sir William."

Chapter Nine

At first they could scarcely credit the boy's story. To begin with, John was a smallish lad, no match for a seasoned knight such as William Booth.

But the lad continued to sob out his account, in bits and pieces. "'Twas Sarah's screaming brought me there," he explained. "Sir William had 'er against a tree, with her skirt pushed up and her bodice torn right down her front."

Ellen clasped her hands to her chest, her face widening in horror.

Connor put a steadying hand on the boy's shoulder. "What happened then, John?"

"When I yelled at him, he just laughed and said, 'Get away, boy, my business is with your sister.' So I jumped on his back, but then he smashed his arm across my face and flung me backward like a bothersome fly."

For the first time Ellen saw that a rivulet of blood trailed from the side of John's mouth. "Are you hurt?" she asked.

John shook his head impatiently, unconcerned with

his own injuries. Now that the tale was half-told, he appeared eager to finish the telling. ''While he was throwing me off, Sarah tried to run, but he caught her and slammed her back against the tree. His arm was pressing into her throat and I saw her go limp. There was a knife on the ground. 'Twas ours, I think, that had been broken. Sarah must have fetched it from the ironsmith.''

Ellen felt as if she were about to be sick. Connor reached out an arm to steady her, then turned back to John. ''What happened then? Tell me *exactly*, John. 'Tis important.''

''I shouted 'let her go!' Sir William laughed again, and his eyes looked wild, darting around, black and beadylike. So I picked up the knife and held it out toward him.'' The boy's eyes were glazed as he seemed to be reliving the fatal moment.

Connor nodded, calmly. ''Did you lunge at him?''

John shook his head. ''He took his arm from Sarah's neck and she slumped down the tree. I was afeared that he'd killed her. Then he drew a hunting knife from his belt and said, 'I'll deal with you first, annoying toad.'''

''He had his own weapon, and he drew it?''

''Aye. He thrust it down toward my chest, but I jumped to one side, and as I did he fell forward.'' He took a big gulp. The sobs had stopped. ''The tip of my knife slid up under his chin as he fell, smooth as biting into a wheel of cheese.''

Ellen shuddered, and Connor looked grim faced.

John rubbed his eyes and spoke in bewildered tones. ''He caved to one side, pulling the knife from my hands, and then he was dead. 'Twas that simple. 'Twas that quick.''

Connor took in a deep breath. "Where's the knife?''

John looked confused. "The knife?''

"Your knife, lad. Where is it?''

"I know not. I...'tis still stuck in him, I suppose.''

"And Sarah?''

"She recovered herself just as it happened. I told her to run on home to tell Mother, and that I was coming to find you.''

"'Twas self-defense,'' Ellen said. "Or at the very least, 'twas defense of his sister's honor.''

Connor spared her a brief glance. "That matters not, even if we could prove such a thing. If 'tis discovered that John did this thing, he will hang.''

She shook her head. "We need to tell his story—''

Connor interrupted her with an impatient wave of his hand. "You may be a Norman, but you don't know anything about Norman justice. At least not *English* Norman justice.'' He turned to John. "We've little time. They'll be looking for the culprit as soon as the body is discovered. We've got to try to retrieve that knife.''

"I'll go to my cousin and tell him the real story. He'd not let them harm the boy over such a thing.''

Connor looked at her, his expression calculating and cold. "I'm sorry, but I'm going to have to ask you to come with us for a spell.''

She wasn't sure she had heard him correctly. "Come with you?''

"Aye. I'm afraid you know too much about this incident. Until John and his entire family are safely hidden away, I can't risk the story being told." She began to protest, but he cut her off. "I've not time to argue. You can come with me peaceably on your own mount or ride more uncomfortably with John and me on Thunder."

"I'm not going anywhere," she said, her color heightening with indignation. Her heart ached for John's plight, but she felt a selfish stab of disappointment that the incident had spoiled what was about to happen between her and Connor. All traces of the lover who had moments ago lifted her in his arms was gone. Connor was looking at her as if she were his most bitter enemy.

Connor ignored her and turned to John. "We'll ride to your house, and I want you to get your family and take them into the woods, quickly. Take only what you can easily carry. We'll try to collect more of your things later if we can. When I've left you there, I'll go back for the knife. At least that should give us time before they discover that your sister had been to the ironsmith today."

"Aye, Master Brand," John replied, his voice confident and trusting. Telling his story to the horse master seemed to have allowed him to regain his self-control.

Once again addressing Ellen, Connor said briskly, "Shall I help you mount, milady? Or do you ride with me?"

"I'm not riding anywhere," she said again, her own voice stiffening to match his tone. "You need not fear that I'll reveal any of this. By the holy rood, I'd not cause Sarah or her family harm."

Connor seemed to hesitate, but finally said, "I'm

sorry. 'Twill be safer to have you with us.'' He reached to take her arm and move her toward the horses. She pulled out of his grasp.

"You have my word, horse master," she said angrily. "I suggest you get started with your plans. Good luck, John," she added to the boy in kinder tones. "Once you and your family are safely hidden, I'll do what I can to get this matter resolved."

Then she turned and started toward the castle. Connor followed her with two long strides and lifted her in his arms. He'd done the same thing only minutes before, but the tension between them now was of an entirely different nature. "I'm sorry, milady," he said again. Then he asked John, "Do you think you can ride Thunder?"

John nodded and stepped toward the big stallion without hesitation. Connor continued, "Lady Ellen and I will ride her mount."

John cast a doubtful glance at the sidesaddle on Jocelyn. "I'll take that one if you like."

Connor gave the boy a brief smile. "Thank you, lad, but I'll manage. Thunder's less skittish with a new rider than Lady Ellen's mount."

Ellen had been struggling in his arms during the entire exchange over the horses, and he'd been ignoring her sputtering protests. Now he looked down at her and said, "If you're not quiet, I'll tie a rag around your mouth. There may be guardsmen within earshot, and I don't want them unduly alarmed. We need all the time we can get."

"Let me go," she gasped, fighting him in earnest. "You can't take me with you. It's outrageous." She could have called out to raise an alarm, but though she was furious with Connor, she didn't want to be the cause of John's capture.

"Will you mount peaceably?" he asked, loosening his grip slightly. She took advantage of the slack to wriggle out of his arms and once again dash toward the castle.

With a grunt of exasperation, Connor hauled her back once more, then threw her up on Jocelyn's back, face-down, and mounted behind her. She kicked at his legs in protest. "Hold still, princess," he said, keeping her in place with a firm hand on her back. Then he nodded to John to begin to ride.

For the sake of her pride, she continued squirming all the way out to the road, but she remained silent until they were well out of earshot of any Norman guards. The truth was that her indignation had faded the moment he'd called her princess. The incident might have reminded Connor of their differences, but she had the feeling that it would not be easy for him to forget what had almost happened between them.

Ellen's body was a mass of aches from being bounced along hanging upside down like a sack of onions. Her ribs were bruised and perhaps even broken, she decided, gingerly running her hands over them. They'd ridden for what seemed like hours, finally stopping in the middle of nowhere. Connor had unceremoniously dumped her from the horse and said curtly, "Wait here. Don't move," then had disappeared, horse and all, into the thick trees.

She looked around the clearing and up at the sky, where the nearly full moon was now directly overhead. It was the middle of the night and the clear air had turned cold.

She rubbed her arms, shivering. Surely the horse master hadn't abandoned her out in the forest? Though at this point, she couldn't be certain of anything. There'd been no repetition of the slip of the tongue when he'd called her princess. He'd treated her roughly, without mercy, eventually even carrying out his threat to tie a kerchief around her mouth until she'd begun coughing so badly that he'd relented, upon her promise of silence.

He'd never once relaxed his vigilance long enough to give her a chance to escape, even as he talked with the Cooper family and several other villagers who'd volunteered to take the family and their belongings into the woods.

Connor had resaddled the mare when they arrived at the village, and holding her firmly had allowed Ellen to sit awkwardly in front of him. They rode toward the spot where the killing had taken place, but before they reached it, they could hear horsemen and shouts. Sir William's body had obviously already been discovered. It had been then that Connor had tied the kerchief over her mouth, before he'd wheeled Jocelyn around and headed in the opposite direction.

Ellen had no idea where they had ridden. All she could see was the circle of dark trees and the sky overhead. She had a feeling that they'd ridden toward the coast. Indeed, there was a tang of salt in the air. But from where she was, she could see nothing but forest. If Connor had left her here, she'd have no choice but to find a place to curl up and try to keep warm until morning.

She walked toward the nearest tree, slowly feeling the numbness drain from her legs. She was angry with the horse master, of course, but she was worried, too. She'd seen Sarah when they'd stopped in the village, and the girl's anguished eyes haunted her. If young John Cooper was executed for saving his sister from that dirty toad of a man, Ellen, too, would never again trust Norman justice.

The ground was mossy and soft. It would not make a bad bed for the night, if not for the cold. She knelt down next to the big tree trunk, feeling around with her hands for any jagged rocks. There was a crunching of branches behind her, someone walking toward her.

"Lady Ellen!" It was Connor's voice. She let out a sigh of relief, then felt a renewed surge of irritation at her horse master. He'd frightened and abused her enough for one evening, and it was time she told him so. She stood and put her hands on her hips, waiting for him.

"There you are."

He came from the opposite direction of the sounds. She whirled around to face him. "I demand that you take me back to Lyonsbridge. It has been a tragic night, I'll warrant, and I'll not hold your deeds against you, but this has gone far enough. Take me back now, or my cousin shall hear of this treatment. 'Twill but compound the problems."

Connor walked up to her, with a semblance of his old, mocking smile. "'Tis late, milady. Best let me show you to your chambers. We'll talk things over in the morning."

Ellen looked around, confused. "My chambers? We must be miles from the castle by now."

"Aye. But our friends here have kindly offered us shelter for the night." He stopped and stepped aside so she could see that in the dark shadows of the trees were others, watching her. "The Coopers are already installed in their quarters. I daresay they're exhausted, poor souls."

"How is Sarah?" Ellen asked, concerned in spite of her anger.

Connor's smile turned sweeter. "The girl's fine. It appears that..." He hesitated. "The knave was interrupted in time," he finished simply.

"Blessed St. Mary be thanked," Ellen breathed.

"And blessed John Cooper," Connor added dryly.

Ellen nodded. "Aye. 'Twas good fortune."

"A good fortune that will alter the lad's life forever," Connor pointed out, his voice grim. "He'll be hunted from this day forth."

"There must be something we can do."

Connor shook his head. "The thinking will keep until morning. Come."

He took her hand and she went with him willingly, not seeing any other immediate option. None of the people who had come with him to the grove spoke. They appeared to be peasants, poorly dressed and thin. Had they come upon a band of gypsies? she wondered.

"What is this place?"

"Our home, for this night, at least. Have no fear, milady. No one will harm you here."

They emerged from the trees at what appeared to be the top of a cliff. With the moon now behind the clouds, the night was too dark to see beyond the rock in front of them, but the sea air was now unmistakable, and she could hear the crashing of the surf in the distance. One by one, the men who had accompanied Connor disappeared over the edge of the rock.

"Can you climb?" Connor asked her, a smile in his voice.

"Where are we going?" she asked.

He ignored her question, saying, "Follow me." Then he pulled on her hand and led her over the lip of the cliff. The path down was not as steep as it had appeared, and she had little trouble keeping up with him, though her slippers slid a couple of times on loose rocks.

When they reached the bottom, she looked around. All she could see were trees in front of her and the rock face behind her. But the men who had descended before them had disappeared.

Ellen looked at Connor, mystified. He simply smiled, pulled on her hands and led the way around a simple bend in the rock. Suddenly they were within a large cavern, lit by cookfires that cast long, spidery shadows on the limestone walls.

Ellen looked around in awe. "What is this place?"

Connor stopped and let her survey the scene before them. "This, princess, is what is left of free Saxon England."

"Welcome, milady," said one of the ragged peasants from behind them, with a cackling laugh.

"You should never have brought her here, Connor." Walter Little scowled at his former liege lord. He'd been a squire under Connor's father, and his

special duty had been to teach the three Brand sons
the art of combat. But when Geoffrey Brand died,
Walter had had a falling out with Connor, disagreeing
with his decision to seek peace in the struggle with
the Norman conquerers.

Walter had been the leader of a group of malcontents who had tried to continue the fighting and had
been outlawed for their efforts.

"I had no choice but to bring her, Walter," Connor
explained patiently. His former tutor was an old man
now, and Connor had learned to be tolerant of his
hotheaded ways. "If she'd returned to the castle to
give alarm, we'd not have gotten the Cooper family
away from the village."

Both men looked over to a corner of the cave,
where Agnes Cooper and her children were setting up
their campsite. The cold walls of a sea-carved cave
were poor replacements for their cozy cottage back at
the village, but at least here they would be safe from
retaliation for William Booth's death.

"They'll be harrying us all the more with the chit
missing," Walter grumbled. "And now what are ye
planning to do with her?"

Connor had been asking himself the same question.
In the scramble to get John safely away, he'd not
made plans beyond the moment. Now, thinking with
a cooler head, he realized that he could have seen the
Coopers off to the cave shelter and ridden with Ellen
somewhere else until it was safe to take her back to
the castle. Instead, he'd been intent on seeing that
John and his family were safe, which meant he'd
brought the mistress of the Norman castle right into
the heart of the Saxon hideout.

"I should not have brought her here," he agreed finally, meeting Walter's accusing stare. "But 'tis late to rethink that. She's here, though I doubt that she could find the place if we let her go."

Walter shook his head and squinted his one good eye. The other had been destroyed in a joust many years before. That and his matted gray locks gave him a fearsome appearance, but Connor held no fear of his old teacher. "Ye cannot let her go, boy. She may not know the road, but she can smell the sea and hear the surf. All they would have to do is search the coast and eventually they'd find this place."

Damnation, but he was right. Connor restrained himself from spewing a string of oaths in self-anger. Walter had ever been strict about such abuse of language. "I don't think she'd reveal our secret," he said, but there was uncertainty in his voice.

"Are you sure enough of that to risk seeing every living soul in this place hanging from a gibbet?"

Connor leaned forward to warm his hands at the small fire they were sharing. He sighed and said, "Nay."

"Ye have a dilemma, boy," Walter pointed out. "If we kill the girl, we could as well start the war all over again."

Connor straightened up. "No harm will come to her," he snapped.

The old man cocked his head and regarded Connor through an eye that was still sharp within the aged folds of skin. "What is this maid to you, Connor?" he asked.

"By the rood, Walter, she's the lord's daughter. If we so much as harm a hair on her head, we might as well set a torch to the entire shire, 'twill be that devastating the Norman's vengeance.''

The old soldier shifted uncomfortably on the cold stone floor. "I've no more stomach for battle," he said.

Connor's eyes took on a glint of amusement for the first time since he'd arrived at the cave. "Nay, I'll not believe that, you old warhorse."

Walter nodded across the cave to where Connor had left Ellen with a nest of blankets, bidding her to sleep. She was still awake, seated upright on the blankets, her back propped against the cave wall behind her. She was watching them. "She's a beauty, that one. I trow she's started more than one conflict in her short years."

Connor followed his gaze across the room. He tried to give Ellen a reassuring smile, but her expression remained hostile. Turning back to Walter, he said, "I'll take her back at daybreak."

Walter shook his head in disgust. "I'm too old for fighting and too old for loving. And there are days when I thank God that both those forms of madness are behind me."

"I'll make her pledge not to reveal this place."

"Aye, and make her pledge to turn your stable straw into gold as well, for she'll be as likely to carry it out. She's *Norman*, lad."

Connor stood. "'Tis almost dawn, old man," he told his tutor. "You can still get some sleep."

Walter shook his head sadly. "None of us will sleep easy until this is resolved, Connor," he said sadly. "But go to her now, for I read from your eyes into your heart, and I see her there."

Connor gave him a sad smile, then walked across the echoing cavern toward Ellen.

Her gold eyes, which had laughed up at him, melting and warm, only hours before, were now as glittery and hard as the metal itself. "I was hoping you'd sleep," he said to her, dropping down to one knee beside her on the blankets.

"I'm not accustomed to sleeping on the floor."

He had sympathy for her plight, but the resumption of her imperious tone rankled, making his voice more caustic than he had intended. "I suspect most of these people were not accustomed to sleeping on the floor before they were forced to flee here by Norman justice."

Ellen looked around the room. "Who are they?" she asked, her animosity momentarily replaced with curiosity.

Connor shrugged. "Just folks. Most were from regular families from the area. Many of them lost loved ones, which influenced their decision to fight on after the Normans were already firmly entrenched. They were outlawed by William's son, and have been so ever since. Some of their families have joined them here, since all their possessions were forfeit as well."

Ellen's eyes grew wide. "Then they've been living like this for *years?*"

"Some of them."

"But how do they survive?"

"As you see them. The caves are their shelter. They get food from poaching, when they can, or from thievery, and from contributions from Lyonsbridge."

"The villagers help them?"

Connor nodded. "Aye. They are their friends, their relatives, some of them."

Ellen was quiet and appeared to be affected by the outlaws' plight, but after a moment, her haughty expression returned as she said to Connor, "None of this explains why you've brought me here. I demand that you take me back to the castle."

As Connor had told Walter, such had been his intention, but looking at her now, her aristocratic face turned up in disdain as her gaze swept around the cave, he was beginning to think that his mentor had been right. Could he afford to risk the lives of all the people here by allowing her to return home? On the other hand, keeping her here would surely bring down upon them the wrath of her father's men. Connor had a dilemma on his hands, and he was too tired to deal with it this night.

He jumped to his feet. "Princess," he said with a smile, "give the floor a try. You might even find that you like it. I've heard that a hard bed gives one a nice straight back." Then he gave a mocking bow and left her.

Chapter Ten

She'd fallen asleep, after all. She'd intended to stay awake, watching for a moment when she could steal away unobserved, but the one-eyed man Connor had been talking with earlier continued to sit by the fire, glancing her way often enough to let her know that she was under surveillance. Finally exhaustion had taken over, and she'd curled up on one of the blankets, pulled another over her and slept.

When she awoke, the eerie cavern of the previous evening had an entirely different aspect. The fires still burned, but daylight filtered in through the mouth and several overhead cracks in the walls. A mist from the nearby sea gave the air a salty smell that combined with the odor of salted pork cooking at a fire across the way. To her surprise, her stomach rumbled with hunger.

As she sat up, rubbing the sleep from her eyes, Sarah Cooper approached, holding a twin's hand in each of hers. "Good morning, milady," she said shyly.

Ellen glanced quickly around the cave, but saw no

sign of Connor. The old man who had been watching her the previous evening was also gone. "Good morrow," she answered. She would not inflict any of her exasperation on Sarah, who was not the cause of her plight. In fact, her servant girl had been a victim, as well. "How are you, Sarah? You're suffering no ill effects of the attack?"

Sarah waggled her head nervously and glanced down at Karyn. "I'd not speak of it, milady," she pleaded.

Ellen nodded. "Of course." She looked at the two younger children. "This is an adventure, is it not, coming to a big cave like this?"

Karyn nodded, her eyes grave and wide, but Abel spoke. "She wonders if this is where the dragon lives, 'lady. The one you was to bring her."

Ellen had forgotten all about her promise to the child. "No, sweetling. I'm sorry that I came away without the dragon I meant to bring you. We all had to leave fast. I wager you and your brother had to leave some of your things behind, as well."

Karyn's blond head bobbed.

"But the dragon I have for you is a little wooden one, not real, remember? And there are no dragons here in this cave."

"If there were, Connor would slay them," Abel said.

Karyn looked at Ellen for confirmation, which she gave with a hint of irony. "Aye, I trow Connor would slay any dragons that came along."

Her answer seemed to satisfy the little girl, who dropped her big sister's hand and moved up against Ellen, clasping her tiny arms around her thigh. Ellen reached over and enveloped her in a hug. "She feels cold, Sarah," she said, straightening up. "This place is so damp. Shall we go out into the sunlight and warm up?"

Sarah looked doubtful. "Beggin' your pardon, milady, but I don't think we can go without permission."

Ellen drew herself up and once again searched the cave for some sign of Connor. "Permission from whom?" she asked, growing indignant anew. Other than her father, she'd never sought permission for anything from any man.

"We're not to leave the cave unless they say we can—Connor and Walter Little and the others. We came to ask you to our fire to break your fast. We've bread and thick pork grease."

The inhabitants of the cave appeared to be a mixed rabble, mostly men, broken-down soldiers from the look of them, but here and there she could distinguish a family group, like the Coopers, huddled around one of the fires. It did not appear that anyone was paying the slightest attention to Ellen or the Cooper children.

"I don't see anyone keeping us from leaving," Ellen said after finishing her inspection. "Let's go out into the sun for a few minutes just until we all warm up a little." She reached down and took the little girl's hand. "Come on with me. It'll be all right."

Abel let go of his sister and took Ellen's free hand. "I'd like to go," he said.

Sarah nodded reluctantly and said, "Very well then."

They started toward the cave entrance, and no one made a move to stop them. Abel gave a little skip as he walked along beside her, and Ellen, too, felt her spirits rising as she contemplated leaving the gloom of the cave for the out-of-doors. Sarah quietly followed along behind.

It was misty, but it appeared that the sun was trying to break through the haze. Ellen and the children emerged from the mouth of the cave and automatically turned their faces toward the sky. At least the day was mild.

"May we climb the rocks?" Abel asked, pointing up the face of the cliff behind them.

Ellen hesitated. Though she wasn't used to asking permission for her own actions, neither was she used to being responsible for the actions of children. Abel was a sturdy little fellow, but tiny to be trying such feats, in her opinion. She looked at Sarah, who appeared to be deferring to Ellen in this instance.

She stepped out from the cliff and surveyed it. A few feet above the ground, a ledge jutted out from the rest of the stone with a scraggly pine growing diagonally out from it. "You may climb to the tree, Abel, no farther," she told him. There was a tug at her other hand, and she looked down to see Karyn's eyes pleading. Ellen turned back to Abel and said, "We will stay here watching you, and when you've reached it safely, you can help pull your sister up."

The solution seemed to be acceptable to both children. The little boy scrambled up the rock and reached the ledge in seconds, then peered triumphantly down over the edge and said, "C'mon, Karyn, don't be afraid. I'll pull you."

With a tiny grin, the girl followed her brother's example, climbing up the rock. Sarah watched a little wistfully, as if she wished that she were still young enough for such play.

"What are ye doing?" roared a voice from behind them.

Ellen whirled around and jumped to find the one-eyed soldier standing not a yard from her, his uneven features twisted in anger. "Ye foolish wench, do we not have enough new trouble with that maggot-brain's killing without you running off and taking the children in the bargain?"

Ellen felt the blood drain from her face. She'd never been talked to in such fashion in her life. She drew herself up and said, "The children and I wanted some air. We're causing no harm to anyone."

The man brushed by her. He was fully a head taller than she, tall enough to reach up to the ledge and snatch Karyn down. When he'd deposited her on the ground, he did the same for Abel. Both children were shaking with fright, which heightened Ellen's fury. "Unhand them," she yelled at him. "Can't you see you're frightening them?"

He didn't even look at the children, but turned to Sarah. "I thought you, at least, had more sense than this, girl. Take these bairns back to your mother."

Sarah did not appear to be intimidated by the man, but she looked remorseful. She gave a nod and reached for the twins' hands, then led them quickly back into the cave.

The minute they disappeared into the shadows, Ellen turned back to the soldier. "How dare you?" she spat.

The anger faded from his eyes, replaced with an amusement infuriatingly like the kind she'd seen too often in Connor's expression. "I beg your pardon, *milady*," he said with an exaggerated bow. "No one leaves the cave without permission."

"I'm not accustomed to asking *permission* to walk out in the fresh air," she replied, using her most imperious voice.

The old soldier was not impressed. "I warrant not. Ye'll have to learn new ways here."

"I'll not be here long enough to learn new ways. In fact, I demand to be taken back to Lyonsbridge immediately. Where is Connor?"

The soldier's eyebrow went up at her use of the horse master's given name, but he answered, "He's gone back. With luck, he'll find that they've not been able to discover the identity of Booth's murderer."

"'Twas not murder," Ellen protested. "The boy acted to save his sister and then in his own defense."

For the first time a glint of admiration lit the old man's good eye. "If 'twere a fair world, that story would save the lad, but we all know 'tis not a fair world. Our only hope is that they don't discover the connection with the knife."

"When is Master Brand returning?" she asked.

He shrugged. "He'll be back when he can. In the meantime, milady, I'm Walter Little, at your service. Ye'll let me know if our hospitality is lacking any of the amenities ye require."

His voice was still mocking, but warmer than before, and his visage was less fearsome now that the anger was gone.

"The only amenity I was looking for was a bit of sunshine. Is that too much to ask?"

Walter gave a half smile. "We have a signal for

leaving the cave so that no one blunders outside when there are others about. 'Tis the only way to keep our secret.''

"Children need to be able to play—"

"Children need a lot of things they don't get in England these days, milady," he interrupted. "What we can't afford is to let them scramble around the cliffs and get hurt. A dank cave is not an ideal place for curing wounds."

His interruption of their morning play seemed more reasonable than it had at first, but she still resented the way he had yelled at them and frightened the children. He'd frightened her as well.

She looked around the small area where they were standing. Near the mouth of the cave was a straight row of pines trees, making it impossible to see unless you were right on top of it. To the north the path they'd descended the previous evening led up the rocks behind them. She couldn't see the ocean, but she could hear the surf pounding somewhere around the bend of the cliff.

"Are you in charge here, Walter Little?" she asked. "Surely you must have some kind of a leader?"

Walter grinned. "We're an independent lot, mum, but we've a leader of sorts. He's not here at the moment."

"Well, I want to speak to the man," she said firmly. "My cousin will be looking for me by now. Our men will be everywhere, and 'twill simply make things worse for everyone."

Walter looked gloomy. "I reckon ye be right about that, mum."

"Will you take me back?" she asked hopefully.

He shook his head. "Nay. And I'll have to warn ye, highborn lady ye may be, but if ye try to leave the cave again without asking, I'll haul you back inside like I did the children off that cliff."

Ellen had to admit that the morning had not passed unpleasantly. After her encounter with Walter Little, she'd gone back inside and had accepted the Cooper family's offer of breakfast. The thick slabs of bread and grease had tasted better than many a feast she'd had in Louis the Fat's court, and she felt her spirits begin to recover.

Surely Connor would come back soon, and she could convince him to end this madness and return her to the castle. By now Sebastian would be scouring the countryside for trace of her. If these people wanted to keep their precious hideout a secret, holding her prisoner would not be the way to do it.

In the meantime, she was enjoying watching the twins' antics. The night in the cold cave had so far not affected Agnes Cooper's health, and she looked on fondly as Abel, Karyn, Sarah and John played counting games with the rocks from the cave floor. They appeared unconcerned that they'd just had to give up their home and most of their possessions.

"You have a remarkable family, Mistress Cooper," Ellen told her.

"Aye. They be good children," she answered. "I know not what I would do if aught happened to any one of them." A shadow crossed her face.

"I'm so glad Sarah's all right," Ellen said in a low

voice. "And sorry that 'twas one of my family's retainers who put her in such a situation."

"'Tis not your fault, milady. The children and I know that. You've been more than kind to us."

Ellen marveled that the woman's voice was devoid of bitterness. The Wakelin bailiff had attacked her daughter, had almost killed her son and had put the entire family in danger of their lives, yet her lack of blame was obviously sincere.

Ellen looked around the cave. She'd had a little contact during the morning with a few of its disenfranchised inhabitants, enough to know that Agnes Cooper's generosity of spirit was not shared by all. She suspected that there were even some here who would be happy to slit her Norman throat.

Once again she searched the cavern for sign of Connor. Though he was the one who had brought her here, she knew she would somehow feel safer in his presence.

As if in response to her thoughts, Agnes Cooper suddenly said under her breath, "Now here's an unsavory crew."

Four men whom Ellen had seen earlier talking with Walter Little were walking toward the spot where the Cooper family had set up their camp. The children stopped playing and fell silent as the men approached.

She'd heard Walter Little call the man in the front of the group Humbert. He stopped in front of her with a sneering smile. The others lagged a step or two behind.

"Is this the high-and-mighty mistress of Lyonsbridge sitting in the dust like a pauper?" the man asked.

Before Ellen could reply, Agnes Cooper drew herself up and said, "Humbert White, where are your manners? Your departed goodwife will be moaning in her grave."

Humbert hesitated a moment, but then said, "My goodwife is in her grave thanks to the likes of these." He gave a disgusted nod toward Ellen.

"Marjorie died long before the Lady Ellen's family came to Lyonsbridge, Humbert. And you'll answer to Master Brand if you mistreat her."

White's bluster died a little at the last comment. "What's he going to do with her?" he asked sullenly.

Agnes looked over at Ellen, who was recoiling in distaste from the rude stares of the three men behind Humbert White. Their leering gazes roamed freely over her body in a fashion she'd never before had to endure.

"That'll be Master Brand's decision, I warrant," the widow said firmly.

"Mayhap not. Brand's not here, and we've been thinking that 'er cousin would pay good money to get 'er back," he said.

Ellen looked up suddenly. Was it possible that these men would escort her back to the castle if she offered some kind of reward? But as soon as the idea entered her head, she dismissed it. It made her shudder to think of being out on the road alone at the mercy of such knavish characters.

Agnes shook her head and waved at the man standing in front of her as if he were a pesky gnat. "Leave us be, Humbert. Nothing's to be done with Lady Ellen until Connor Brand says so, and well you know it."

Humbert looked around at the men behind him.

One of them shrugged; the others looked away. "Mayhap we're tired of listening to Brand," he muttered. "He's not lord around here anymore."

But after another curious glance at Ellen, he turned and the four men wandered away. Ellen sagged against the rock wall in relief. The men had made her skin feel crawly.

"Don't mind them," the widow said, patting her hand. "They've too much time on their hands here, I trow, and find it easy to get into mischief."

"What did he mean about Connor?" Ellen asked. "When he said that he's not lord here now?"

Agnes looked away at the children. "'Tis just Humbert's grumblings. He was ever a troublemaker, and worse since he lost his wife."

"What happened to her?"

"Marjorie died in childbirth, but Humbert blames the Normans, begging your pardon, milady. 'Twas during the worst of the fighting, and they were forced to flee the village just as the child was about to arrive. He lost them both, and some say he's not been the same man since."

Ellen's eyes followed the four men as they made their way toward the back of the cave, where another group of idle men were sitting around a fire and passing a jug among them. She shivered. The widow was right. It was not a healthy situation for men to be cooped up in a place like this day after day with no gainful occupation.

"When will Connor—Master Brand—be back?" she asked, hoping Agnes might have better information than Walter Little.

The widow gave her a gentle smile of understanding. "Connor's a comely man, is he not? 'Tis a shame that the two of you are from such different worlds. You'd make a handsome couple."

Ellen's thoughts flashed back to the moment in the stable yard when he'd lifted her in his arms. It seemed a lifetime ago. At the time, in the throes of their passion, it had made sense to her, but now as she looked around at the scraggly Saxon residents of the cave, she couldn't imagine anything more absurd than a liaison between her and this stable master.

"I'm only interested because it seems that everyone's waiting for Master Brand to determine what's to become of me."

Agnes nodded. "Be patient, child, and have no fear. No one here will dare harm you when they know you're here by Connor's orders."

She spoke the words with absolute certainty, making Ellen wonder once again what the horse master's relationship was to these people that they deferred to him on such matters.

She gave an irritated sigh and got to her feet. "I'm going to go ask Walter Little if he'll arrange the signal or whatever they have to do so that we can walk outside for a few minutes. If I have to spend much more time in this cave without seeing the sky, I'll go mad."

With the children trooping behind her, she went off in search of the one-eyed man.

After Walter Little consulted with his mysterious network of lookouts, he allowed Ellen and the children to walk outside for a spell, though he'd cautioned gruffly, "No climbing up the cliffs."

They followed the sound of the water around the rock and were rewarded when they emerged to find a length of sandy beach. The twins clapped their hands in delight over the sight of the vast water stretching out in front of them. They had a good hour of play, running back and forth to keep from being caught by the teasing waves, before Walter came to fetch them back inside.

After the brief freedom, the cave seemed even gloomier. How could people continue living in a place like this year after year? Ellen thought. Would the Coopers be condemned to such a fate? The thought kept her sober all through the simple supper she shared with the family.

Connor had not returned all day, and she could get no response to her questions about him. Once again she began to consider escape. She had no idea how she would find her way back to Lyonsbridge, but if she got away from this place, there must be people around who would help her find her way home, especially if offered a nice reward.

She'd noticed that most of the men in the cave had spent much of the afternoon and evening drinking from their jugs of ale. It might be easier to slip away at night, when most of them were sleeping or in a drunken daze. If only Walter Little would stop watching her. She hadn't seen the old soldier take so much as a sip of the brew that was being passed so freely among the others.

"Bring your blankets over to sleep with us, milady," Agnes told her. "I'd not trust some of these men after the show Humbert White put on earlier."

The older woman's skin had taken on an unhealthy

sallow tone, Ellen noticed, though perhaps it was the dimness of the cave. "How long do you and the children plan to stay here?" she asked gently.

The widow looked distressed for just a moment, then the usual serenity returned to her eyes. "As long as God wills, child. Forever, if 'tis needed to keep my Johnny safe."

Ellen shook her head. "If I could just go back and speak with my cousin, mayhap we'd settle this and you could go back to your home."

Agnes smiled. "Bless you, child. I've often thought that if they'd only leave things to us women the world would be a saner place. But we have to await Connor. He'll say what's best."

Ellen looked across the cave. Walter Little was propped upright against a cave wall, apparently asleep, but mysteriously, when she looked at him, his good eye opened and he gave her a nod.

"Who's to say that Connor will even come back? He may be worried about securing his own position at the castle."

"He'll be back." There was utter conviction in the widow's voice.

Ellen heaved a sigh and stood to go fetch her blankets. In truth, the thought of stealing out into the night to make her way alone across England was not appealing. She picked a path across the cave, careful not to disturb some already sleeping inhabitants. "Connor will be back," the widow had assured her. Aye, but *when?*

The next day passed much as had the previous one. Walter Little allowed Ellen and the children to leave for short walks at midmorning and again at midafternoon. The rest of the day Ellen stayed close to Agnes Cooper, hoping to avoid any further confrontations with the men of the cave.

By evening, the widow had begun coughing again. Sarah was watching her mother with worried eyes, and John had started pacing back and forth the length of the cave. "Where's Master Brand?" he asked, reaching the end of one of his trips. "I want to know what's happening back at Lyonsbridge. Maybe I should head back there myself."

His mother looked stricken at the idea, and with surprising forcefulness, Sarah turned on her brother and said, "Don't talk like a dimwit, John. You're the one they'll be looking for. What's the point of any of us being here if you walk right back into their arms?"

Ellen expected that Agnes would say something to stop the fighting between her two oldest children, but she looked too weary to speak.

"Sarah's right, John," Ellen said gently, reaching up to put a hand on the boy's sleeve. "You of all people have to stay hidden. I'm sure Master Brand will be back before too long to let us know what has transpired."

But sundown came and then a mostly silent dinner, with Agnes eating next to nothing, and still there was no word of the horse master. Walter Little claimed he had heard nothing from the village or from the castle.

The twins fell into an early sleep and Sarah insisted that her mother lie down, though the older woman protested that she had no need of pampering. Ellen, John and Sarah stayed awake, staring into the tiny fire. No one spoke, as it seemed there was little to say. There was little to do but wait.

Most of the cave fires had been banked and the inhabitants seemed to have settled down to sleep when John suddenly jumped up and said, "I can't stand this anymore. I'm going. It's dark and I'll take care that no one sees me."

"John, no!" Sarah said again, sharply. "Mother's worse, and if she wakes to find you gone, who knows what it'll do to her."

"I'll come back before dawn," he said. "I've got to know."

Ellen looked across the cave toward Walter Little. The old soldier had stretched out on the ground with a blanket and appeared to be sleeping. If John was intent on leaving, perhaps this was her opportunity to leave as well.

"If you go, I'm going with you," she said.

John looked at her doubtfully. "I couldn't let you do that, milady."

"You can't stop me," she answered smugly.

"I intend to go running."

"Then I'll run, too."

John made a harsh sound of exasperation.

"You see, John," his sister said. "It's impossible. Why don't you just lie yourself down and go to sleep? Mayhap by morning Master Brand'll be here."

John looked down at Ellen again, hesitant. "I can't stand it here anymore," he said.

Ellen jumped up before he could have time to think better. "Then let's go. It'll be safer with two of us keeping watch. And if the worst should happen and they catch us on the way back, I'll be there to be sure that nothing happens to you.''

"What will you do when we get there?" John asked.

"I'll go back to the castle and start working to get things straightened out so that you and your family can leave this cave.''

"I know not what Master Brand would say.''

Ellen was utterly sick of hearing people wonder what Connor Brand would say or do. "It's not healthy here for your mother,'' she said firmly. "Her cough's returning. We need to do something to get her some help. At the very least, she needs some of the tonic that worked for her before.''

This finally seemed to convince John. "All right,'' he said, with a quick nod of his head. "Don't wake Mother,'' he added to Sarah. "I'll be back before dawn, I promise.''

The two young people moved silently around the edge of the cave and out into the night air, which was damp and chilly. John put his finger to his lip to urge Ellen to stay quiet, and motioned to her to follow him. "We'll take a shortcut up the cliffs,'' he whispered.

Ellen hiked up her skirts and held them awkwardly with one hand while she used the other to help boost herself up behind John. The climb was almost straight up, and it was all she could do to keep up with the nimble young lad. It felt so good to be free that she didn't care about her bursting lungs or the scratches on her soft palms, but she was happy to see the top edge of the cliff finally come into view.

"Just a couple more feet, milady,'' John told her in barely audible tones. He disappeared over the top for a moment, then his head reappeared and he held his hand out to her.

She let him help pull her up the final steps and collapsed on the ground, her legs and arms shaking from the exertion.

"Well done, milady," he told her with a note of admiration.

She grinned over at him. "Aye, we made it, John."

"You're tickle-brained fools, the both of you," said an unmistakable voice from a few feet away in the dark.

"Master Brand!" John exclaimed, and Ellen's exhilaration fled.

Chapter Eleven

Connor's voice was icy with fury. "What were the two of you doing?" he asked. "Trying to break your necks out here in the middle of the night so they'd find you washed up by the waves on the morrow?"

John scuffed his feet and did not meet the horse master's eyes. "You didn't come back, and I wanted to find out what was happening," he mumbled.

Connor shook his head. "I'd given you credit for more sense, John Cooper."

"Aye," the boy said sadly.

"I'll make no apology," Ellen told him.

She could see the glint of his smile in the moonlight. "I'll warrant you won't, milady, but that doesn't mean this wasn't an addlepated stunt."

"'Tis an easy climb," she said.

"No," he said firmly. "'Tis not." He turned to John. "And you, lad, what did you expect to do once you reached the top? The countryside is swarming with Norman soldiers who'd vie for the prize of putting a skewer through your gullet."

"I'd thought to find you."

"They're looking for me, too," Connor said.

"For you?" Ellen asked in alarm.

"Aye. It seems that my disappearance the night of Sir William's murder was noted. I've been declared an outlaw as well as John."

"They can't accuse you, Master Brand," John said. "If 'tis so, then I'll go to them and confess."

"Don't be a dolt, boy," Connor said harshly. "No one's going anywhere, and particularly not tonight. I've not slept these two nights past." He gave a low whistle and Thunder came walking toward them in the dark. "I'll have to take the path with my horse, John. Can I trust you to make your way back down the cliff and into the cave without diversion?"

John nodded, then looked uncertainly at Ellen.

"The lady Ellen will ride down with me," Connor said. His tone brooked no argument. "Milady," he said, with a gesture toward his horse.

Ellen gave a nod of reassurance to John, who then turned and disappeared over the edge of the cliff. "I'll go down to the cave with you tonight," she told Connor, "but tomorrow you must take me back or release me to my own efforts. 'Tis only complicating the problems to hold me here."

Connor's face was as hard as the stone cliff beneath them. "'Tis complicating more than you realize, milady, but I'm not prepared to let you go and put all who inhabit this place at risk of being slaughtered by your father."

"My father?"

"Aye. Lord Wakelin himself is crossing the channel this very hour with a force large enough to lay waste to this land in a way not seen since the days of the Conquerer himself."

"Because of Sir William?" she gasped.

"Nay, milady." His voice was suddenly weary. "Because of you."

"I told ye 'twas a grave mistake to bring her here," Walter Little said, smiting the rock behind him with the edge of his hunting knife.

It was barely past dawn, but most of the men in the cave had gathered around as Connor, Walter, Humbert White and others discussed the arrival of the new Norman troops. John Cooper stood at the edge of the circle, his face drawn and pale.

Connor looked over Walter's shoulder toward the Cooper campsite, where Agnes, Ellen and the other children still slept. "Keep your voices low," he warned. "I'd not upset the women and children among us."

"They'll be upset soon enough if a horde of Norman soldiers comes riding into this place," Humbert White said.

There was a murmur of assent from the other men in the group.

"Connor's right," Walter said in conciliatory tones. "They haven't discovered this place for years. There's no reason they will now, and there's no reason to excite the little ones."

John spoke for the first time, his half-man's voice squeaking with the effort. "'Tis because of me, all this trouble. I'm going to go back today and turn myself over to them."

Humbert White shot him a look of disgust.

"'Twould but make their first victim an easy one, and we'd still be slaughtered for all that."

"'Tis not just because of you, lad," Walter Little said more kindly. "The real frenzy is because of the lady, I'll warrant. I knew there'd be trouble the minute I saw her."

Connor rubbed his eyes, which stung from the smoky cave and the lack of sleep. "I'll take her back today," he said.

"So that she can tell the Normans exactly where we live?" someone shouted from the back of the group, and several others added their protests to the dissenter's.

Walter looked at Connor. "They're right, Connor. Ye can't take her back, not until we find a place to move all these people." He gestured around the cave at the sleeping families. "We can't take the risk."

Connor looked around the group of men. Except for John, who was watching with eyes full of anguish, they were all nodding in agreement with Walter. There had been a time when these men would have obeyed his orders without question, but whereas most of the outlawed men treated him with respect, his authority was no longer automatic.

"Very well, but it must be soon. Once her father arrives they'll be combing every bush on the coast looking for her."

Walter pointed at two men across the circle from him. "Godwin and Arthur, you know this coast better than any of us. Do you think you can find us a new sanctuary, one the Normans won't find?"

Before they'd become wanted men, the two had been fishermen. Now they scrounged from the forest like the rest of the outlaws and only occasionally risked setting out in the small boat they still kept hidden in a nearby cove.

"There's naught to the north. We'll have to move south," Godwin said. "But I think 'tis possible."

"Aye," his companion agreed. "By Lydey's Cay there are caves like this 'un. Mayhap not as large."

"As long as it will give adequate shelter for the time being," Connor told the men. "Go quickly and report back as soon as you can. Wakelin's soldiers will not wait to begin their campaign."

Humbert White stepped to the front of the group, shouldering Connor aside. "I say it's time we stopped sniveling in caves and took back what's rightfully ours. If Lord Wakelin's so almighty fond of his daughter, we bargain for it. We tell him to clear out of Lyonsbridge Castle or the girl dies."

The man tried Connor's patience, but he could tell that Humbert's sentiments were shared by a number of the others. It would not be wise to dismiss him out of hand. "And then what, Humbert?" he asked calmly. "The Wakelins leave and King Henry sends someone else to take over, mayhap even more tyrannical than Sir William was."

"He'd have a sight of trouble doing so if we held the castle," Humbert argued.

"Lyonsbridge has no fortifications for battle, White. 'Tis a home, not a fortress. And Henry would send ten men to our one." For once it was easy to keep his pledge to his mother to argue for peace. When he looked around at the scraggly outlaws who were all that remained of the rebelling Saxons, he realized that any contest with the well-armed-and-trained Norman soldiers would be nothing short of suicide.

"A good Saxon can outfight ten mewling Normans any day," Humbert barked.

Connor's efforts to keep the discussion quiet were in vain. The volume of the discussion had heightened, and by now most of the women and children were awake. Some had even ventured close to the circle of men. It was time for him to test how much power he still held over these people.

"The matter is decided, Humbert. Godwin and Arthur are going to scout a new location for us. With luck we can move on the morrow, and I'll take the lady Ellen back to the castle the moment we leave here."

A few of the men looked as if they were ready to continue the argument, but the two fishermen obediently nodded and headed out of the cave.

Walter Little said to the men nearest him, "We'd best make a foray to find some food before the countryside's swarming with Normans." He picked up his bow and quiver from the floor and started to leave, joined by a number of the other men.

Humbert stood for a moment, watching them go, then looked across the room at Ellen, who was sitting up on her blankets and watching the group of men. There was a sneer in his voice as he said, "I wonder if it's really *our* safety you're worried about, Brand, or if you have more interest in the Norman tart than you're admitting."

Peacekeeper or no, Connor had an urge to drive his fist through the man's face.

"Watch your tongue, White," he said tersely. Then

he turned his back on the man and started walking with long angry strides toward the Cooper fire.

John caught up to him and clutched at his arm. "Are you sure I shouldn't give myself up, Master Brand?"

Connor barely gave the lad a glance as he said, "Nay, John. Leave it be." His eyes were on Ellen, who had drawn herself up as she noticed his approach. She sat awaiting him on the blankets as if she were a queen on a golden throne. In spite of three days living in the primitive conditions of the cave, she looked as regal as when he had first seen her, galloping toward him on Jocelyn. He felt a quick stab of admiration, and something more primal.

"Good morrow, milady," he addressed her.

"I see nothing good about it, horse master. I'm ready for you to take me back."

At her side, Agnes Cooper had not risen from her bedroll, but was watching them with open eyes. She looked much weaker than she had when Connor had last seen her. He turned back to Ellen. "I hope to be able to grant your wish on the morrow. For now, I'll have to ask you to be content with our continued hospitality."

Ellen appeared to have been expecting his reply. She jumped to her feet, dragging with her a rough gray cloak. "May I borrow your wrap, Mistress Cooper?" she asked, ignoring Connor. "The day is cold, and I know not how long I'll be walking."

Agnes looked from Ellen to Connor, then moved her head back and forth with a little sigh. The effort made her cough.

Connor reached out and snatched the cloak from Ellen's hand. "You're not walking anywhere."

She glared at him. "You will stop me by force?"

"Aye."

Sarah, John and the twins were watching the exchange wide-eyed.

Ellen clenched her jaw and sat back down. "'Tis obvious that you're stronger than I, horse master. I'd not win a match of muscles. But I *shall* leave this place, and my father will hear of my treatment at your hands."

Her eyes were sparked with fury, her hair streaming out around her beautiful face. Connor focused on her lips and felt his body awaken at the sudden memory of the kisses they'd shared. He leaned toward her and said in a voice intended for her ears alone, "I trust you'll give your father a *full report* of your treatment at my hands."

Her face flamed red. Connor gave a nod of satisfaction, then spun on his heel and walked away.

The fishermen hadn't returned, and Connor's temper was frayed. He'd spent the day trying to reestablish his ties with the bullheaded rebels who'd remained at the cave, but, unlike the villagers at Lyonsbridge, who still regarded Connor as their leader, these men had lived as outlaws too long to recognize the authority of any man.

He'd hardly touched the supper Walter Little had brought him. It was past sundown, and he was having trouble keeping from succumbing to the need for sleep as he sat with his back against the wall of the cave and his legs stretched out in front of him. His eyes had drifted closed when he felt the gentle tug at his sleeve. It was Sarah Cooper.

"Master Brand?" she whispered.

"What is it, Sarah?" he asked sleepily.

"I wasn't sure if I should disturb you, but I don't know what to do about Lady Ellen."

This brought Connor bolt upright. He'd asked Walter to watch her until midnight and then awaken him to keep guard, but he never should have given such duty to the old squire. "Has she escaped?" He squinted in the gloom of the cave and relaxed as he saw Ellen, still seated next to the widow Cooper's bed.

"Nay, she's been helping me nurse. Me mum's growing poorly again, Master Brand."

"Aye, I've heard her coughing. Somehow we'll get her some tonic on the morrow. But what about Lady Ellen?"

"I thought I should tell you, she won't eat."

Connor blinked in surprise. "Won't eat?"

"No, nor drink. She's refused all the day long. She says she'll perish first and let Master Brand carry her bones back to Lyonsbridge."

"The bloody fool."

"I just thought you should know, Master Brand."

Connor gave a great sigh and heaved himself to his feet. What he needed was sleep, not a stubborn female to deal with. "You did right, Sarah," he told her.

"Me mum could probably change her mind, but she's not been entirely right in her head this afternoon."

Connor looked at her sharply. "Your mother's having the delirium?"

"I warrant. She's hardly spoken, but her words don't seem to be going together too well."

Lord, he had not only a stubborn female to handle, but a seriously ill one, as well. "We'll tend to your mother first, Sarah, then I'll speak with the lady Ellen. Run to Walter Little and tell him I have need of him at your campfire."

The girl slipped quietly away, and Connor made his way across to the widow and Ellen. He spared the latter barely a glance as he knelt beside Agnes and took one of her frail hands. "Can you hear me, mistress?" he asked. "How are you feeling?"

The woman's only response was a tossing of her head. In the glow of the firelight, her face looked bright scarlet. "How long has she been like this?" he asked John, who knelt at his mother's other side.

"Since sunset. 'Tis the cough again. She's spitting blood every time."

Connor swore softly. "We've got to stop it." He knew that she should be home in a warm, dry bed, but that was impossible. "There's so much smoke," he said, his voice trailing off on a note of hopelessness.

"And these damp walls," Ellen added sharply. "'Tis as I've been saying these several hours past. I tried to tell your watchdog, Master Little, but he wouldn't listen. We need to get her out in the fresh air."

"'Tis cold—" Connor protested, but she interrupted.

"That matters not. We'll bundle her well in blankets, but she can't have the damp and the smoke. And she needs a potion of mead and honey."

"Mead?" Connor asked.

"We have ale," John suggested.

"Ale, then," Ellen said briskly. "Bring it to me."

Before Connor even had time to consider another protest, Ellen had recruited two men from the neighboring fire to help John lift his mother, blankets and all, and carry her out of the cave. Connor followed along behind, feeling once again as if his authority meant little.

Walter Little came up beside him. "Where are they taking her?" he asked, nodding at the procession carrying the sick woman.

Connor shrugged. "To the fresh air, so they tell me."

Walter grinned. "I'd never taken you for one of those males who lets his woman wear the pants, Connor."

Connor rolled his eyes. "Shut up, old man, and help me find a sheltered spot for their sickroom that won't give us away to the Normans prowling about."

They'd found a copse of trees to one side of the path, about halfway up the cliff. It was not visible either from above or from the beach below.

Though they couldn't risk a fire, they'd laid the widow on a leather saddle blanket and wrapped her well against the cold night. She'd begun breathing more easily almost at once.

Miraculously, a pot of honey had been found, and Ellen had mixed it with ale and spooned the mixture bit by bit into the sick woman's mouth. It had quieted Agnes's coughs enough to allow her to fall into a deep sleep.

Connor's desire for sleep had fled. The nap he'd had sitting up against the cave wall had refreshed him for the moment. He sent Walter and the children back to the cave to their beds, but Ellen insisted on staying by the widow's side.

"You could come to bed, too," Sarah had told her as she prepared to leave. "I've seen me mum like this before. The coughing's worn her out. She'll sleep the night."

"I'll stay with her," Connor added. "You should go get some sleep, milady."

She'd looked at him coldly. Now that the crisis with the widow was past, the tension between them was rising once again. "I'm not sleepy," she said.

"Do you intend to go without sleep as well as food and drink?"

"Mayhap."

He ground his teeth. Sweet Jesu, but the woman was infuriating. He nodded at the children and Walter. "Go on down. The two of us will keep watch here."

After the group's footsteps on the path faded, the only sound was the distant crash of the surf and the widow's deep, even breaths. Neither Ellen nor Connor spoke for several minutes.

Finally Connor reached for the flask of ale that Ellen had used earlier to make her potion, pulled out the stopper and took a long drink. He held it out to her. "Thirsty, milady?"

She turned up her nose at him. "Nay."

"You've had neither food nor drink since breakfast, they told me."

"I'm not thirsty," she repeated.

He jammed the stopper back on the flask and tossed

it to one side. "You're a stubborn wench," he grumbled.

Ellen raised her eyes to look at him. Even in the dim light he could see the sweep of her long lashes. Once again, the memory of their kisses crept unbidden into his head.

"I just want to go home. Once I'm back there, I'm sure I can straighten out this coil so that poor Agnes and her children can return to their home where they belong. From where I sit, you're the stubborn one, horse master."

Connor stood and paced to the edge of the clearing. He was not used to explaining his actions, particularly not to a female, but Ellen of Wakelin was no ordinary female. "We'd have a rebellion on our hands if I took you back," he told her. "There are those who fear that you'll betray this place to your father's men."

"I'd not," she said indignantly.

He regarded her steadily for a long moment, then replied, "Mayhap you don't think so now, but when your father presses you for details, who knows what you might reveal?"

"I'm not some blathering fool who can't control her own tongue, horse master."

She'd raised her voice, and Connor cautioned her to lower it with a nod toward the sleeping woman, though it appeared that the widow's sleep was deep.

"Even if I wanted to take you back, they'd stop me," he told her. "I'm one and they are many."

"We could steal away now and no one would even know of it until morning."

"And leave the widow out here alone, exposed to any predator who might come along? Wild wolves,

mayhap?'' There had not been wolves in that part of
England for years, but Ellen did not know that. The
truth was, much as Connor wanted to believe her pro-
testations, he couldn't take the risk when the lives of
so many of his people might be at stake. But he knew
it would only aggravate her further to let her know
that he doubted her word.

Ellen looked down at the sick woman. ''No,'' she
said, her voice subdued. ''I'd not leave her here.''

''Well, there you have it,'' Connor said, relieved.
''So if you insist on keeping watch with me all night,
you might as well do so comfortably.'' He reached
over and retrieved the flask he'd discarded and extended it toward her. ''Slake your thirst, milady.
'Twill take the chill off the night.''

Ellen appeared to be doing battle with her earlier
resolution, but finally she snatched the flask from him,
tore off the plug and took a long, long drink.

''Slowly,'' Connor warned, his eyes amused.
''You'll choke yourself.''

Ellen finished her drink and with a little more dignity replaced the stopper and set the flask on a nearby
rock.

''Feel better?'' he asked her after a moment.

She nodded with obvious reluctance, and to his surprise, Connor could see that underneath her aristocratic demeanor, she was on the verge of weeping.
These past three days must have been difficult for her,
he realized. She'd been torn from her home and carried off in the middle of the night, forced to sleep on
the ground and eat poor food in the company of rough
men who were sworn enemies of her people.

Connor's roots had been torn from under him years

ago. He was used to hardships, but Ellen was a gently bred noblewoman who undoubtedly had never experienced anything remotely like this in her entire life. All in all, she'd handled herself with courage and dignity, and she didn't deserve his mockery.

He moved closer to her and took her hand. "Shall I fetch you some food as well, milady? I've promised to take you back to Lyonsbridge as soon as I can. There's no need for you to go hungry in the meantime."

She said nothing, but shook her head. He studied her more closely. He'd been right. Her big eyes glistened with unshed tears in the moonlight. The sight gave him a quick stab of sympathy, which was followed by a desire to comfort her that overwhelmed every other vestige of sense.

He reached toward her face and rubbed gently under her eye with his thumb. "Don't mar these beautiful eyes with tears, princess," he said softly.

"I'm not crying," she said firmly, but a little hiccup at the end of her statement belied the words.

Connor looked down at Agnes, who still slept soundly. Then he stood, picked Ellen up in his arms and moved a few yards away to a mossy hillock at the edge of the circle of trees, where he knelt and placed her on the ground. "Your eyes are wet from the night air, then," he said, gently teasing.

She gave him a watery smile. "Mayhap." She wiped the end of her sleeve against her nose and gave an undignified sniff. "I'm sniveling like a coward," she said with some irritation.

"Ah, sweetheart, you've comported yourself more

staunchly than many a soldier I've known. I find thee
a wondrously brave lady.''

Her tears had disappeared and a different emotion
was in her eyes as she looked up at him. He took in
a jagged breath. His head swirled, banishing all
thought of the sick woman behind them, the Normans
prowling the countryside, the rebellious men asleep
in the cave beneath them.

His own eyes must have reflected his desire, for
hers suddenly widened and became unfocused. She
lay back against the gentle slope of the hill and held
her arms up to him.

''I find thee wondrous as well,'' she whispered.

Chapter Twelve

This time Ellen couldn't say what had filled her with such a mixture of longing and emotion. If she could stop to reason, she'd probably realize that she was altered by the distress of her capture, the lack of sleep, the poor conditions. But as she looked at Connor's striking, tawny head looming over her in the night, all she could think of was that she wanted to feel his lips once again on hers.

"Wondrous," he'd said. *Aye, wondrous,* she thought, as he lowered himself beside her and took her in his arms. His mouth was soft, yet insistent, and she gave herself up to it completely while all conscious thought fled.

She lay against the soft ground, and he moved his body over hers so that they pressed together chest-to-chest and leg-to-leg. His tongue probed her mouth, magically, sending sensations rushing down through her midsection. She moved restlessly beneath him and moaned softly.

He pulled away, letting the moonlight stream over her face. "Art wondrous brave and wondrous fair, milady,'' he rasped. ''You've bewitched me, I vow. 'Tis madness for us to be here like this.''

At his words, Ellen lifted her head to peer down the small hill toward the sleeping woman. ''Agnes?'' she asked.

He shook his head and pressed her back, stopping her question with gentle, nipping kisses. ''You heard Sarah. She said the widow will sleep through till morning. But this is madness nonetheless.''

His hand had traveled down her bodice and ended up resting just over the portion of her body where all the feelings from his kisses had radiated. The heat of it burned through the cloth of her dress. She wanted more of him. She wanted it more than she could ever remember wanting anything in all her pampered life. But she was afraid, too.

''I've not known the love of a man, horse master,'' she whispered, averting her face from his hooded gaze.

He took her chin gently in his fingers and turned her face toward his. ''Say my name, Ellen.''

''Connor.''

The word was almost inaudible, but it was enough for him. He bent toward her and brushed his lips along her mouth, then feathered kisses down the side of her neck until chills ran up and down her back. Her very bones seemed to have melted.

'''Tis madness,'' Connor said again, and she nodded in agreement. ''But I want thee, if you'll have me.''

He stopped kissing her and waited. She'd hoped he would continue the relentless onslaught, sweeping her up in the passion she sought without giving her choice nor time for thought. But he waited.

Her throat filled. The tears that had threatened earlier returned. The ache inside her was undeniable. She wanted him, too, but it was, as he said, *madness*. She was this man's captive, this arrogant servant who insulted her way of life and defied the rule of her people.

He saw the answer in her face and his expression stiffened. He sat up, looked away from her, brushed the palms of his hands together. He didn't speak.

"I'm sorry," she whispered finally.

He shook his head, but remained silent.

"I'll check on Mistress Cooper," she said in a small voice. She tried to get up, but found that her skirts were still caught underneath him, pinning her to the ground. She tugged at them, suddenly desperate to put distance between them.

Obligingly, he moved to one side, still without looking at her.

Ellen stood, shook out her dress and walked with wobbly legs down the little incline to where the widow lay peacefully asleep. Kneeling at the sick woman's side, she said, "I'll sit with her awhile."

She could no longer see Connor's face in the darkness. His voice was gruff as he answered her, "As you will. I'll keep to this bed for the night, but lest you get ideas about running off, be aware that I'll wake at the slightest noise."

"I'll not run off," she said. "Not this night."

He gave kind of a grunt, then rolled over and lay back to sleep.

Ellen sat listening to the widow's breathing and

stared into the darkness. Her body was slowly cooling, the heated frenzy over, but she felt shaky inside and empty. She'd needed something from Connor, and not just the completion of her physical desires.

Her entire life, she'd had whatever she desired at the snap of her fingers, the raising of her voice. She'd never had to give of herself in return. As long as she could remember, she'd accepted the admiration of men as her due. But now, when once again the gratification of her whims was offered without price, she hadn't been able to agree.

She knew of other noblewomen who had taken their pleasures with underlings. Indeed, some of the more shameless in Louis's court kept servants for that very purpose. But somehow she'd known that surrendering herself to Connor would require more of her soul than she was willing to give.

The widow stirred and gave a little moan in her sleep. Ellen leaned over and rubbed the back of the sick woman's hand with her fingertips, feeling the veins through the paper-thin skin. Her touch seemed to calm the woman, and her breathing became deep once again. Ellen looked over at the mound where Connor lay, but he hadn't moved.

What strange irony, Ellen thought. She'd come to England hoping to impose her Norman world on a land of savages and then depart. Instead she was finding herself ensnared with the people here in a way she had neither anticipated nor desired.

She shivered and hugged her arms around her knees as the night winds rustled the trees around her. The tears that had sprung to her eyes earlier began to come in earnest. She rocked back and forth and let them fall, tears such as she had not shed since the day they'd told her that her mother was dead.

Agnes was definitely better the following morning. They brought her back inside for the daylight hours, moving the Cooper campsite to the front of the cave where the air was the purest. It boosted everyone's spirits to see the woman's smile again, wise and gentle. But by late afternoon, when there was still no sign of Godwin and Arthur, the two fishermen, tempers began to flare anew.

Ellen had given up her vow not to eat, though she had little appetite. Connor had not mentioned their encounter of the previous evening, and had avoided her company for most of the day.

When she finally went near him just as the final rays of sun were slanting through the opening of the cave, he stiffened as she approached.

"Do you think my father's here in England by now?" she asked him.

"Aye."

"Where do you suppose the fishermen are?"

"I know not."

"What will you do if they don't return?"

He scarcely glanced at her. "We'll send out others."

She sighed, a little piqued. After all, *he'd* been the one to stop their lovemaking the previous evening. If he'd been persistent, she imagined they would now be lovers. The deed would be done.

"Are you annoyed with me, Master Brand?" she asked finally.

This got his attention. His eyes fastened on her

face, intense and, yes, angry. It gave her a perverse measure of satisfaction. "Angry at you?" he asked slowly. "Nay."

"What, then?"

She could see a muscle clench in his jaw. "At myself mayhap. 'Twas ill done yestreen."

The knowledge that he'd been affected by their kisses as much as she was a balm to the confusion and depression she'd been feeling all day. It even allowed her to offer a small smile. "Parts of it were not ill done," she said, gently teasing.

A light flickered deep in his eyes. "Aye," he agreed. "Parts were not."

His gaze shifted over her shoulder and the light died, replaced by wariness. Ellen turned around to see the same four men whom Agnes had scolded the other day at her campfire.

Their leader, Humbert White, spoke. "Godwin and Arthur haven't come back," he said to Connor gruffly.

"I'm aware of that, White."

"The boys and I have been talking, and we're ready to put my plan into action."

"Your plan?"

Humbert's hair was wild and matted, no worse than that of many of the men in the cave, but as he started talking, flailing his arms around, he suddenly seemed to Ellen to take on the look of the madmen one sometimes found wandering around public squares. "About the girl. We're going to send a messenger to her father and tell him that unless he leaves this land, he'll get her body back in a box." He said the words with relish, flashing a twisted smile at Ellen as he finished.

Ellen expected Connor to get angry with the man, but he stayed calm. "Which one of you is going to be the messenger?" he asked. "Because I guarantee there won't be enough pieces left of *that* man to put in a box."

The men looked at each other uncomfortably. "We could send a woman, mayhap Sarah Cooper," Humbert offered, but the others didn't seem to think much of his suggestion.

From the back of the group a smaller man whose appearance was a little neater than the rest stated in a quiet voice, "You're still lord of the Saxons, Brand. What do you think we should do?"

Ellen looked at Connor in surprise. His glance went to her briefly, then he turned back to the men. "We wait for Godwin and Arthur one more day. If they don't come back, I'll ride back to the village and recruit some of the men to find us a new site. There are many there who know this coast as well as the fishermen."

The man at the back who had spoken said, "The masons have quarried on these cliffs. They know them well."

Humbert White's expression was thunderous as he turned back to his companions. "How much longer are we going to sit here and wait for Wakelin's men to find us?" He reached out and roughly took hold of Ellen's upper arm, drawing her so close to him that she could smell his fetid breath. "I say the girl's our best hope."

In an instant Connor stepped forward, picked Hum-

bert up by his armpits and threw him several yards
into the center of the cave. His voice was deadly.
"Touch her again, White, and I'll break my oath of
peace long enough to knock your head from your
shoulders."

White lay sprawled on the floor for a moment,
looking dazed, but then he picked himself up and
said, "No one's good enough to touch 'er but you,
eh, *milord?* Well, you'd best think again. You're not
master of Lyonsbridge anymore. You're master of
nothing more than a stable full of horse dung. If
you're good enough for the Norman bitch, so's any
man here."

Then he turned and limped away.

The rest of his companions were silent as he left.
Finally Connor said to them, "Humbert's mind is getting more unstable. You men would be better off finding someone else to follow."

The slight man who had spoken earlier said,
"You're still the one we follow, sir."

After a slight hesitation, the others nodded in
agreement.

"Then stay away from him. His kind of poison
only leads to more troubles."

With White's departure, all sense of confrontation
had disappeared. Two of the men even made a slight
bow as the group began to move away. Ellen watched
them go, trying to make sense of what had transpired.
That odious man had called Connor *milord,* and now,
as she looked at the tall Saxon, she realized with sudden clarity that Connor Brand had never had the bear-
ing of a servant, because he was *not* a servant.

"Who are you?" she asked when the last of the

men had left them. She'd asked him the same question shortly after they first met, and he'd replied with impudence. But now she was determined to get the answer.

He regarded her with his steady blue eyes. "I'm the past, milady. The last Brand of Lyonsbridge. The last of the lords who ruled over this place since the days when England was naught but legends and mists."

Then he turned on his heel and walked away.

Connor sat on a rock ledge looking out over the sea. He'd begun to feel the damp walls of the cavern closing in around him and had decided to take over the afternoon watch from Walter Little. He also wanted some solitude to think.

When the Normans had come to England, Connor's life had turned upside down, but after his parents' deaths, he'd managed to achieve some sort of peace with his new existence. He'd expected to live out his life with his horses, seeing to the needs of the villagers and ensuring that war would never again erupt in his beloved home.

Now it seemed as if the upheaval was beginning all over again, and it had begun before William Booth's death. From the moment Connor had seen Ellen of Wakelin, the worm of dissatisfaction had begun to gnaw.

He shifted his position on his uncomfortable perch, then gave a laugh of irony. Once he'd sat in his great hall in cushioned luxury, but today his seat was a hard rock, his bed a bare cave.

He leaned his head back against the cliff wall, trying to keep his mind on the problems he and his people faced. As he'd told the men earlier, if the scouts they had sent out didn't return, he'd find another way to search for a hideout, but he had a feeling that wouldn't solve the problem in the long run. The Normans had left the renegade Saxons alone because the peace had held, but now that Sir William had been killed, they weren't likely to give up searching until they'd brought someone to task for the deed.

Then there was Ellen. Her golden eyes danced before him as he closed his own. The previous night they'd almost made love. His experience told him that if he'd pressed the issue, they would have. But he hadn't wanted her on those terms. He shouldn't want her on any terms. It was madness, just as he had said.

His eyes popped open at the sound of a voice calling his name. His brother's bald head came into view just below Connor on the cliff. "What are you doing perched way up here like a seabird waiting to swoop?" Father Martin asked irritably, puffing at the exertion of the climb.

Connor moved to make room for the priest and greeted him without much enthusiasm. "Martin. What brings you here?"

Father Martin carefully wedged himself next to Connor on the narrow rock, then answered, "I've brought more bad news, I fear."

Connor's bout of self-pity dissipated and he became instantly alert. "From Lyonsbridge?"

Martin nodded. "Lord Wakelin's installed himself in the castle and the grounds are spilling over with men."

"They want William's killer."

"Aye."

"But no one has told of this place?"

"Nay…" There was hesitation in the priest's voice.

"What is it then?" Connor asked.

"They've issued a warrant for Johnny Cooper."

"They can't arrest him if they can't find him," Connor argued.

Martin's eyes were grave. "They say the villagers are hiding him. Lord Wakelin has decreed that one villager a day is to be flogged until the boy is surrendered and his daughter is safely returned."

"Flogged?" Connor felt as if the air had gone out of his gut.

"Harry Mason's to be the first. Tomorrow at midday."

"Sweet Jesu," Connor whispered.

Martin crossed himself. "Aye," he said.

Both men sat and stared out at the dark blue ocean. From this distance the violent waves looked like gentle swells. "I know not what course to take, Martin," Connor admitted after a long pause. His voice was uncharacteristically shaky.

Father Martin looked over at his brother and gave him a gentle smile. "Mayhap 'tis time to look to the Lord."

Connor did not return the smile. He continued to stare at the water for several minutes, then slapped his palm against his thigh and stood, bracing himself against the wall behind him. "If the Lord had time for Saxons, we wouldn't be in this coil. But 'tis time for action, that much is certain. I'll not let my people's flesh be torn from their backs."

He slid around his brother, causing the priest to clutch the rock for safety, and started down the cliff at a reckless pace. "'Tis your own flesh'll be torn by the rocks if you don't have a care, Con," Father Martin called after him. Connor did not slow his descent.

The priest sighed, then turned around and, hand over hand, carefully began to pick his way down the embankment.

"I'm taking you home," Connor said.

Ellen's head came up sharply. She was kneeling next to Agnes Cooper, helping the widow drink some broth Ellen and Sarah had prepared earlier in the day. "Now?" she asked.

He nodded, then crouched next to the sick woman. "Are you better, mistress?" he asked gently.

Her eyes had regained their sharpness. "Don't worry about me, Master Brand. You have more important things to concern you."

He turned to Ellen. "Bring Mistress Cooper's cloak," he said curtly. "The night air is chill."

Ellen looked at Agnes, who smiled and said, "Run along, child. 'Tis well to undo this thing that should never have been done."

Ellen handed the mug of soup to Sarah, who took her place at her mother's side and said, "Godspeed, milady."

"Hurry," Connor urged.

Ellen looked around the cave. Most of the men had settled down to their nightly drinking around the fires. Without further argument she followed Connor's lead around the edge of the cave walls and out to the mouth.

They were almost to the outside when Humbert White stepped in front of them, swaying, obviously the worse for drink. "Where are you taking her, Brand?" he asked in slurred tones.

Connor shoved him aside and continued toward the entrance, but Humbert grabbed his shoulder and spun him around. "You're not going anywhere. The girl's our hostage."

Connor gave a deep sigh, then pulled back his fist and slammed it into Humbert's midsection. The man crumpled to the floor at once and lay without moving. Ellen stood gaping at him.

"Come on," Connor said, beginning to move.

"But…" Ellen gestured to the fallen man.

"He'll be all right. Let's get out of here before I have to do the same to a half dozen of his comrades."

Ellen was still sputtering, "He's not moving—" when Connor grabbed her arm and whisked her out of the cave.

"Thunder is just down the beach," he told her.

He held her arm to keep her walking along beside him, and it was all she could do to keep up, but finally they reached his horse. While he saddled his mount, she had a moment to catch her breath and ask him, "Are you truly taking me back to the castle? Why the sudden change in plans?"

He finished tightening the saddle, then leaped on the horse's back and reached down to pull her up behind him. "I'm trying to save lives, milady, including yours."

"Has something happened at Lyonsbridge?"

"Your father's there and fighting furious, from the

sound of it. Unless something's done, we're going to set off another war.''

''I thought you were worried that I'd reveal this place to my father.''

''I am. But I'm going to take your pledge not to do so.'' He twisted in the saddle to look at her. ''You'll give it?''

''I've told you so, horse master. Though it's not really horse master, is it?''

She'd been waiting all day to question him further about his morning revelation. His family had been lords of Lyonsbridge before the arrival of the Normans. The discovery had both relieved and confused her.

She'd been relieved to think that she had not, after all, been attracted to a mere servant. She'd been confused because for reasons she couldn't fully understand, the knowledge had somehow saddened her.

He hesitated awhile before answering her. ''My position is master of your father's stables, milady, or it was before John Cooper's troubles.''

''But you are not really a servant.''

Thunder was making his way up the sharp incline to the top of the cliff, and Ellen had to hold tight to Connor's waist to keep from slipping off.

''Would you have let me make love to you last night if you'd known I had noble blood in my veins?''

The remark was cruel, and it cut more deeply because she'd been wondering the very same thing. Stung, she replied in the same caustic vein. ''No Saxon blood is noble in Norman eyes.''

Connor gave a humorless chuckle. ''Then 'tis well

I did not contaminate you with more than a few Saxon kisses."

"Aye. 'Tis well."

They rode in silence for several minutes, then Connor said, reluctantly, "I need to make peace with you, milady."

"It must gall you to admit it. I have no quarrel with you, horse master," she replied.

"Your father has threatened to whip the men of the village unless John Cooper is turned over to him."

Ellen drew in a sharp breath. "'Tis not like him," she said.

"That may be, but Martin brought the word this afternoon."

"Your brother was here?"

"Aye, but I'll have to ask your pledge not to reveal that, either."

"I'm not heartless, horse master, nor dimwitted. I'll say nothing about this place."

"We'll be in your debt. And you will speak to your father about the floggings?"

"Aye," she said, her voice subdued.

"Sometimes a flogging can kill even a strong man," he told her. "Lyonsbridge village needs no more widows and orphans."

Ellen shivered and pulled the widow's cloak more securely around her. "I'll speak to him," she said.

Connor nodded, then urged Thunder ahead into the night.

Chapter Thirteen

Brian, Baron of Wakelin, shook his head sadly at his only child. "The shock of your capture has unbalanced you, child. I'll never forgive myself for exposing you to the rough treatment of these outlaws. You'd best keep to your room for a few days and leave this matter to me and your cousin."

Ellen clasped her hands in front of her and tried to remain calm. It was true that she was not recovered from her ordeal of the past few days, but her exhaustion was from lack of sleep, not rough treatment. "In general, I was treated well, Father," she explained for the tenth time.

They sat in the great hall after breaking the morning fast with a rich meal of stuffed capons, thick bacon and almond cakes her father had brought from Normandy. As she sat down to the table, Ellen had thought of the Coopers, still back in the gloomy cave, dining on bread and grease.

"We'll not ask for details of your treatment, Cousin," Sebastian said, leaning toward her across the table. "We can only imagine the horrors a beautiful woman like yourself would be subjected to at the hands of these Saxon barbarians.'' His oily smile made Ellen feel as if she hadn't bathed.

"I was subjected to no horrors, Sebastian,'' she said again. ''And remember, the outlaws, as you call them, returned me safely to my home.''

"After four days,'' her father pointed out. His tawny eyes, so like her own, were grave with concern. ''And only after they realized that their acts would have serious recriminations among their people. Now we must continue on the same course to bring Sir William's murderer to justice.''

"Sir William wasn't murdered. The boy was acting in defense of his sister and of himself.''

"Nonsense,'' Sebastian snapped, with a sniff of disdain. ''This is a story they've concocted to cover the crime. William Booth was no lecher.''

"I myself saw his eyes on the girl at the examination of the horses,'' she argued.

Lord Wakelin stood and walked over to her chair. ''Go to your quarters, my daughter. I'm going to send Sylvianne to give you a tonic and sit by you while you sleep.''

Her father had brought one of her attendants from Normandy, a robust woman who was utterly loyal to her master and had never had much time for Ellen's girlish whims.

Ellen pushed back her chair and stood, facing her father. ''If you do this thing,'' she said, ''if you flog that man in the village today, I'll leave your household and not return.''

Wakelin's smile faded. ''You know not what you say, child. You've been altered—''

She interrupted him. "I know exactly what I'm saying. Mayhap I've been altered, but 'tis not in the way you think. Call off this punishment today, or you'll see me no more. I'll join a holy sisterhood, if needs be. Do *not* doubt me on this."

Her father's face had gone white, but before he could argue further, Ellen pushed by him and fled from the hall.

"The girl is addled," Sebastian said, rising to his feet as well.

Lord Wakelin continued to stare after his departing daughter. "I'm not entirely certain."

"She'll be better on the morrow, and the sooner we capture this boy and see him hanged for William's murder, the sooner Ellen will return to normal."

After a long pause, Wakelin said slowly, "Postpone the flogging for the nonce."

"But, my lord—" Sebastian began.

"Postpone it," Wakelin barked. "Make another round of questioning among the villagers. Offer a reward for information, but don't hurt anyone."

Sebastian gave a little bow, his face a mask. "As you will, milord," he said. He waited stiffly until Lord Wakelin had left the room, then he picked up the carcass of a half-eaten capon and smashed it against the wall behind him, narrowly missing a kitchen boy who had come scurrying up to clear the table.

The rich breakfast rolled around like a great lump in her stomach as Ellen returned to her chambers, and her mind was equally agitated. Her final words to her father had not been planned. In truth, she couldn't imagine leaving his household forever, nor did she feel herself destined for a life of sacrifice and contemplation in holy orders. But she'd been able to think of no other way to stop his abuse of the villagers, and time had run out.

Her old nursemaid, Sylvianne, tried to offer her a sleeping potion, but she refused and snapped at the woman when she insisted on remaining at Ellen's side.

"Lord Wakelin's orders," the woman pleaded, until Ellen shrugged with exasperation and let her stay. The dour-looking woman sat in the corner of the room, watching her charge, her hands in her lap.

"Have you not some stitching to accomplish?" Ellen asked finally.

"Nay, milady. I'm only to attend to your needs."

Ellen had worked hard since arriving at Lyonsbridge, and she'd forgotten how much of the time she as well as her attendants back home had idled away without productive activity. "I have no needs, Sylvianne, as you can see. My father wants me to sleep, and I trow I can do so without anyone's assistance."

"But if your ladyship should awaken and require something—"

"If I require something, I'm capable of raising my voice to call, or mayhap I could even use my legs to get it myself."

The woman looked as if she thought her mistress had lost her mind.

"Go on," Ellen said to her with a sigh. "Go find something to do."

Obviously reluctant, the woman stood and started to leave the room, but Ellen called her back. "First I want you to find me a page boy. His name is Rolf, and he was out in the bailey a few minutes ago.''

"Rolf, milady?''

"Aye. Send him to me.''

Sylvianne left the room, shaking her head, but in a few minutes there was a soft knock at the door, and Ellen opened it to admit Rolf.

He tugged at his forelock and bowed several times, waiting for her to speak.

"Come in, Rolf,'' she said, holding the door.

His eyes opened wide, but he did as she bade him.

When she'd closed the door behind him, she turned to face him and said, "Don't be afraid, Rolf. I wanted to know if you had word of Sarah Cooper.''

It was as if a shutter had clapped down over the boy's face. "Nay, milady,'' he answered, a little too quickly.

Ellen smiled. "Sarah's my friend, Rolf,'' she told him, surprised to realize as she said it that it was the truth. She no longer thought of the Coopers as tenants, but as friends. "I was with her and her family until last night, and I've not revealed their hiding place, nor will I.''

She could see Rolf's shoulders relax. "She's safe from that bastard,'' he said bitterly. "'Tis all that matters.''

"From Sir William?''

"Aye, he been after 'er for months.''

"She's told you this?''

"Aye, and I've seen it. Nearly everyone in Lyonsbridge has.''

Ellen tucked the information away in her head, but

she had more pressing matters to deal with first. "Do you know about the flogging in the village?"

"Aye, milady, but they say 'tis not to happen, after all."

"Who said?"

"Everyone's saying it. By order of Lord Wakelin, they say."

"Thank God," Ellen said with a deep breath of relief.

"Aye, milady."

She studied the page for a moment, tapping her finger against her mouth. He appeared to be a bright lad, and comely, as Sarah had blushingly confided to her. The two young people would make a good match, if the Coopers were ever allowed to resume a normal life.

"So you know where the Coopers are hiding?" she asked him.

He looked at the floor and appeared reluctant to answer.

"I'm not asking you to reveal anything, Rolf. But I want you to go to them and let them know that the floggings have been called off."

He lifted his head. "My duties—"

"I'll cover for you here at the castle, if need be. Stay with her as long as you like. But be sure you tell Master Brand about the floggings. And tell him…" She hesitated.

What exactly did she want the boy to tell Connor? What message could communicate the jumble of feelings that had been inside her since the Saxon had left her the previous evening at the gates of the castle? Aye, and if she could somehow let Connor know her feelings, what would be the sense of it? He was being sought as an outlaw along with John Cooper. It was likely that she would never see him again.

"Just tell him that I arrived safely," she said finally.

Rolf's face had brightened in anticipation of seeing his sweetheart. He gave an eager nod of agreement. "Aye, milady. I'll give Master Brand your message."

She let him out of the room, then walked slowly back to her bed and sat. The boy was eager and reliable. Connor would no doubt receive her message. The only problem, she decided as she flopped backward on the bed, was that it hadn't been the message she really wanted to send.

She'd stayed in her chambers all day. Sylvianne had brought her food at midday and in the early evening, and Ellen had tried to eat, but her thoughts were too much on the Coopers, still in the clammy cave by the sea. Was little Karyn getting used to the dark shadows at night? Was Agnes coughing again?

Ellen had sent the maid away each time with a nearly full tray, certain that her lack of appetite would be reported to her father. It was probably just as well. It would let him know that she was serious about her vow to stake her own welfare against that of the Lyonsbridge villagers.

On the morrow she would ride to the village herself, she resolved. She wanted to let the people know that the days of abuse by Normans were over. She'd not stand for it. If they could only get the matter of William Booth's death resolved, they could work together to return peace to this place.

On that optimistic hope, she changed to her night rail without summoning Sylvianne to help her. She'd had enough of the woman's obsequious company for one day.

A fire was laid. The chamber's small fireplace was a luxury she'd been delighted to discover at Lyonsbridge. In Normandy only the great hall and the kitchen had hearths. For the first time in her life, she took the tinder box to light the fire by herself and gave a smile of satisfaction at her independence when the shavings ignited.

When the thicker branches began to catch, she crossed the room, hopped up onto the high bed, tucked her bare feet up under the skirts of her nightgown and stared at the flames.

The licks of gold reminded her of the color of Connor's hair in the rays of the setting sun.

"I've come to thank you, milady," came a voice out of the shadows.

It was *his* voice, and for the briefest moment she thought she'd conjured him from the fire by some strange witchcraft, but then she realized that he was indeed here, in this very room, standing by the far wall, watching her.

"How did you get here?" she asked with a gasp, drawing the covers up against her thin dress.

"'Tis my bedchamber," he answered, stepping into the light. "Or it was. I slipped in through the casement as I did countless times in my youth after the castle was shut tight for the night." His grin held vestiges of that long lost boy.

"You climbed up the wall?" she asked, amazed.

"Aye." He discounted the feat with a wave of his

hand and walked toward her. "Circumstances forced me to leave you at the gate last night instead of escorting you to your door as would a true gentleman. 'Twas not the way my mother raised her sons."

"But you knew I was safely arrived. Did not Rolf go to the cave? I sent him—"

"The boy came this morning," he interrupted. "He brought your message that the floggings had been cancelled, which I trow was your accomplishment. I came to see you safe with my own eyes and also to thank you."

"I need no thanks. I couldn't believe my father had ordered such a thing in the first place. Sebastian sometimes holds ill influence over him."

Connor walked a step closer to the bed. "But his daughter holds good influence."

She thought for a moment. "I'm not sure I've ever tried much before today."

"How did you get him to change his mind about the floggings? John Cooper is still at large."

"'Tis not important," she said. "The important thing is that they're stopped." She gave a little shudder.

The covers had slipped down from around her as they spoke, and Connor reached to lift a blanket over her shoulders. "I should not keep you sitting up," he said. "You'll take a chill."

"I'm not cold," she said. Her voice came out a whisper.

He looked down at her a long moment, and she felt the now familiar closing of her throat, the plunge in her midsection. His blue eyes burned more brightly than the fire.

His knee slipped onto the bed beside her, then his arms went around her, and without conscious thought, she encircled his neck with her own arms and offered up her lips.

"I didn't come for this, I swear," he murmured.

But their union had been preordained, Ellen decided as he laid her back against her pillows. It was as if the mists of this wild land had swirled into her body and carried away her will and reason, leaving her wanting only the feel of her Saxon knight in her arms, his lips searing her skin.

He rolled away briefly to disrobe, then stood next to her by the bed, naked and splendid in the flickering firelight. She'd seen men stripped of their clothes, prisoners and others, but the sight had never before caused this flush of heat to her face, the throbbing all the way to her legs.

"Now you, sweetheart," he said. "I'd see thy fair body."

With amazingly little self-consciousness, she let his big, roughened hands strip away her nightdress, and she lay quiet beneath his slow gaze.

His teeth caught his lower lip as he looked at her. After a moment he said, "On my oath, Ellen of Wakelin, thou art the most beautiful woman I've ever looked upon."

Then he moved over her, finally skin against skin, his warm and hers cold. She felt the roughened hair of his legs against her smooth, sensitive thighs. His hard chest gently flattened her peaking breasts as his mouth joined hers in a long, silken mating.

She moved underneath him, restless and longing

for deeper contact. "In truth you have never known a man?" he asked, low in her ear.

She shook her head and turned her face away from him for a moment, but her need was stronger than her embarrassment, and when his lips sought hers again, she gave them willingly.

"Then we must go gently, my sweet," he murmured, "though my body races."

He held her upper arms to still her movement as he kissed a trail from her chin to her breasts, then tenderly drew a nipple into his mouth and suckled. She lifted her head to look down at him. His lashes swept up as his eyes met hers, heavy-lidded and sensual. The sight sent a shaft of longing to her loins.

Just as her nipple was beginning to sting from his rhythmic sucking, he let it loose and switched to the other side. She let her head fall back and concentrated on the rush of feeling centered in the tiny nub.

"Ah, Saxon," she moaned after several moments. "What have you done to me?"

Connor pushed himself up to face her once again and regarded her with a lopsided, sensual grin. "Saxon? I'll hear my Christian name on your lips, my Norman enchantress, before we become lovers."

"Are we not yet lovers? Is this a dream that I lie naked in your arms?"

He shook his head slowly, then crooked his leg to allow his thigh to brush that most sensitive part of her body. "We've only begun, sweetheart, but I'd hear my name. Say it. Say, make love to me, Connor."

It would be a declaration of surrender, and both knew it. He would no longer be a servant, nor yet a conquered Saxon, but Connor, her lover, her equal, her master even, in the age-old way that men had always mastered women.

She withheld a long moment while his husky voice whispered in her ear and his tongue made swirls around her earlobe and the top of her neck. Then, slow and sure, his hand stroked along her stomach and lower, finding the soft folds of her and sending wild waves of sensation rocking upward.

"Love me, Connor," she groaned.

The slowness was over, replaced by frenzy. The movement of his fingers became faster, more assured, and she let her legs fall open and called out to him again, needy and searching for release. He moved quickly, filling her, with a whisper of apology. But her horsewoman's body was strong and ready. The brief discomfort turned to an exquisite fullness, then an urgency and she dug her nails into his back as their rhythm became frantic.

Finally, he stiffened and gave a small moan. Deep inside she felt the pulsing, and it triggered an answering crash that rocked throughout her body, leaving her trembling and weak.

Connor's arms had collapsed beneath him and he lay, apparently equally stricken. But he was the first to move, sliding to one side and gathering her in his arms. "I didn't hurt you, sweetheart?" he asked, nuzzling her neck.

She shook her head.

"'Tis a wonder," he marveled. "I daresay 'twas vigorous for first-time lovemaking. You made me lose myself."

"You weren't overly lost, horse master," she said

with a teasing smile. "I knew where you were the entire time."

He gave a deep laugh and reached down to gently swat her bare behind. "'Tis lucky for you I like my wenches saucy. But I told you to call me by my name."

"'Twas the price of becoming your lover. But now the deed is done."

"Are you thinking I'll slink back to my stables then, and things will be as before?" His tone was half-serious.

They had been said in jest, but her remark and his reply set a sudden chill to the room. Ellen looked over to see if the fire had died. It burned brightly.

"Things will not be as before," she said slowly, "but in truth, I know not how they will be."

He was quiet a long moment. When she lifted her head to see his face, he was looking around the room as though remembering when this place had been his by right of law and of birth.

"Connor?" she prompted.

He finally turned his head back to her. His smile was brittle. "We said 'twas madness, this thing betwixt us. Mayhap we've tamed the madness, for the nonce."

"What do you mean by that?" The chill had reached up to her throat.

He was already putting on his clothes. "My very presence here puts my life at risk, milady."

"You're leaving?" she asked, unable to believe what she was seeing.

"If I'm caught, your father will have my head on a pike. 'Tis that simple."

Somehow she knew that fear for his life was not at the core of Connor's sudden change in mood. He was anything but a coward. He certainly had had little fear when he'd climbed three stories to reach her room. There was something more to his departure.

Suddenly shy of her nakedness, she covered herself with blankets as he finished dressing. "When will I see you again?" she asked, feeling weak for posing the question.

He stood gazing down at her, his expression stoic. "Did you like living in a cave, milady? Are you eager to join me in that romantic, dank bower by the sea?"

She could not reply.

After a moment, he nodded. "I thought not." He took a final look around the bedchamber. "'Twas madness, in truth," he said softly, as if talking to himself. "A most wondrous madness."

Then she felt a whoosh of chill air as the casement shutters opened and he was gone.

Chapter Fourteen

Ellen had changed her mind at least a dozen times throughout the night. One moment she'd punch her mattress in fury and vow that first thing in the morning she'd go to her father and tell him the Saxons' hiding place, so that his soldiers could clear out the entire lot, starting with their arrogant leader.

The next moment she'd consider making her way to Father Martin at the abbey and asking him to take her to Connor.

She couldn't remember her mind ever being in such a muddle, and it kept her tossing until shortly before dawn, when she fell into an exhausted sleep, still feeling the traces of Connor's fingers on her skin.

It was midmorning when she awoke, and then only because Sylvianne had knocked on the door to check on her mistress's welfare. She'd sent the woman away and dressed herself, still no closer to a decision about her next move.

The most sensible thing would be to put the night of love out of her mind entirely, and the horse master along with it. She should ascribe it to a fit of madness, as he had apparently done with such ease, and forget it ever happened. But how was she to banish that memory of his eyes, heavy with desire? Of his kisses, melting the strength from her limbs?

Connor had been right about one thing. If her father discovered what he had done to her, he would have his head. And if he knew the whole of it, how after taking her virginity, his stable master had discarded her like a broken pitcher, he would see Connor's limbs torn from his body.

She gave a deep sigh as she descended the twisting stairway to the great hall. It was well past the hour to break fast, and the room appeared to be empty, but as she went into the buttery for some ale to cut the morning chill, she encountered Sebastian, filling a cup for himself.

He raised it in a mock toast. "So you've decided to rejoin society, Cousin, now that you've unmanned your father with your childish tantrum."

"I see nothing manly about a leader flogging his vassals," she said. "If 'twas my doing that changed my father's mind, then I'm grateful for it."

"You know not the ways of men, Ellen. A leader who threatens and then doesn't carry out his threats is seen as impotent."

"A leader who is capable of admitting a mistake is seen as wise," she snapped.

"Verily, Cousin, I think the damp English air has sickened your brain. In France you were never one to meddle in affairs that were best left to men. No lord worth his salt would let the murder of his reeve go unpunished."

"Sir William was not murdered."

"So say these Saxons you seem to have grown so fond of. Are you going to listen to them before your own kinsmen?" His sharp black eyes narrowed as he studied her. "Mayhap 'tis *one* Saxon in particular you listen to."

"'Tis justice I listen to," she insisted, but she couldn't help the telltale flush that ran up her cheeks.

Sebastian cocked his head, considering. "The horse master," he said slowly, comprehension dawning. "How like a female to be swayed by a handsome face and form," he sneered. "In case you hadn't heard, Cousin, Connor Brand is declared outlaw, too."

"He's done nothing," she said. Nothing but smash her heart asunder not twelve hours ago.

A light of glee danced in Sebastian's eyes. "I believe Lord Wakelin needs to know of this, my dear cousin. You must be protected from your own misguidance."

Ellen felt sick at the pit of her stomach, but she refused to let her cousin see the weapon he held over her. "Tell my father what you will, Cousin," she said breezily. "He's not likely to believe you over his own daughter."

Sebastian's smile didn't waver. "We'll see whom he believes, Cousin. And we'll see how resolute he becomes in finding this stable master when he learns that his precious daughter lusts after the man like a village strumpet."

The two fishermen had finally returned, weary and on foot after their boat had been smashed on the rocks in a cove far to the south, where they'd ventured in an unsuccessful search for a cave large enough for all the Saxon refugees. In the end it was decided to split the group and disperse to smaller caves, which were plentiful all along the coast.

"Mayhap 'tis a better plan, anyway. 'Twill be more difficult to find several smaller sites than one big one," Walter Little had said, trying to put a good face on things.

Connor had been unusually silent all morning, just at a time when his leadership was needed more than ever.

Humbert White and his companions had already taken their things and moved, and several of the families had left as well. The Coopers remained, waiting for Connor, along with a number of the other outlaws who remained loyal to their former lord. With the Coopers was the castle page, Rolf, who had vowed to join the outlaws rather than return to a Norman rule that could so endanger John and Sarah.

Connor raised his gaze from the fire where he'd been staring for the past several minutes. "Aye, 'tis as well," he agreed. "In truth, 'tis time to end this thing of hiding in caves and in the forest. These people belong at Lyonsbridge, raising their families, going about their occupations, leading normal lives."

Walter looked skeptical. "Aye, and Normandy should sink into the sea, but I doubt either of those things will happen."

Connor stood and picked up the bucket of sand to douse the fire. "Let us leave this sodden hole," he said brusquely.

Walter kicked at the sticks that had fallen from the fire, watching Connor with troubled eyes. "We're but exchanging this hole for another, my lord. You can't go back to the village, nor can the Coopers. Sometimes I worry over your lack of fear, lad. It goes against good sense.''

Fear? Aye, Connor thought with another twist of his gut. He *was* afraid. Not of Lord Wakelin's men. He'd face them twenty to one if need be. But he couldn't answer for his bravery if he ever again had to lay eyes on his daughter.

When his parents had died and left him the trust of caring for his people, he'd thought his destiny had been chosen. He'd never looked beyond that to a re-awakening of any sense of a life for himself. In one hot, magical encounter that had all changed. This morning, after lying awake the night through, he'd realized that he'd give over his trust, let every other cause and England along with it fester and rot, if he could but have her. The knowledge had shaken him more profoundly than anything since he'd lowered his mother into the ground.

''I'm not a fool, Walter,'' he said. ''The Coopers and I will find another cave to hide away like the rats we've become, and you're welcome to join us.''

They helped the Coopers gather their things, leaving what they couldn't carry, and set off. Miraculously, the sizable group of people who had inhabited the cave seemed to have melted into the sand cliffs of the coast like so many snowflakes.

Connor, Walter, the Coopers, Rolf and the four outlaws who had chosen to join them settled on a small cavern a scant two miles from the original cave. Walter had urged more distance, but Connor had seen that Agnes Cooper was once again flagging, and had decreed that they would camp there, at least for the time being.

John had spent a lot of time in the past few idle days listening to Humbert and the other malcontents, and had almost decided to journey with them, until Sarah had told him that their mother needed him. But now, as they settled into the cramped new quarters, he was fidgety and ill-tempered.

Finally Sarah turned on him and said sharply, "'Tis to save your hide we've left our home and come to this place, John. The least you could do is try to be pleasant."

"Aye, sister, and 'twas to save your virtue that I put my hide at risk," he snapped back. "I'll not be chastened by—"

Agnes held up a shaky hand, stopping her children in midargument. "We've enough trouble with the Normans without turning on ourselves," she said with her usual firm serenity.

Sarah looked instantly contrite, but John turned away muttering and left the cave.

Connor watched him go without trying to stop him. The boy reminded him of himself in earlier days, when he still had the faith to rail at the lot fate had cast him in sending conquerers to his beloved land.

He'd long since lost that faith. Martin may have come to some kind of peace by turning to his God, but Connor held on to one creed only—his people. He'd sworn to keep them safe and away from the ravages of war. His night with Ellen at the castle had been a betrayal of that creed. It was a mistake he had no intention of repeating.

* * *

"Is there truth to your cousin's words, my daughter?" Lord Wakelin asked, his voice disbelieving. "Have you developed a fondness for this stableman?"

Ellen wanted to tell her father that Connor was more than a horse trainer, but any attempt at defending him would surely be taken as confirmation of Sebastian's charges. "My cousin has ever been fanciful, Father," she said, looking at Sebastian in disgust. He stood hovering over her father's shoulder, like some kind of ill-fed vulture ready to swoop.

Wakelin twisted around to look up at him. "What gave you this odd notion, Nephew?"

Sebastian's smile came too quickly. "'Tis known among the villagers, milord, that this man has set every maid in the shire a-swoon."

"For shame, Sebastian," Wakelin snapped. "Ellen's not a village maid. She has the best suitors in Europe at her feet. What care has she for a lowborn Saxon lout?"

Ellen remained silent.

Sebastian moved around the chair so that he was facing his uncle more squarely. "Mayhap 'tis but a fancy, as she says. I hope so, for the men I've set to investigate Booth's murder tell me that 'twas surely done with the complicity of the horse master. Mayhap at his instigation."

"'Tis a lie," Ellen cried.

Her father turned his head sharply to look at her. "Daughter?" he asked mildly.

She forced herself to remain calm and lowered her voice. "I was with these people, Father, immediately after the incident. Connor Brand knew nothing about the killing until John Cooper came to him. The boy acted alone, and that only in defense of his sister.''

"There's long been bad blood 'twixt this stableman and Booth," Sebastian insisted. "And he fled immediately after the murder, which is proof of guilt in itself.''

"Connor was only helping the Cooper family to get away for fear revenge would be taken by Booth's men before the full story was revealed," Ellen told her father.

Lord Wakelin pushed back his chair and sighed. "'Tis for a court to decide the truth of it. But both the boy and this horseman must be brought to justice.''

"Aye," Sebastian agreed with a sly glance at Ellen. "And if my fair cousin cares naught for the man, she won't demur if we put a reward on his head.''

"The matter should be settled," Wakelin said. "You have my permission to offer a reward. Post it in the village as well. I'm sure the people there know more than what your troops have been able to wring out of them.''

"Father, you cannot—" Ellen began.

But her father stopped her with a shake of his head. "Leave it be, Daughter. 'Tis not your affair, and if you continue to meddle, I'll have to send you back to Normandy, where I should have kept you in the first place.''

Sebastian cast a look of triumph at Ellen. "By your leave, Uncle, I'll see to your orders.''

Her father turned back to his papers as Sebastian left the room, bringing the audience to a close, and leaving her no choice but to retire to her room and hope that the unity she had witnessed among the Saxon villagers would withstand the temptation of Sebastian's Judas gold.

By late afternoon, the worry, combined with her lack of sleep the previous evening, had given her a fierce headache. She wished there was some way to find out what was happening back in the caves, but the page boy Rolf had not returned to his duties at the castle.

She even considered trying to ride out herself, but she was sure that her father would never consent to her traveling abroad while troops still combed the countryside. So she stayed in her room, paced the floor, snapped at Sylvianne and tried to banish the thought of Connor's kisses from her throbbing head.

It was nearly sundown when Sylvianne knocked, timidly, her voice apologetic.

Ellen pulled open the door and asked rudely, "What do you want now?"

"'Tis the priest, milady, asking for you."

"Father Martin?"

"Aye, he's in the chapel—"

Before the poor woman could finish her sentence, Ellen had pushed past her and was making her way down the winding stairs and across the great hall to the chapel at the opposite end of the castle.

Father Martin was kneeling at the altar, his eyes closed in prayer. She hesitated, then cleared her throat.

He took another few moments before he crossed himself and stood to face her. "Good afternoon, milady."

"My handmaid said you wanted to see me," she said, faltering a little at the end of her sentence. In the candlelight of the chapel, the priest's resemblance to his brother was startling—those same intense eyes, the same long nose and square line of his jaw.

He walked down the aisle toward her. Close-up, it was easier to banish the apparition of Connor. The priest's round form under his robes was nothing like the strong, lean body she'd seen above her in the fire-light of her bedchamber the previous evening. Heat flooded her face at the memory.

Father Martin nodded, as if appreciating her abandonment of the polite preliminaries. "Aye. Your father's soldiers are searching the caves along the coast for the refugee Saxons. 'Tis likely they'll find John Cooper. Methinks the lad will not flee and leave his family to face Norman wrath."

Ellen felt a swift stab of disappointment. So the villagers had not held firm against the temptation of easy money. After witnessing how they all worked together to help one another, she'd been virtually certain that not a soul would reveal the outlaws' whereabouts. "Who told them of the caves?" she asked.

Father Martin winced. "No Saxon soul, as God be my witness. One of Phippen's men discovered the large cave where you were kept. 'Twas an easy deduction that they'd sought similar refuge farther down the coast."

Ellen sighed, but it was satisfying to know that it had not been her father's reward that had made the difference. Nevertheless, Father Martin was right. If the soldiers were searching the caves, it was likely that they could stumble upon both John and Connor at any moment.

"Will you take me to them?" she asked Father Martin.

"I beg your pardon, milady?" he asked.

"Will you take me to where your brother is now so we can warn them?"

Father Martin bent his head and looked deep into her eyes. "The soldiers will be there before we could ever reach them," he said, then added gently, "and in any event, I don't think it would help my brother's case to be found with the daughter of the Norman overlord."

She turned away from his searching gaze.

"What is between you two, milady?" the priest asked.

He was a holy man, and she could not lie, but he had not asked her for details. It would be the truth to tell him that there was nothing between them, for Connor had made it plain in his rejection of her the previous evening that their encounter had been the swift satisfaction of their lust, nothing more.

"We may be able to prove Connor innocent of Booth's death," the priest continued. "But what will be his fate if 'tis proven that he, a humble servant, has cast his eyes upon the lord's daughter?"

"There's naught between me and your brother, Father," she said, meeting his eyes.

"By the holy rood, you swear it?"

"Aye. There's naught between us now, nor ever will be."

Father Martin nodded, his expression relieved. "If

John and Connor are arrested, I beg my lady to use her good offices to see that they're not mistreated."

"Of course."

"And I shall begin to gather evidence to prove their innocence. 'Twill not be easy in John's case. Though Booth was a known lecher, we have only the girl's word that he attacked her, plus that of the accused. There were no bruises on her body."

Ellen drew herself up indignantly. "Does a woman have to be battered and broken before she can be defended? Methinks not, Father Martin."

The priest smiled. "I agree with you, my child. We'll just have to hope that your father's court is of like opinion."

When she came to attend her mistress the following morning, Sylvianne informed Ellen with a sniff of disdain that perhaps things could finally return to normal in this godforsaken castle, now that the miscreants had been brought in and thrown into the belly of the keep.

Ellen pressed the woman for details, and she reported that the entire family of the boy-murderer, as well as the estate's former stable master, had been arrested and chained in the donjon.

"Chained?" Ellen exclaimed in horror. "Not the widow, surely? Nor the twins? They're yet babes."

The woman gave an annoying shrug and, when Ellen once again refused her help to dress, shuffled away with an air of insult.

It took less than ten minutes for Ellen to dress herself and make her way to the lower floor of the castle, below the great hall, where a maze of storerooms was occasionally used as a castle prison.

It was one area of the castle that Ellen had not yet reached in her cleaning campaign. The place smelled of the offal of animals and rotted food. Light filtered in from the outside around the periphery, but as she ventured into the interior of the maze, she found almost total darkness. Good lord, she hoped poor little Karyn Cooper was not in one of these cubicles.

One of the men who had ridden with her and Sebastian from Normandy was on guard at the end of a narrow passageway. He lifted a torch from a nearby bracket and held it up to determine the identity of the newcomer. When he saw Ellen, he gave a slight bow, then said, "You're not to go in there, milady. We've prisoners."

"That's why I'm here," she said curtly. "I've come to see them."

The man looked uncomfortable, but did not move out of her way. "'Tis your cousin's orders, milady. I'm to let no one near them."

"What's your name, soldier?"

"DeGuerre, milady."

"Are you aware that I am mistress of this household, DeGuerre?"

"Aye, milady, but your cousin said—"

She pierced the man with her most intimidating stare. "My cousin is here at my father's will, not by right of birth. If you want to jeopardize your position at this castle by naysaying the rightful mistress, then let it be on your head."

Uncertain, DeGuerre shifted back and forth, causing the heavy armored vest he wore to creak. While he was still evidently deciding what he should do, Ellen plucked the torch from his hand and slipped around him down the hall.

She found them in a small room at the end of the passageway. The tiny space was crowded with barrels. Abel and Karyn perched side by side on two of them, their wide eyes looking haunted.

Along the far wall Sarah, Agnes, John, Rolf and Connor were tied together. The bonds were rope, thank goodness, not chain, but nevertheless the sight made Ellen grow pale.

"Milady," Sarah called with a shout of joy.

But Ellen went first to Karyn, who had burst into tears at the sight of her. She found a wall bracket for the torch, then gathered the child into her arms and cradled her. "This is outrageous," she said, when she could speak over the fullness in her throat.

"'Tis your Norman justice of which you spoke so highly, milady," John Cooper said bitterly.

"Hold thy tongue, John," his sister chided.

Karyn's sniffles subsided as she rested her head against Ellen's shoulder. "She was 'fraid of the dark shadows." Abel, as usual, interpreted for his sister. "She thought they were dragons."

Ellen kissed the top of her head. "There are no dragons here in Lyonsbridge, Karyn. Nor any wild beasts."

"Other than your cousin's dragoons." Connor spoke for the first time. His voice was tinged with the old mocking amusement, in spite of the gravity of the circumstances.

Agnes had not spoken, and now that Karyn was no longer clutching her neck so desperately, Ellen turned her attention to the widow. In the dim torchlight, her face was haggard and she looked suddenly like a very old woman.

"Are you all right?" Ellen asked her. The widow appeared too weak to answer, but she mustered one of her gentle smiles.

Ellen gave Karyn a final squeeze, then set her back on the barrel. "Sit right there for a minute, sweetling, while I talk to your mum."

Abel reached across from his barrel and took his sister's hand. "I'll take care of her, 'lady," he said, his little voice solemn.

Ellen walked toward the five prisoners. Connor's eyes had not left her since she'd entered the little room. It was the first time they had seen each other since the night they had made love, but she pushed the thought away. This was not the moment to think about Connor's rejection of her.

She studied the thick rope wrapped around each individual, linking them together in a sinister chain. "Mistress Cooper, you're going to be ill again. We've got to get you out of here," she said. With a despairing glance at the heavy rope, she added, "To get you all out of here."

"My thought precisely," Connor agreed, and before she knew what had happened, the rope seemed to have dissolved from around him and he'd bounded up to stand by her side, almost knocking her off her feet in surprise.

"How...what...?" she sputtered.

Connor rubbed his wrists where the rope had chafed. "I've something of a facility with knots, sweetheart. I've been free of the bonds this hour past, but I'd not yet thought of a plan for leaving this place safely with the widow and the little ones. At least not one that didn't involve killing any guard that got in our way.''

"I'd kill them all," John muttered, "for what they've done to my family."

Connor turned a reproachful glance on the lad. "More killing 'twould but lead to further reprisals and more bloodshed, John. You're young, you've yet to learn that lesson." He turned to ask Ellen, "How many guards did you encounter in coming here?"

"Just one. A man named DeGuerre."

"He let you pass freely?"

"More or less."

Connor gave her a quick smile of approval. "Then the man's a fool and should not be difficult to pass. The problem will be once we leave these stinking catacombs. We're sure to encounter more guards, mayhap some not as easily swayed by a pretty face."

Ellen thought for a long moment. "What if the guards were all sent off on another mission?"

"What mission? Now that they've caught us, they've ceased hunting for the rest of the outlaws. They care naught for that ragged crew."

"Nay, but they would care about the daughter of the lord, if she were kidnapped by the outlaws who remain."

Agnes lifted her head from the wall long enough to protest. "I'll not have you making foolish plans, milady. I'd not exchange our freedom if it meant harm to you."

But Ellen had warmed to her plan. "I won't be in the least danger. I'll simply ride away, disappear, and when my father receives a message that I'm once again being held hostage, he'll send every soldier out in search of me. Once you're safely away, I'll come back and say I was released unharmed and that I want to forget the whole incident.''

Connor shook his head. ''You're not to become involved in this again.''

''I won't be involved. I'll merely be going for a ride, as I have done dozens of times. 'Twill be a diversionary tactic, nothing more.''

Connor smiled at her use of the battle terminology, but he said, ''I've told you before that I like not the idea of you riding out alone.''

She looked first at the children. Karyn's little face was peaked and haunted. Abel offered her a wobbly, but brave smile. Then she turned her eyes to Agnes, who had slumped weakly against the wall.

With a grim smile of resolution, she turned back to Connor. ''Horse master, it appears to me that you are not in a position to have much choice in the matter.''

Chapter Fifteen

He argued with her for fully five minutes, but Ellen did not waver from her plan. Finally, realizing that she was as stubborn as she was beautiful, he agreed, and they began to discuss the details of the escape. Both realized that it had to be done quickly, before Agnes Cooper became too weak to flee.

"Escaping from this place won't solve the dilemma," Connor pointed out, frustrated. "They'll just start looking for us again."

She told him of his brother's search to find evidence of Sir William's lechery and added that she needed additional time to talk to her father. As she made ready to leave, she said, "No matter what you may think of Norman justice, Connor, my father's a fair man."

"If he's anything like his daughter," he replied, "I'd trust my fate in his hands."

Then he grasped her shoulders and brought her against him for a quick, almost violent kiss that left them both shaken.

The sting of it stayed on her lips as she made her

way to the stables. She'd set the stage, left the note where Sylvianne would find it when she came to see if her mistress needed help preparing for supper. All Ellen had to do was slip away without being seen, so that no one would know that she'd gone of her own volition.

Jocelyn was waiting peacefully in her stall and gave a soft whinny as she recognized her owner's scent. Would kidnappers make her take her own horse? Ellen wondered suddenly. She would just have to hope her father and Sebastian would think so, for she had no other way to get far enough away from Lyonsbridge so that she wouldn't be easily found.

She started to lift her saddle, looking up and down the aisle of stalls to be sure she wouldn't be surprised by a stable boy wandering in. Her eyes lit on the spiral stairway at the far corner. It led to the quarters Connor had fashioned for himself.

She should have known the minute she'd seen his rooms that this man was not a mere horse trainer. Though lacking some of the amenities of the castle, he'd outfitted the two rooms comfortably, very much like his former chambers in the castle, when his family had been lords of Lyonsbridge.

She remembered how shocked she'd been when he'd told her he lived in the stables. No one seeing him working day after day in the muck would guess that he lived just upstairs in relative luxury.

The saddle was poised in midair, suddenly heavy in her arms. *No one would guess,* she thought to herself again. "Of course," she said aloud. Why should she go riding off, playing hide and seek with her father's troops across the countryside, when she had a perfectly good hideout right here? Everyone knew that Connor had abandoned his former lodgings, and in any event, they certainly wouldn't think to search for *her* here, right under their very noses.

She slammed the saddle back on the fence, gave Jocelyn an apologetic pat and ran toward the stairway. She could stay here comfortably for hours, until the morrow if need be. She'd have refreshment, books to read, even a soft bed if she grew tired.

Skipping with pleasure at her own ingenuity, she hurried up the stairs.

In the end they'd simply walked away. Even the guard Ellen had seen posted at the end of the passageway was nowhere in sight when, shortly after sundown, Connor led his band through the maze of storerooms and out a covered side entrance he and his brothers had used as children.

They'd spent most of the afternoon discussing where they would go to keep out of the way of the soldiers until Martin could come forward with his evidence or Ellen could make good on her promise to sway her father.

Agnes and Sarah had both shuddered when John had suggested returning to the caves.

"I could take you to my people in Baintry," Rolf had offered. "'Tis but a two day's journey. We could walk all night and hide during the day."

Sarah looked as if the page had offered to slay one of Karyn's dragons for her, but Connor had been doubtful. "I'm not sure you would make a two-night walk, mistress," he said to Agnes. "Nor would the little ones."

"I'm stronger than I look, my son," she told him, and, indeed, in her eyes was a shaft of determination he could not deny.

"Rolf and I can carry these sprites when they get tired," John had added, hoisting Abel up on his shoulders.

Once Connor had assured himself of everyone's resolve, he agreed to the plan, but told them that he himself would stay near Lyonsbridge.

"I'd know that the lady Ellen is returned safe," he said, adding, "and I want to talk with Martin about the evidence he has gathered."

He walked with them the first two miles, making certain that Agnes was up to the pace, then he cautioned them one more time to get themselves well hidden before the first rays of dawn, and he left to make his way back to Lyonsbridge.

There was a single candle burning low in its stand on the table in the middle of his bedchamber. One of his blankets had been draped over the window shutters to prevent the dim light from being seen by anyone walking in the stable yard below. She was there in the middle of the bed, curled up like a sleeping child, but the curves of her body were no child's.

He stood in the doorway and watched her for several long minutes. Her black hair streamed back from her beautiful face, sweet and tranquil now in sleep, with none of the arrogance he'd seen the day she'd first come riding into his stable and into his life.

He'd felt a little guilty for leaving the Coopers on the road without seeing them to their destination, but as he watched the gentle rise and fall of Ellen's breasts, he realized that he had somehow expected this encounter. He'd sought and ached for one last meeting with the spirited Norman maid. Their lives would take them on two different roads, but first they would come together one more time.

He walked over to the bed slowly, not taking his eyes from her. His body was already aroused, but there was a feeling beyond the physical, an emotion that made his breathing shallow and fast.

He stood over her and traced a finger along her delicate cheek. She stirred, but did not awaken. Though his body was urging otherwise, he was determined not to hurry. He picked up his lute from beside his bed, then walked into the outer chamber. It had been months since he'd played. He'd told Martin that the coming of the Normans had banished the music from his soul. Mayhap this Norman woman had brought it back.

Taking a seat on his window bench, he idly plucked the strings, remembering how Ellen's slender fingers had looked playing the instrument on the day he'd caught her in his rooms. Those same fingers had explored his body, tentatively at first, then more boldly, during their one night of love. The memory stirred him again, but still he waited, and began to pick out a tune. It was a ballad about a wood sprite who'd met and made love to a mortal man. Their union was impossible, but the faeries of the forest had agreed to give the lovers one more night of magic before they had to part.

He'd learned the ballad from a wandering troubadour, who'd claimed that the man had been none other than he himself. His lute had seemed to come alive as the story unfolded, and the handsome young man had left every lady in Lyonsbridge, even Connor's mother, swooning at his romantic tale.

Connor gave a little smile at the memory. Those had been good days, before the troubles, days when his parents had expected to live to an old age, reigning over their castle and their lands, watching their sons marry and produce strong grandchildren.

It was not to be. His parents and Geoffrey were dead, Martin sworn to the church and Connor to his people. But like the troubadour song, he'd been given one more night of enchantment.

The music seemed to be part of Ellen's dream. She'd fallen asleep restlessly, her head full of caves and leering outlaws and dreadful images of John Cooper's thin back being torn to ribbons by the flogger's lash. But in midsleep the dream had changed to a forest clearing, that faerie circle where Connor had first kissed her, and her body had stirred at the memory.

Then the faeries were there, dancing to the music of a lute, and she came awake with a start as she realized that the music was not a dream at all.

She lay still a moment, listening, though she knew it could be none other than he. As the notes filtered in from the next room, she smiled and stretched sensuously. She'd *known* he would find her here. Subconsciously, she'd been waiting for him all afternoon.

The music stopped and he appeared in the doorway, looming like a giant in the shadows cast by the single candle. A deep throb had begun within her from the moment she sensed his presence. She had to force herself to think about the world beyond this haven they'd found.

"The Coopers?" she asked, sitting up.

He approached the bed. "They're away safe. I won't tell you where—" When she frowned he added quickly, "'Tis not because I don't trust you, Ellen, but only so that you can say with all truth that you know naught of their whereabouts."

"Should you not be with them?"

His eyes were hooded. "I wanted to be sure you were safe."

She smiled. "I trow my father's men are searching for me far and wide, but I've never left home."

Connor looked around the room. "'Twas a wise plan. On the morrow you should be able to return to the castle and tell your father that the outlaws released you."

"Aye." She swallowed hard as he continued watching her with those sleepy eyes, but made no move to come closer to her. "On the morrow," she ended in a whisper. The last time they'd been alone together, he'd rejected her, had in fact seemed to resent their coming together. She bit her lip, looking up at him. Had he truly come only to see her safe, and would he now leave to join his friends?

Then he smiled, slowly and sensually, and she felt it as a swift plunge through her midsection.

"On the morrow," he repeated, his voice husky.

She nodded.

He lifted the lute he still held in one hand. "Would my lady like some entertainment to make the hours fly by on faster wings?"

"Mayhap," she answered with a dry mouth.

He sat beside her on the bed and gave a tuneless strum across the strings. "Do you prefer adventurous ballads, milady, or sweet songs of love?"

"Prithee make the choice for me, Sir Minstrel."

He plucked out an intricate series of notes, haunting and wild. "Ah, if the choice is left to me, milady, 'twill be the music of seduction." His spoken words were as melodious as the music itself.

A pulse beat steady and strong behind her ears. She closed her eyes and swayed lightly with the unworldly melody, feeling it seep into her. The music of seduction, he'd said. She remembered Sebastian's words about the horse master's effect on the village maids. How many had he seduced with his magical fingers?

Yet at this moment it mattered not. 'Twas likely this one night alone was all the love she and this Saxon would ever share. She'd not think beyond it, nor of the past. There was only this night, the strains of his lute, the flicker of the candle, the smell of fresh herbs from the smooth coverlet of his bed. She lay back against the mattress and opened her eyes. "Come to me, Connor Brand," she said.

Connor's fingers on the lute slowed into an off-key chord, then another, then stopped. He set the lute carefully down on the floor and said with another slow smile, "At your service, milady."

Waves of feeling radiated up her neck at the mere sound of his voice. He put his hands on her shoulders, pressing her deep into the bedding, and lowered his lips to hers. The flare of passion was instantaneous. There was no time for teasing or tenderness. Her mouth opened to his searching tongue and she groaned in impatience.

His urgency equalled her own. In a frenzy of cloth and laces, they shed their clothing until they lay together skin on skin, the ridge of his manhood already hard against her most sensitive parts. His warm hands made circles on her breasts as he continued his deep, needy kisses. "I'm desperate for you, my love," he murmured. "I've been ready since the moment I came here and saw you asleep in my bed. I'm not sure I can wait any longer."

She let her legs fall open and moved her hand to the very lowest portion of his hard back to show her own readiness to receive him. She had no skill in the ways of lovemaking, but the movements came naturally, and soon their two young, strong bodies rocked together in spiraling ecstasy. All feeling pooled into the lower part of her body as he moved into her more deeply and she quaked in completion.

His head fell heavily on her chest, and she idly trailed her fingers through his soft blond hair. She was filled with an inexpressible emotion. She wanted to burst into tears and laugh with joy at the same time.

He didn't move for so long that she finally whispered his name.

When he raised his head to look at her, it was *his* cheeks that held the glisten of tears in the light of the candle. The sight made her heart swell inside her chest.

"I love thee, Ellen of Wakelin," he said. He sounded shaken.

Ellen couldn't answer. Her throat was too full.

"I'm too heavy, my love," he said, sounding more like his normal self. He moved off her to one side.

She pulled him back close to her and shook her

head, then finally found her voice to say, "I like to feel you there. I like the heaviness of you against me."

His head went down on her chest again and they lay in silence for several contented minutes until she asked softly, "Did you mean it?"

He rolled off her once more and boosted himself up on his elbow to look down at her. "Mean what?" he teased.

"What you said. You said you loved me."

His smile turned brittle. "Aye, vixen. You can add me to your list of conquests, if it pleases you. When you return to your land, you can tell the great lords who worship at your feet that they're none better than a humble Saxon horseman you once knew."

His sarcasm stung after the emotion of the previous moments. "I'd not cite humility as one of your traits, horse master," she retorted.

He grinned at her. "Not humble then, say just poor."

Ellen thought for a moment before she replied in a more serious vein, "I'm not sure poor is an apt description, either. You've books and music and the wild countryside to ride your beautiful horses. I'll be going back to the stifling court of Louis, where they'll set me to prattle with his ladies and sew fine stitches the day long."

She turned and lifted herself on her own elbow so that she could look directly into his eyes. "Is Sarah poorer than I when she has a wise mother to give advice, brothers and a sister to provide laughter and love, and the devotion of a handsome young man to turn her head?"

"Sarah and her family are running from the law with their bellies empty of food these two days past. Most would hardly count them as rich."

"I would," Ellen said softly.

There was an answering gleam in his eyes. "I do love thee, Ellen," he said again, "though it make me thrice a fool."

She loved him, too. She'd known it for a long time, mayhap since the day he'd kissed her at the faerie's ring of trees. But something kept her from saying it aloud.

His own declaration had been circumscribed. There had been no pledge of undying devotion, no talk of a future or, indeed, anything beyond this one night. Even if her father would ever countenance such a match, Connor would never agree. She was one of the hated Normans who had deprived him of his birthright and more. Indeed, in spite of his protestation that he loved her, it was possible that his taking of her had been carried out callously, as some kind of personal revenge.

"What do Saxon men do when they love a maid?" she asked, keeping her voice carefully neutral.

He sat up suddenly and pushed himself to the top of the bed so that he was leaning against the wall. Then he picked her up and nestled her on his lap. "Same thing as Norman men, I warrant," he said, beginning to kiss her neck. "Something like this."

She could feel him swelling again against her bare bottom, and her body responded to the signals. Desire rose in her anew and she twisted in his arms to give herself over to a new round of passion. But even as she melted under his kisses, deep inside she felt the beginning of an ache.

Connor Brand was a remarkable man. He had indeed seduced her with his sweet music and his hard body and his masterful lovemaking. He'd said that he loved her, at least for this night, but she found herself wanting more. Her Norman people may have conquered Connor and his fellow Saxons, but it was he who had taken possession of her heart.

He'd left her shortly after dawn, the emotion of the previous evening nowhere in evidence with the harsh light of morning. She could almost believe that she'd imagined the shine of tears on his cheeks.

He'd touched her own cheeks once with his callused fingers, and had looked at her a long, hard moment, as though memorizing her features, then he'd gone, silently, like the forest wraiths of his songs.

She waited the entire morning, wandering dispiritedly, back and forth from his antechamber to the bed they had shared. She tried to interest herself in one of the Latin tomes he kept, but her mind would not focus on the carefully drawn letters.

By midday she decided that her ruse had continued long enough. She peered carefully from the window of Connor's room to see that the stable yard was empty, then she descended the stairs and crept out of the stable. When she reached the gates of the castle, the yeoman at the round tower shouted out, and almost immediately his cry was joined by several others. A group of soldiers rushed toward her, exclaiming over her safe return.

She learned with a flush of guilt that her father was

riding in the hunt for her, had in fact been out all night. Sebastian had remained at the castle, to supervise the search efforts, the yeoman guard had informed her.

"More likely so that he would not miss a good night's rest," she muttered to herself, then told the guard to report her safe arrival to her cousin. "I'll await my father in my quarters," she told the man, rejecting his suggestion that he immediately escort her to her cousin.

She had no desire to see Sebastian and listen to more of his oily insinuations, especially when his charges about her feelings for Connor were true. She cared nothing for Sebastian's opinion, but she loved her father and did not like deceiving him.

But once she'd enclosed herself inside her bedchamber, she almost regretted the decision not to await her father in the great hall or some place where the normal activity of the castle would keep her thoughts from returning again and again to the night she and Connor had shared. Indeed, the sight of her chambers and her own bed was like salt on her wound. It was here that Connor had first introduced her to the sensual pleasures a man and a woman could inspire in one another.

She lay back on her mattress and sighed. She'd come to England with the idea of bringing culture and discipline from a more civilized land, but instead she'd found in the strength of the people here something that went beyond rich tapestries and intricate court dances. And she'd found what it meant to feel one's heart soar at the sight and sound and touch of a man.

But she could never be part of a family like the Coopers. To her, she would always be their liege lady, due deference and respect, but never affection, and she and Connor had made it plain that, though he professed to love her, their love was destined to remain unfulfilled. His duty and his heart were with his people, and she was a foreigner, a usurper, in his land.

She turned her face into the mattress, pulled the covers over her head and willed herself to sleep.

Chapter Sixteen

"By the law of the land, the feudal lord is obliged to hold an open court and hear evidence in a capital offense," Father Martin told his brother.

Connor was reclining on the hard cot in the friar's bare cell in the abbey complex. "I doubt that Lord Wakelin will put the word of two Saxon children over the reputation of his late, lamented bailiff."

"Nay," Father Martin agreed. "But mayhap 'twill not be just the Cooper children's word. There are others in the village who were subjected to Booth's lechery or were witness to it."

Connor shrugged. He knew he should be encouraging Martin, and, indeed, taking as active a part in the investigation as his outlaw status would allow, but he couldn't seem to muster much enthusiasm for the effort.

The truth was, he didn't want to think about the Coopers' plight, nor Booth's perfidy, nor Martin's fact-finding. He wanted to close his eyes and once again picture Ellen's face as it had looked at the height of their passion. The very thought stirred his body all over again, and he sat up on his brother's celibate bed and pushed himself against the cold cell wall so that his arousal would not embarrass them both.

"It's worth a try, I suppose," he answered Martin finally. "Though they won't have a trial without an accused, which means John would have to be taken into custody again. I think I'd put more faith in his chances if he flees the country."

"John's young and able, but what about the rest of the family? And what about you, Con? Are you prepared to live the rest of your life in exile from Lyonsbridge?"

Better in exile than to live here as a servant and wait for Ellen to arrive one day as the pampered wife of some high French nobleman, Connor thought. "Forgive my desultory response to your efforts, Martin," he said finally. "I believe the days of hiding and imprisonment have wearied me."

Father Martin studied his brother. "What I see is a weariness of soul, brother, not of body, and I know not what remedy to prescribe. You've already rejected my suggestion to cleave more closely to the ways of the Lord."

Connor forced a smile. "That be your path, Martin, not mine. If my soul's weary, 'tis only from the pain of seeing the people of Lyonsbridge continue to suffer injustice after we'd thought to put all that behind us. The Coopers are a good family and not deserving of such travail."

"Then get up off that bed and help me see that things are set to right, Con." The challenge in his voice reminded Connor of the brother he'd squabbled and competed with as a child, before Martin had taken his vows and become sometimes irritatingly serene. Before the Normans had turned their world upside down. Before a beautiful Norman woman had so seized his head and his heart that all other considerations seemed to pale in comparison.

He swung his feet around and planted them on the floor, clapping his hands on his knees with sudden resolve. "Aye, brother, you're right, as usual. 'Tis past time things were set to right."

"I'll have no argument, Daughter," Lord Wakelin said sternly. "I can't put you at risk of another such terrible adventure. You're going back to Normandy on the morrow. Sebastian will escort you while I stay here to settle this matter of Booth's murder."

Ellen had pleaded, cajoled, threatened once again to flee to a nunnery, but since her father considered her security at risk, he had refused to budge.

Sebastian had sat in on the discussion with a quiet smile of satisfaction. He'd assured his uncle that he'd see his dear cousin safely back home and then return to aid in bringing to justice the outlaws who were still at large.

Sylvianne, morose and silent as ever, had come to her room to help her pack. The maid's only words were an expression of gratitude that she would be accompanying her mistress back to Normandy. "Finally I'll be quit of this infernal place where even the garderobe smells of pigs," she'd said with one of her incessant sniffs.

Ellen's head throbbed, and she considered a dozen courses of action without deciding upon any. She could run away again. Her father had posted guards at her door, but once she was on the road heading to the coast, she could make a break. Jocelyn could outrun any of her cousin's horses, she was sure. But then what? Her father would only begin the search again, until they found both her and the fugitive Cooper family.

She had a fleeting thought of somehow finding Connor. The two of them could run off together to a faraway land where it would no longer matter that he was a servant and she a lady, he a Saxon and she a Norman. But as soon as the fantasy entered her head, she dismissed it. Connor had made it plain that he would not run away and leave his people to what he considered the injustices of Norman rule.

In the end she hadn't come to any decision by dawn, when she and Sebastian set out, accompanied by a heavy guard.

Ellen barely spoke to her father at the farewell, and the hurt expression on his dear, lined face stayed with her as they made their way along the road to the coast. For one of the few times in her life, Ellen felt ashamed of her behavior. It wasn't her father's fault, after all, that she'd come to England and changed her thinking on so many matters. It certainly wasn't his fault that she'd fallen in love with a Saxon and that circumstances had conspired to make that same Saxon into an outlaw.

"Don't look so glum, Cousin," Sebastian said, riding up beside her. "Soon you'll be back to your parties and your suitors. You can forget all about this place."

She wanted to ignore him, but the guilt she felt

over having spurned her father in the morning made her give him the courtesy of a reply.

"I've no longing to return to a life of idleness, Sebastian, nor to the fawning suitors of Louis's court."

"Perhaps you've developed a taste for rougher men. I'm not yet convinced that your head was not addled by the handsome looks of the crude Saxon who worked at our stables."

"I care not what you think, Cousin."

"To all appearances your close association with the villeins of Lyonsbridge has altered your manners. You scarcely spoke to your father this morn as we left."

She shrugged. "He knew my displeasure at his decision to send me home."

Sebastian was silent for a long moment, then he gave his cousin a sly glance out of the corner of his eye and said, "I trust my cousin won't regret the insult should anything happen to Lord Wakelin."

Ellen sat up straighter in her saddle. "What do you mean by that?"

Sebastian's thin lips were clamped in a tight line, but she could see a gleam of triumph in his eyes. "Nothing," he said. "I'm merely pointing out that children should always respect their parents."

He spurred his horse ahead, leaving Ellen to ponder his words with a troubled expression. Her father had sent a heavy guard to escort her to Normandy, but he still had the majority of his men with him. In any event, she knew that Connor had every intention of solving the current problems without bloodshed. Her father should not be in any danger.

Still, she realized, as she watched Sebastian ride off, if something were to happen to her father, it would be quite convenient for her cousin. With Ellen back in Normandy, that would leave dominion over Lyonsbridge to Sebastian alone, and, in fact, give him a base of power from which he might wrest from her the entire Wakelin inheritance.

If she'd thought of Sebastian at all these past few years, she'd considered him weak. She'd certainly never suspected him capable of the kind of treachery that sometimes went on in noble families when great riches were at stake. But the past few days had taught her to be less carefree about her approach to life, and since arriving in England, her cousin had shown a side of himself she'd never before suspected.

He was riding up ahead with two of his guards, telling them something that evidently amused him, since she could see his back shaking with laughter. Suddenly one of the guards glanced back at her sharply. It was DeGuerre, the man who had been guarding the prisoners. His eyes were troubled.

The breeze had picked up, and Ellen felt the prickling on her skin like an omen.

Her cousin's conversation with his men drifted back to her as indecipherable murmuring, but a sudden gust of wind brought DeGuerre's words clearly. "You have our loyalty, my lord," the soldier told Sebastian. "When's it to be done?" Then the wind dropped and she could no longer hear.

She shifted in the saddle. The words could mean nothing. She was probably giving them a sinister connotation that they did not deserve. But DeGuerre had distinctly called her cousin "my lord." Of that she had no doubt.

Was there a possibility that Sebastian might be plotting against her father? She remembered his sneering words earlier and became increasingly alarmed. Perhaps it was a mistake for her to go meekly back to Normandy.

She strained to hear further snatches of her cousin's conversation, but the wind had shifted and the words were inaudible. She sat up straight in her saddle and surveyed the countryside.

With Jocelyn beneath her, she knew she could escape the escort if she chose, but she'd not known where she would head once she was free. With sudden determination, she knew with absolute certainty where she would go. To Connor.

She waited until they'd almost reached the coast. The soldiers had relaxed their guard, and even Sebastian seemed to be paying his cousin little attention. Ellen knew that they must be near the large cave where she'd been taken the night of Booth's death, but Connor had brought her there and taken her away in the dark. She didn't recognize any landmarks.

Nevertheless, the increasingly salty tang of the air told her that they'd soon be at the sea, and her opportunity might be gone, so she chose a moment when a sharp bend in the road had the soldiers paying attention to their mounts. When half the group had rounded the corner, temporarily out of sight, she made her move.

Jocelyn was as fresh as when they'd left the stable, and, as usual, responded instantly to her mistress's command. She turned her off the road and headed directly up a steep incline, slippery with loose rocks. The mare didn't hesitate, charging up the hill as if the devil was behind her. Ellen hugged to the saddle closely and let the horse do her job.

It was several moments before the men on the road even realized what had happened, but at a furious shout from Sebastian, they spurred their mounts to follow her. Several of the horses balked at the treacherous terrain, but three men on heavy warhorses managed to keep close to her pace.

Ellen looked over her shoulder to see them pounding up behind her, and prayed that when she reached the top of the cliff, she'd find an even stretch where her lighter, faster horse could leave them behind.

Jocelyn plunged up the final steps without slowing, and Ellen breathed a great sigh of relief as a grassy lea came into view, similar to the one she and Connor had raced across when she'd first come to Lyonsbridge, an eternity ago.

She straightened in her saddle, loosened her hold on the reins and let Jocelyn race. The meadow stretched out for a couple of miles, then ended at a thick forest. If she could make the safety of the trees, she could probably elude her captors. If they caught her in the open stretch, there was no place for her to hide.

Jocelyn galloped along, smoothly and evenly, but Ellen could hear the pounding of the three powerful horses behind her. She had half the meadow left to cross before reaching the forest refuge. What had Connor told her that day? An easy middle makes for a lightning finish.

She put a hand on her horse's neck as Connor had

that day, said, "Easy, girl," and felt Jocelyn slow almost imperceptibly, marshaling strength. They continued that way for a long, agonizing minute as the hooves behind her became louder, then she once again leaned her body close to Jocelyn and whispered, "Now, girl. Fly with me."

Jocelyn leaped forward in a burst of speed such as Ellen had never before witnessed. Her hooves seemed in fact to be flying above the ground. In seconds they reached the trees, and Ellen pulled on the reins, turning sharply into the depths of the forest. The overcast sky provided little light among the thick trees. In the distance she heard the shouts of her three pursuers, who had halted their horses at the entrance to the forest. They seemed to be discussing their next move.

Ellen let her mount continue to wind among the trees, quietly and carefully, as if following the steps of an elaborate court dance. Were the soldiers following? She could no longer hear their shouts, nor did she hear horses moving through the woods.

She stopped Jocelyn for a moment to listen. All was quiet. Perhaps the soldiers had turned back to report to Sebastian that his cousin had eluded them. She smiled briefly at an image of apoplectic rage on his face.

She let Jocelyn continue to pick her way through the trees. The thick forest had served to befuddle her captors, but she feared that by now she was equally disoriented. She had no idea which direction would take her toward the coast. In fact, she didn't even know how to leave the woods. For all she knew, she might be traveling around and around in circles.

She sighed and said to her horse, "What do you think, girl? You've gotten me this far."

"She probably thinks her mistress is a foolhardy young woman, and she'd be right," said a voice practically in her ear.

She whirled around in the saddle to face Connor, mounted on Thunder, directly behind her.

"How... How did you get here?" she sputtered. "I heard nothing."

"Thunder can move like a forest cat when I bid him," he said with a grin. "But let me be the one to question. What in the name of St. Jude are *you* doing here? Is there some odd potion you take that makes you continue to put yourself at risk?"

She sat in her saddle and stared, her gaze taking in his handsome face; his lips, which had sent trails of magic down her neck; his strong hands, which had turned her easily to his will. She'd thought never to see him again.

"Milady?" he asked, when she continued without speaking.

She gave herself a little shake. "Two nights ago you did call me Ellen," she said, her voice barely audible.

His smile died. "Two nights ago we were kidnapped by the faeries of the forest, remember? They left us helpless and at the mercy of their magic."

"Aye, 'twas magical," she replied, stiffening.

He nodded. "Would that the real world were so as well. Now tell me, Lady Ellen, what are you doing here, lost in the forest?"

"Mayhap I came looking for those faeries." She gave him a sad smile, and he returned one in kind.

"Nay, I was on my way home, sent by my father. It seems he thinks England too dangerous a place for his only daughter."

"I don't blame him for wanting to keep safe something so precious."

She blushed, but told herself that now was not the moment to let herself be once again carried away by Connor Brand's easy charm. "I ran away from Sebastian and his men," she explained.

"To what purpose?" Connor asked in surprise.

She took a deep breath. Now that the deed was done, she wasn't sure she could even explain to herself. Sebastian hadn't said anything definite. She couldn't accuse her cousin because of a sinister look, a few words carried on the breeze. And was Sebastian the only reason she had fled? Or had she run because she was not yet ready to leave this Saxon land and in particular the one Saxon in it who had captured her heart?

"I'm not sure," she said, but she knew that she would never admit to Connor that a desire to see him again had had anything to do with her decision. "But I'm worried that Sebastian is planning harm to my father."

"Have you knowledge of such a plan?"

"Not specifically, but after I bade my father farewell this morning, my cousin implied that it would be the last time I would see him."

Connor frowned. Ellen hoped he would not think her a hysterical female, but he seemed to regard her words seriously as he asked, "What would happen to Lyonsbridge if your father died?"

"My father intends to leave his estates to me, but

since I am female, that inheritance may be challenged in the courts.''

"By your cousin."

"Aye."

"Mayhap you should return to your father and tell him this. It would put him on his guard."

"He refuses to believe anything bad of my cousin, and I'm afraid Sebastian has convinced him that my wits have been addled since arriving in this country." Her face colored, and Connor did not ask for details about the exact nature of her cousin's charges.

He sat for a moment, lost in thought. Finally he said, "The men who were following you turned back, but I warrant your cousin will be sending more in their place soon. The first thing we have to do is find a safe place for you."

"Your apartments again?" Ellen asked, a bit wistfully.

He smiled. "With the wood faeries? Nay, eventually someone will get the thought to look there. This time I have in mind a more sanctified place."

The Abbey of St. John was much less imposing than the stone church it faced across the courtyard. A spartan wooden structure with pens for animals built on each end, it housed thirty monks of the Benedictine order, along with three kitchen helpers, all male. The abbey had never before housed a woman.

Brother Augustine had not been pleased at the suggestion that Ellen take up residence in one of the inner cells, even when Father Martin had prevailed on him in the name of Christian charity. His agreement had come only after a gentle reminder that the land upon which the abbey stood belonged to Lord Wakelin, and that the lord would undoubtedly not look kindly on the monks turning away his daughter when she was seeking refuge.

From the moment they'd arrived at St. John's, Connor had taken pains to keep her at a safe distance from him, determined not to allow the sparks that had flared between them in the forest to ignite.

As Father Martin and Brother Augustine discussed arrangements, he tried not to notice how the tendrils of her hair had escaped from her headdress somewhere during her breakneck ride. The black curls blew gently in the wind, caressing the white skin of her cheeks. He tried not to focus on how she ran her delicate tongue over her full lips, chapped red from the wind.

"Connor!" his brother said sharply. "I asked for your opinion."

For all he knew the priest and the monk had been discussing the price of pepper berries at the market fair. "Sorry, brother," he said.

Father Martin looked from Connor over to where Ellen stood next to her horse. "Brother Augustine thinks we should inform her father that the lady Ellen is here seeking a spiritual retreat and that we intend to allow her to stay with us for some days."

Connor considered the idea. It would avoid having her father send soldiers out combing the countryside for her, but they ran the risk that Sebastian would disregard the sanctity of the abbey and come to take her back by force. "Not just yet," he answered finally. "First we need to see if 'tis true that Sebastian has plans against her father. Ellen's running away might force his hand.''

His brother lifted an eyebrow at Connor's use of her Christian name, but Brother Augustine appeared not to notice.

The two clerics stood discussing the details of the arrangements for several more minutes, and Connor finally grew impatient. "We could wait until this thundercloud opens up and gives us all a good soaking to see if that would help matters," he snapped, pointing at the ominous sky.

Brother Augustine waggled his head nervously, but finally stood aside and let Connor lead Ellen into the darkened interior of the abbey. One of the monks was already busy clearing a room for her. She thanked the man with a gracious smile that made him blanch, then quickly duck his head and disappear into the corridor.

"Will you be all right here?" Connor asked, looking around the barren room.

"No wood faeries have visited this place, I trow," she said with a rueful smile.

"Nor have these walls heard ballads of love," he agreed.

They stood watching each other for a moment.

"Then 'tis just the place for me at the moment," she said airily.

Connor laughed, but grew serious as he told her, "Nay, milady. You don't belong in such a setting. Your beauty was made for love, and you shall have it again someday soon."

"Will you not call me Ellen?" she asked again.

He took a step closer and bent close to her ear. "Ellen," he whispered. "Ellen of my heart."

Tears brimmed in her eyes, and he wiped at them with his thumb. "Weep not, fair Ellen. My heart is but a trophy for thy collection. I give it to thee freely."

Her lips trembled. He kissed them softly and tasted the salt there. Then he pulled away and forced himself to address her in a normal tone of voice. "Stay hidden here, milady. Do not venture out for anything unless my brother is with you."

She nodded her head, watching him with eyes luminous with silent pleading.

Connor turned his back on them and walked briskly away.

Chapter Seventeen

Ellen spent the day restlessly in the tiny cell, reconsidering her decision to run from her cousin. Perhaps she should have confronted him with her suspicions on the spot. Perhaps it would have been better to return to the castle to warn her father. Here, tucked away like an egg in a chicken coop, she could do nothing. She felt powerless and unsure, both feelings foreign to her nature.

Father Martin brought her a simple meat pie for supper, but she saw no one else throughout the day. Finally the monotonous cadence of the monks' evensong made her eyelids heavy, and she lay down on the cot to sleep.

When she awoke it was pitch-black. For a moment she didn't know where she was, but the scratch of the monk's rough blanket beneath her brought back the events of the day. She was still in her cell. The lone candle they'd left her had blown or sputtered out.

The chanting of the monks had ceased, leaving a silence so total that it gave her an eerie feeling of otherworldly beings. As soon as the thought entered her head, a cold grip of fear seized her throat. There was something moving in the darkness. Black on black, moving the air around her like some kind of night phantom. She lay paralyzed against the bed, not wanting to move until the spirit had passed from the room on its unholy quest.

Suddenly it was descending on her. She sat up and pushed into the darkness with all her strength, but her arms were caught and pinned to her sides, not by a spirit, but by a mortal man.

"Sweetheart," Connor said. "I'd not meant to startle you. I thought you asleep."

A great rush of relief flowed through her, followed by something more, a sudden elation at the sound of his voice. "Connor," she breathed, collapsing against him.

His arms folded around her and of one accord they fell back against the bed. "Are you all right?" he asked in a husky whisper. "You've had good treatment?"

She hardly heard his question, so intent was she on the feel of his body against her once again. "I'm well, my love," she said. The endearment slipped out without conscious thought, and he answered it with a kiss that in the blackness landed unerringly on her lips.

Ellen felt the instant response of her body, but her head hammered for information. "Where have you been this day?" she asked eagerly. "Is there news of the castle? My father?"

He kissed her mouth to silence, then answered gently. "Your father was about to send word to the king informing him of your disappearance, which could have brought legions of soldiers to the shire.

We decided it would be best for Brother Augustine to tell him that you are here, on a ten-day retreat, inviolable. No one will come here.''

''Sebastian?''

She still couldn't see Connor's face, but there was satisfaction in his voice as he answered, ''Mayhap your father's faith in your cousin is finally being tested. Sebastian had convinced your father that you had fled to my arms. When Brother Augustine arrived to tell him of your presence here, he caught Sebastian in the lie.''

''Mayhap 'twas not a lie,'' Ellen admitted. ''I wasn't sure what I was going to do when I fled from him, but I think somehow my heart knew that it was to you I was running.''

''That's an admission that might be best kept to yourself, sweetheart.''

''Aye.'' Ellen's eyes stung with disappointment. The other night in his chambers, Connor had said he loved her, but he seemed firmly against admitting any possibility of legitimacy to their union.

''I can't see you,'' he said with a little chuckle, and proceeded to let his hands do the work his eyes could not, moving them over her face and down to her breasts.

''I look none different than I did this morn,'' she answered, her voice catching.

''As you looked this morn with the wind teasing the curls around your fair cheeks and the midmorning sun striking gold fire in your beautiful eyes? Then that is the vision I'll keep in my head as I make slow, sweet love to you,'' he whispered.

They might have no future, but again it seemed that

they'd been granted one magical moment out of time. She struggled to clear the troubled thoughts from her head, and before long all consideration had given way to the wonder of his fingers and his mouth on her body.

"At least you could be a little more discreet about your dalliance," Father Martin grumbled.

Connor slammed his ax into another log, splintering it into firewood for the abbey kitchen. "'Tis not a dalliance."

"What will you call it, then? I trow you'll not hold that you are sneaking into the maid's chambers each night to teach her the catechism."

Connor stood another thick log on end and cleaved it cleanly in two. "Ellen's no milkmaid, and my time with her is not a dalliance."

"By my faith, 'tis not a holy union sanctified by the bonds of matrimony," Father Martin chided. "Nor will it be. *Dalliance* is a kind word compared to what some others would use."

Connor straightened up to mop a sheen of sweat from his brow. He sent his brother a sideways glance. "Others such as the good brothers who, having themselves forsworn such earthly pleasures, are quick to begrudge any man who does not hesitate to unsheathe his sword when the occasion warrants."

"You'd do well not to mock them, Con, since they keep your presence here a secret at risk of their own freedom."

"Aye, Martin, forgive me, and I appreciate your concern on this matter. If I be overly churlish, mayhap 'tis my own guilt that makes me so."

"'Twas a mistake from the beginning, Con," Father Martin said with a shake of his head.

"Mayhap."

"Mayhap? What possible good can come of this? You have no lands. At the moment, you're a declared outlaw. You have neither status nor wealth for a union with the likes of Ellen Wakelin."

Connor turned back to the log he had just split and in several more violent blows whacked it into kindling. "I don't need you to tell me that, brother," he said, huffing as he finished and kicked the pieces of wood over onto the pile.

The exasperation went out of Father Martin's expression and his eyes softened in sympathy. "You need to find a young woman of the village, Con, who will comfort you and foster your leadership among the Saxon people."

"I need no young woman, Martin. When Ellen returns to her father, he'll send her back to Normandy, and that will be the end of it. Things will return to normal."

Father Martin looked doubtful. "I never thought to see my wayward big brother with a broken heart."

Connor rested his ax on a log and leaned on it pensively. After a long moment he looked up at Martin, smiled sadly and said, "Nor did I."

Now that her presence at the monastery was no longer a secret, Brother Augustine had given Ellen permission to attend chapel and move around the quarters and the courtyard. Except during the prescribed hours of silence, she was allowed to talk to the brothers as they worked about the kitchen or in their gardens just behind the main abbey building.

At first they had shied away from her, averting their eyes and scurrying in the other direction at her approach, as if she were a rain cloud about to give them a dampening. But after two days, some of the bolder ones met her gaze and even offered a mumbled acknowledgment to her greeting.

By the third day, there were at least half a dozen whom she could recognize and call by name. One was the kitchen supervisor, who personally brought her meals to her cell. Brother Alphonse was short in stature, coming only to her shoulders, but his girth was almost the equal of his height, evidence that he took his culinary duties seriously. Indeed, after a couple of meals in which she showed appreciation of his skill, he'd begun staying with her while she ate asking her questions about food preparation in the fancier Norman court circles.

She shared gardening knowledge with the gardening monks and engaged Father Martin in a lively discussion of theology, carefully steering away from any talk of his brother or what the two of them might be doing when, as had become open knowledge, Connor sought her out in her tiny cell each night after the rest of the abbey was at rest.

In general, she realized, she was happier than she'd been at any time in her life. She found her days spent in the company of the simple country brethren charming compared to the jaded court back home, with its backstabbing and political intrigue. But, she admitted to herself, the pleasant days were nothing in comparison to the nights. Forgetting the rest of the world in each other's arms, she and Connor managed to make each coming together more magical than the last.

She refused to think about what would happen when the days of her supposed retreat were over. Nor had Connor mentioned the subject. In the long hours of their nights together, sometimes they had serious discussions about their respective childhoods and the influence of their parents. Other times they dealt with lighter themes, the foods they liked or their mutual passion for horses—the easy banter of lovers. But there was no talk of the future beyond the darkened cell they shared.

The morning of her sixth day at the abbey, Ellen awakened alone. Connor had, as usual, left before dawn, but this day he'd not roused her with his accustomed kiss of farewell. She frowned a little as she ran her hand over the indentation in the straw pallet where he'd lain. They'd had few nights together, but already she felt hollow inside at the thought of nights stretching out before her without his warm body by her side.

Suddenly morose at the thought, she decided not to wait for Brother Alphonse to arrive with her breakfast, and wandered out of her cell, intent on seeking him out in the kitchens and saving him the trip.

It looked to be a fair day, mild with all the promise of spring. From across the courtyard drifted the chant of the monks in the church at morning-song. Ellen stopped and lifted her head. Above the monotonous strains she thought she heard an unaccustomed sound—the laughter of children.

It seemed to come from the direction of the kitchen

outbuildings, just to the west. Curious, she made her way quickly in that direction.

"'Lady!" a childish voice shouted as she rounded the corner, and suddenly she was engulfed by two whirling bodies, Abel and Karyn.

She knelt down and let them throw their tiny arms around her neck, deeply touched at their open display of affection. "Ah, sweetlings," she said. "I've missed you."

"I missed you, too, 'lady," Abel said, close to her ear. "And Karyn, too."

The little girl nodded in vigorous agreement. Ellen noticed that her wheat-colored hair, which had become matted and dirty in the caves, was once again clean and silky. "You've been well?" she asked, raising her eyes to address the question to Agnes, who was coming up behind the twins with a smile of apology for her children's exuberance.

"Aye, milady," she answered. "We've been well attended by the folks of Rolf over to Baintry."

Ellen knelt more securely on the ground so that she would not drop the twins, who continued to hold tightly to her neck. "But what are you doing here? Are you not in danger? And where is John?"

Agnes's smile wavered. "Master Brand said 'twas best. We'll trust in his judgment and in the Lord."

Sarah was standing by the kitchen door, holding a bowl in her hands. Ellen looked up at her, questioningly, and she explained, "John has turned himself over to your father, milady, to await the king's justice."

"They've arrested him again?"

Agnes took over the tale. "Master Brand and Father Martin have evidence to present in his favor. They asked us to come here so that Sarah will be available to tell her story on the day of the trial.''

Connor had told her nothing of this, and Ellen felt hurt by the exclusion. He might profess his love to her in the dark of night, but during the day he went about his duties as de facto lord to these people and confided nothing.

She prized Abel's arm gently from where it was pressing into her neck, cutting off her air. "There's to be a trial?" she asked, trying to keep her voice from betraying any resentment over her lack of information.

Sarah put the bowl she'd been carrying on a nearby trestle and walked over to pull Abel away from Ellen. "Aye, milady, there's to be a trial, at the market fair three days hence. Master Connor says he thinks there's a good chance they'll find the deed 'twas self-defense. Then John would go free.''

Her eyes were troubled, and when Ellen looked from her to her mother, the widow's expression mirrored her daughter's unease.

Karyn watched as her brother scampered over to the bowl Sarah had deposited and reached in a finger, which came out coated with pudding. The little girl gave Ellen an unexpected, wet kiss on her cheek, then let go her hold and ran to follow her twin's example.

Both children giggled as they slurped the sticky sweet from their hands, but Ellen exchanged worried glances with the other two women. None voiced the unspoken question: *If they find self-defense, John will go free, but what if they find him guilty?*

* * *

"What if they find him guilty?" Ellen asked Connor that night. In the light of the single candle in her small cell, his eyes looked shadowed with fatigue.

"Then we'll be close to having another bloody war on our hands, because the villagers will not easily let them hang one of their own, a young lad at that." His voice was weary, and he seemed more distant than on previous evenings.

Ellen had not asked him why he had not told her of his plans regarding the Coopers, but she'd hoped he would offer something in the way of explanation. Instead, he seemed reluctant to talk at all.

"I just want to know what I can do to help," she told him, trying to break through his sudden reserve.

"You could tell your father to pack up his men and head back to his own land," he said. "But I suspect that course would not be to your liking." His tone was light, but with a touch of his earlier bitterness, which she'd hoped was over between them.

She ignored the gibe and continued, "I'd like to aid the Coopers, if I can. If you think it would help for me to go to my father, I'll go this very night to plead John's case."

He reached for her. "I have better use for your lips at the moment," he said, and kissed her to dispel any doubt about what use he had in mind.

Ellen pulled away, insisting on staying with her subject. "I couldn't bear it if anything happened to John, Connor. Just the look in Agnes's and Sarah's eyes today…"

Connor gave up his efforts to kiss her and sat up. "There's naught you can do except cause more complications, Ellen." His voice was sharp.

Hurt anew, she hugged her arms around her. "As I've caused complications in your life, Lord Saxon?" she asked.

He studied her, the tenderness of their past nights together nowhere in evidence. "We've complicated each other's lives, I fear, sweetheart, as well you know. Remember, we said from the beginning that our coming together was but a form of madness."

"'Twas madness and that's the end of it?" A trembling had begun somewhere in her middle, but her pride didn't want to let him see how terribly the widening breach was affecting her.

He took in a deep breath. "We knew the end would come and soon. If you'd as lief it be now, I'll honor your wishes."

How had they come to this? Ellen wondered, her stomach twisting with sudden anguish. She should have kept quiet and let him kiss her, let him make love to her. But if he was unwilling to share any part of his life with her beyond this bed, of what use was their coming together? Perhaps he was right. If her heart was to be split apart, it might as well be like a knife thrust, quick and sure.

He awaited her answer without speaking, sitting beside her stiffly on the hard cot.

"So be it," she said in a low voice.

He turned his head toward her. "You'd have me leave?" There was not the least softening of his features.

"Aye," she said.

Without a moment's hesitation, he gave a curt nod, then stood and walked out of the room. She waited a full minute, until the echo of his steps in the corridor had completely faded, before she let fall the first tear.

Connor had a number of informants within the ranks of the castle guards, mostly Saxons who had been recruited before Lyonsbridge was given to Lord Wakelin. Some even had families still in the village. When they had come to Connor during the worst days of Sir William's rule, saying that they had decided to resign their posts, Connor had convinced the men to stay. He knew that it helped the Saxon cause to have friends on the other side, even if the men were sometimes forced to actions they didn't want to take.

Connor himself had always been able to move in and out of the castle with relative ease, and continued to do so in spite of his outlaw status. He was familiar with every crack and cranny of the castle complex and knew which gates were manned at which hours.

In the tension-filled days while he and Martin put together a defense for John Cooper, he passed restlessly from the castle to the abbey, then on a secret visit to the village and off to the coast to check with the outlaws who were still hiding out in the caves there.

It was only during the long nights with Ellen, while he and the Norman beauty lost themselves in shared passion, that he'd been able to forget this new crisis facing his people.

Now that was ended. He'd known that their time was measured, a few precious hours in which their divergent lives intersected. There could be nothing beyond. He had his responsibilities in Lyonsbridge, and Ellen's destiny was elsewhere, back in Europe with a rich nobleman, perhaps a prince.

Nevertheless, he hadn't been prepared for the swiftness of the end, nor for the ache it left in his midsection. It had stayed with him all day, nagging misery from the pit of his stomach all the way up to his jawbone.

Hidden in a rarely used outbuilding that had once served as an armory, Connor was waiting to meet a soldier named Werrold, who was cousin to Sarah's page boy suitor, Rolf. Rusted pieces of armor lay in disorderly heaps around him. They should be melted down and put to better use, he thought, suddenly ashamed at how the castle had been neglected in the years since his parents' deaths. Ellen had been right about that, and her campaign to clean up and renovate the place had been laudable.

Perhaps when the issue of Booth's death was resolved, she would agree to stay and finish the task, though Connor knew it would be painful to have her as close as a stone's throw, yet not his, ever again.

He picked up a pike from the pile of metal and twisted it, studying the wicked-looking hooked point at its end. What barbarians men were to use such things against one another, he mused, then blinked in surprise at his own thoughts. He'd always held that his commitment to peace in the land stemmed from his promise to his mother, but all at once he realized that it somehow had become an even deeper part of his spirit.

It was not just a deathbed oath. War brought no good to anyone. He genuinely wanted Normans and Saxons to live together peacefully in this land, to see it grow once again into a happy, prosperous place where young men could live long enough to dandle their grandchildren on their knees.

The thatched door rustled, and Werrold peered cautiously inside. "Milord?" he asked in a whisper.

Connor stood, brushing the rusty flakes of iron off his hands. "Not milord to you, lad. Call me Connor, if you like."

The slender young soldier slipped inside. He looked nervous, as if he wanted to deliver his information quickly and be gone. "Master Brand, then," the boy said, refusing to be less respectful than that.

"How are things in the castle?" Connor asked. "Is Phippen still threatening to storm the abbey to get the lady Ellen back?"

"My lord Wakelin will hear none of it," the soldier answered. "But Sir Sebastian still rages. In truth, there are times I think the man unbalanced. The other day he beat a poor castle guard unmercifully because the man did not immediately offer to see to Sir Sebastian's mount, which was not, after all, the guard's place to do so."

Connor scowled. "I've had my own doubts about the man. 'Tis a wonder Wakelin cannot see his nephew's shortcomings."

"Some say 'tis because the lord had no son. He makes excuses for his nephew because he has no other heir to depend on."

Connor snorted, "He has as worthy an heir as any man should ever wish for."

"Aye," the man agreed politely, but did not look convinced.

Connor had no intention of spending more time

extolling Ellen's virtues. "How's the boy faring?" he asked.

Both knew that he referred to the castle's now closely guarded prisoner, John Cooper.

"Well, Master Brand. I've seen that he's fed well, as you asked. He's nervous about the trial."

"Aye, as are we all. What is the word on it among the castle folk?"

"In truth, sir, they talk more of the market fair that accompanies the assizes than poor John's fate." The man's face became animated. "You've heard that there's to be a chase."

"Aye." Connor rolled his eyes. Back when his family ruled Lyonsbridge, he and his brothers had often ridden in the traditional obstacle race. It had been an annual event in his youth, along with the market fair. The fact that, at the same time, trials were being held sentencing poor thieves and miscreants to gaol or to have their hands chopped off or worse, had never seem to dampen the festivities.

There had not been a chase these several years past, and Connor had been surprised to hear that Lord Wakelin was reviving the custom in the midst of all the turmoil over John Cooper.

"They say 'tis Sebastian who planned the event," Werrold said. "Odd, since he doesn't strike me as much of a horseman."

Connor, too, found it odd. "Is he planning to race himself?" In past years the chase had typically been an event for foolhardy lads who were too young to have any fear of hurtling their horses over obstacles at breakneck speed.

"Not only he, but Lord Wakelin, too. Sir Sebastian

said it would show that Normans and Saxons could compete peacefully.''

This struck Connor as even more odd. Since when had Sebastian Phippen become concerned about fostering Norman-Saxon relations?

When he made no comment, Werrold continued, ''I thought about giving it a run myself. The purse is five gold sovereigns.''

''A princely sum,'' Connor observed, but his voice was distracted. ''Lord Wakelin is putting up the amount?''

''Nay, 'tis said Sir Sebastian made the offer personally.''

After a few more questions, Connor sent the young man on his way, then slipped out of the castle grounds and started walking, taking care to stay out of sight of the road. The news about Sebastian's promotion of the chase stayed with him all the way back to the abbey. Werrold had been right; Sebastian was not a horseman, nor was he a champion of Norman-Saxon peace. Something was wrong here. It appeared that John Cooper's trial might not be the only concern at tomorrow's fair.

Chapter Eighteen

In the days of Connor's parents, the chase had been a competition waged for honor and glory. The only prize had been a battered brass lion that had passed from champion to champion. The trophy had been lost since the days of the war.

Now that the stakes had been raised, the contest took on a more serious vein. For two days, knights and some freemen from neighbouring shires had been arriving, joining peasants from surrounding villages who had come for the annual fair. The grounds around the castle were filled with colorful tents and awnings that billowed in the March wind like sheets flapping on a gigantic laundry line.

The assizes were to begin at dawn so that the proceedings could end before the scheduled entertainment of the afternoon, which traditionally included jongleurs and acrobats, and which, this year, would culminate with the chase.

Connor had spent a restless night on the floor in his brother's cell. Martin had refrained from asking why he did not go to Ellen's chamber as usual. Instead, the priest looked at the sadness in his brother's eyes and tried to cheer him with stories of how the Cooper twins had turned the normally austere abbey into a topsy-turvy playground.

Connor had forced a smile to reward his brother's efforts, but his thoughts were on Ellen, alone in her cell only a few feet away.

Not wanting to miss a minute of the day's events, they'd set out for the castle before dawn, joined by streams of others coming from Lyonsbridge and nearby villages.

Ellen had insisted on walking with the Coopers, though Brother Augustine had offered her one of the abbey's horses to ride. She walked along the road in the predawn darkness, holding a twin's hand in each of hers and carefully avoiding Connor's eyes.

Their only exchange of the morning had been when they first set out. "Won't they arrest you if you show yourself openly at the castle?" she asked, her concern forcing her to break her silence with him.

"My supposed crime is aiding John. If they find him innocent today, my misdeed should no longer matter."

Like the three women, he refused to speculate on what would happen if John was not found innocent.

The children skipped along gaily beside Ellen, unaware of the importance of the day to the future of their family.

Sarah had been joined by Rolf. The page was taking some risk by exposing himself at the castle, but he'd arrived yesterday from Baintry and had insisted that he was going to be by Sarah's side during the proceedings, come what may.

Wooden stands had been constructed to the north of the castle. It was here that the trials would be conducted in the morning, and from here that spectators could view the afternoon's competition. The grounds in front of the structure were already full when the Coopers, Rolf, Ellen, Connor and Father Martin arrived. It appeared that the earlier trials were already underway. Ellen looked at the crowd with dismay.

"How will we get through to the front?" she asked. "Sarah has to be able to tell her story."

"We have plenty of time," Connor assured her. "There's no point in going forward until John's trial begins. Then they'll call for witnesses."

Ellen looked around uncomfortably at the jostling crowd, made up mostly of serfs and villagers.

"Mayhap you'd like to go up with your father so that you won't have to stand with this throng," he said. "I'll clear a way for you."

She looked at his face to see if there was derision there, but his expression was impassive. "I'll stay with the Coopers," she said firmly. "I want to stand with them at the trial, and I want my father to see me there."

Connor gave her a look of approval. "Good girl," he said, then he turned from her and resumed his talk with Father Martin and some of the villagers.

By midmorning, the sun had burned through the mist, and some of the onlookers had wandered off to view the wares of the merchants in the tents, but Ellen still stood patiently with the Coopers. By now the twins had claimed her as their special playmate, and every time they made a discovery or attempted a new kind of trick, their first move was to run to Ellen to call her attention to it and receive her words of encouragement or praise.

Karyn was no longer remotely shy with her. In fact, the little girl seemed more attached to Ellen than to her own sister and mother, a fact that bothered neither of these two women. Sarah was much too occupied with her suitor, and Agnes confided to Ellen that it warmed her heart to see the shine her daughter had taken to the noblewoman.

"There was a time I thought never to see a smile on her face again, milady," she said, gazing fondly at the little girl as she tumbled on the ground with Abel and some of the other village children. "Now if we could only persuade her to talk again, my blessings would be complete."

"Is there no clue as to why she stopped talking?" Ellen asked. She'd broached the question before, but Agnes had always seemed strangely reluctant to answer.

"'Twas a wicked day," she said, shaking her head and avoiding Ellen's eyes. "There was evil abroad. And since that day my baby has not uttered a word."

"When was this wicked day?" Ellen persisted.

"Almost a twelvemonth past, milady. 'Tis best not spoken of."

If something sinister had happened the day that Karyn stopped speaking, just over a year ago, Ellen wanted to learn of it. She was no authority on sicknesses of the mind, nor in spell-making, if indeed 'twas a spell that had struck the child dumb, but she had the feeling that uncovering the secret that the Coopers seemed to want hidden might be the child's only chance to recover.

"I think you should speak of it, Mistress Cooper, for Karyn's sake."

But before she could pursue the subject further, Connor came up beside them, his face tense. "'Tis time," he said. "They're bringing John out now."

It broke Ellen's heart to see John's slender arms and legs weighed down with shackles, metal ones this time. His face was pale and his usually bright eyes were dull.

Karyn and Abel stopped their laughter at the sight of their brother. Karyn crept up beside Ellen, and she lifted the girl in her arms with a whisper of reassurance.

The crowd parted to let the party through, and a number of people reached out to give the two Cooper women gentle pats of encouragement. Ellen's attention was suddenly diverted as she was spied by her father, seated next to Sebastian up on the dais. As liege lord, her father had been conducting the morning trials, but he stood now with an exclamation and walked quickly toward his daughter.

He made a move to embrace her, but stopped uncertainly as he eyed Karyn, still in her arms. Ellen drew herself up and said, "Good morrow, Father. This is my little friend Karyn. 'Tis her brother who stands falsely accused here today."

Lord Wakelin smiled at the little girl, then leaned forward and kissed Ellen on the forehead. "We'll hear what the boy has to say, my daughter, and justice will be served. Would you sit up with me?"

"I'll stay with my friends," she answered stiffly.

Without further comment, he spun around and climbed back up into the stands, leaving her standing alongside Agnes. Ellen turned her head, looking around the crowd for Connor, but he seemed to have vanished.

From up on the stands, Sebastian glared openly at his cousin.

The captain of the guards led John, shuffling in his chains, to the front of the dais and spun him around to face Lord Wakelin. "Defendant John Cooper, accused of the foul murder of milord's reeve and faithful subject, Sir William Booth." The captain's voice boomed out the dead man's name, and immediately Karyn's arms tightened in a stranglehold around Ellen's neck. She struggled to loosen the little girl's grip and looked at her in surprise. Big tears had begun to roll down her face, and her tiny body quaked.

"Don't be frightened," Ellen whispered to her. "The man has a big voice because he's a captain."

Karyn shook her head, and the sudden panic in her eyes seemed to be more than fear over the captain's shouting. Ellen had no time to wonder at the cause, however, since the charges were being read by a clerk. Her father sat leaning forward on one elbow, listening intently.

Ellen made circular strokes on Karyn's back, hoping to calm the girl. She had not thought it wise for the two younger children to attend the trial today, but for some reason Agnes had insisted on bringing them.

As castellan of Lyonsbridge, Sebastian was to present the case against John. Sweat dripped from his forehead and dampened the back of his heavy wool surcoat as he stood in the hot sun, gesturing toward John and accusing him with thespian dramatics.

"In short, milord," he ended with a piercing gaze

at John, "you have the word of two young Saxons, who lied to cover up what was undoubtedly a wicked robbery that went amiss, against the reputation of an upstanding Norman, loyal servant to his king."

Father Martin had requested permission to speak for the defendant. His manner was in stark contrast to that of Ellen's cousin. The crowd had grown bored with Sebastian's harangue, but when the priest stepped quietly to the front, a hush fell and the cleric's quiet words reached to the outermost limits of the throng.

"My lord," Father Martin began, his blue eyes riveted on Lord Wakelin's face, "you have a unique opportunity today. By your decision here this morning, you will be able to show the good people of this shire once and for all that Norman justice is not just for Normans, but is for the good of everyone, Norman and Saxon alike."

Ellen noted that her father straightened up with interest at the priest's words, whereas Sebastian's frown grew deeper.

"You may proceed with your evidence, Father," Lord Wakelin said. "And be assured that justice will be rendered impartially, as charged by the liege lord of us all, King Henry."

With a quiet nod, Father Martin briefly told the Coopers' story of what had happened the night of Booth's death. He then called in quick procession four girls from the village, none older than Sarah. Each told in halting, small voices of being accosted by Sir William Booth. To Ellen their accounts were utterly convincing, and it almost made her sad that the weasely little man was dead. She would have enjoyed seeing him in shackles like the ones weighing down John.

After the fourth young woman had spoken, Sebastian jumped up from the bench he'd occupied opposite the defendant and said, "I must object, my lord. Sir William Booth was a man whose honor had never been impugned until these Saxons came here today in an attempt to besmirch it. Obviously they're in a conspiracy to protect one of their own."

To Ellen's horror, her father appeared to be giving credence to her cousin's words. She broke away from the crowd and walked to the front of the judging stand. "Father, I'd also like to testify," she said.

Her father looked down in surprise. "What do you know of this thing, Daughter?" he asked.

She made a motion to put Karyn down on the ground, but the girl clung tighter to her neck, her body still trembling. So Ellen continued to hold her close as she walked up the three steps to stand on the platform in front of her father.

"I was riding with Master Brand that evening," she said. "I was there when John came to tell him of what had happened. And I saw how shaken Sarah Cooper was shortly after the event. 'Twas no made-up tale."

"My cousin's head has been swayed by too close an association with these people, Uncle," Sebastian said, walking closer to Lord Wakelin so that his words wouldn't be heard by the crowd. "She'll say whatever Brand tells her to say. She knows nothing that can be counted as solid evidence in this trial."

Lord Wakelin turned to his Daughter, "You saw

Sir William on several occasions, daughter?" he asked gently.

Ellen nodded, "Aye, but—"

"And did you ever see the man making improper advances to the Cooper girl or anyone else?"

Ellen hesitated before she reluctantly admitted, "Nay." Then she lifted her head and said loudly, "I believe every word these girls are saying. And I hope Sir William Booth is this moment roasting on a spit in hell."

Karyn pulled on Ellen's head and suddenly said in a childish lisp, "Shure Willem bad man."

Ellen was so startled she almost dropped the girl, but when she fully realized what had just occurred, she whirled around to find Agnes, whose hand had flown to her mouth. "She *spoke*," Ellen gasped.

As if in a trance, Agnes moved to the dais, then slowly climbed the stairs, her arms reaching for her daughter, who let go her grip on Ellen and went to her.

Agnes spoke with difficulty, her voice raspy. "Sir William tried to bother her, too, just like he did Sarah. We didn't want anyone to ever know."

Ellen felt sick in the pit of her stomach. "Booth molested this angelic child?" she gasped.

Agnes continued, "We caught him afore he could do aught to her, but he swore he'd seek revenge if we ever spoke of it." Her voice cracked. "We told my poor baby that she must never talk of it, and from that day to this, she refused to say anything at all."

Ellen turned toward her father, who looked confused. Sebastian flailed his arms and said, "Enough of these histrionics. They've worked up some kind of a play to try to free their kin.''

"Willem bad man," Karyn said again.

Ellen reached over to put her hand on the child's cheek. "Did Sir William do something bad to you, sweetling?"

Karyn nodded, tears streaming down her cheeks.

Ellen's tears were flowing, too, as she turned to her father, her voice shaking with rage. "Are you going to believe that this innocent child is part of a conspiracy? How much longer will you listen to Sebastian's lies?"

One of the Norman soldiers who was guarding John stepped forward and cleared his throat. "Beggin' your lordship's pardon, but it galls me not to speak. 'Tis true what the lassies are saying. Sir William was ever after them, the younger the better. 'Twere well known among us."

Ellen flashed a glance of thanks at the man. "There's your Saxon conspiracy, Sebastian," she said. "Do we have to get every man jack of William's troops to testify to the man's perfidy before you'll believe that this young boy was simply defending his sister's honor, just as any good *Norman* lad would do?"

Lord Wakelin pushed on the table in front of him and stood. "I believe I've heard enough. The boy's story seems to be true, and I'm hereby ruling that Sir William's killing was in self-defense."

Sebastian began to protest, "Uncle, you cannot—"

But Lord Wakelin cut off his words. "I've made my ruling, Nephew. Now I suggest you get your men to loosen the bonds from this boy so that we can all go on to enjoy the day's festivities.''

He bent down to utter a few words to the clerk who was sitting at a side table, recording the event, then began to walk in the opposite direction. His steps were plodding, suddenly like those of an old man, and the sight gave Ellen's heart a twinge, but at the risk of causing him more grief, she had one more matter to put before him.

''Father, there's one more item,'' she called. When he turned back to her, she continued, ''The horse master, Connor Brand, was named outlaw solely for his part in helping John Cooper that night. Now that John's been declared innocent, Master Brand should be freed of such a designation.''

Sebastian shot his uncle a contemptuous look. ''''Tis as I've told you, she's besotted with the man.''

Lord Wakelin looked over to where his daughter stood celebrating her victory with her new Saxon friends. His expression was troubled. ''''Tis a capital offense to aid a fugitive from the king's justice,'' he said after a long moment. ''The results of the trial change nothing.''

Before Ellen could continue to argue the matter, he had stepped off the platform and walked away.

The Cooper family was the center of attention for the rest of the morning as the villagers celebrated John's acquittal. John and his mother made a point of personally thanking the Norman soldier who had come to his defense. Several of the other castle guards gathered around to offer their own congratulations and, when invited, joined in the villagers' celebration.

Ellen was pleased to see the mingling of the two groups. The ordeal had been hard on the Cooper family, but it could turn out that the event was a blessing in disguise if it served as a beginning for Norman and Saxons to come together in peace.

She only hoped that the day had not proven to be too much for little Karyn. The girl had not left her mother's side since the trial, but when Ellen knelt down and spoke to her, she answered, actually answered, in her own shy whisper.

The tears were gone, and when Ellen looked down at her now as they headed out to the course that had been set up for the chase, Karyn gave her a little smile.

"Are you ready to see the horses run, sweetling?" Ellen asked her.

"Aye, 'lady," Karyn said, duplicating her brother's form of address, and even added, "Will 'lady ride on Jocelyn?"

Agnes beamed with happiness to hear her daughter speaking naturally once again, and Ellen gave a laugh of delight. "Nay, sweetling, 'tis but men can race in the chase, though I trow I could beat a goodly number of them if they'd let me try."

"I've no doubt of it," said a voice from behind her. She'd not seen Connor since the start of the trial. She assumed that he'd heard her father's refusal to lift his outlaw status and had decided it would be better to stay well hidden. Nevertheless, she'd found herself looking for his tall form around every corner as she'd wandered with the Coopers through the maze of cookshops and merchant tents, the latter selling bolts of fine cloth, tinware and precious avoirdupois goods from the East—alum for cloth dying, and rare spices.

At the sound of his voice she whirled around to face him, her heart lifting. "Oh, Connor!" she exclaimed. "Did you hear it all? John found innocent? And little Karyn *speaking?*"

He smiled at her. "I heard it all, princess. 'Tis a happy day for Saxon England."

"Aye, and for Norman England, too," she said, gesturing around to where groups of Norman soldiers and Saxon villagers engaged each other in friendly conversations.

"Aye," Connor agreed.

Suddenly she remembered that not *all* had gone well that morning. "'Twill turn out well for you, too, Connor, I promise. My father needs time to consider the matter, but I know he will change his mind on this. He's normally a fair man."

He gave her a rueful smile. "I fear your father is just a man who is afraid for his only daughter, and I blame him not."

"Sebastian has poisoned his mind on the subject."

Connor cocked his head and asked her with a twisted grin, "Was it then a lie that your cousin told, when he said that you were infatuated with me?"

The misunderstanding of the other night seemed forgotten for the moment as he stood not a foot from her, his eyes suddenly hungry. But the physical craving that had flowed between them, almost from the moment they first saw each other, did not alter the circumstances.

Connor seemed not the least concerned over his outlaw status, nor depressed at the thought that her father's strictness on the matter might stem from disapproval of her feelings for him. Obviously, her Saxon lover had neither hope nor desire of a future for the two of them together.

So be it. She took a step back and looked up at him. "'Twas not entirely a lie, as well you know, horse master, but rather a happenstance irrelevant in the large scheme of things."

His mouth quirked and his expression lost none of its amusement. "Ah," he said. "Irrelevant."

Once again, it appeared he was mocking her, and she felt her temper rising. Looking around, she said impatiently, "Aren't you in danger of being seen here? If you don't care about your own safety, you might consider the rest of us. People are having a good time. Wouldn't it spoil the festivities if they had to witness the arrest of their former lord?"

"Would it spoil your day, princess?" he asked, leaning close to her again and speaking in the low, husky voice that made her stomach churn.

"I've no desire to see you in chains," she snapped.

He flashed his grin again and said, "I'm glad to hear it." But he made no move to leave.

"When the chase begins, every soldier who's not entered will be here watching. You're sure to be recognized."

"I'll be gone by then," he said with irritating nonchalance. "I just came to see how the Coopers were faring and to spend a few minutes with you."

"Then what? Will you be heading back to the caves?"

"Nay. I've had my fill of hiding."

She put a hand on his forearm. "Connor, you must

give me time to talk with my father. I can't do it now, because he's going to be riding in the chase. Go away for this night at least, and we'll see what happens on the morrow."

He leaned forward and kissed her quickly on the lips. "You may be surprised what the morrow will bring, princess. Now let me look at those golden eyes of yours one more time before I go to my post."

"Your post?"

"At the course."

"You're going to ride in the chase?" she asked, confused.

"In the past I've ridden it many times, but this year you might say that I intend to serve as a sort of an uninvited official."

He put his big hand at the back of her head and held her steady while, heedless of the crowds moving around them, he gave her another kiss, this time deep and wet and long.

When he pulled away, Ellen's face was flaming, but before she could utter a word of protest, Connor had disappeared once again into the crowd.

Chapter Nineteen

In the olden days, the village folk had often spent the better part of the winter building an elaborate course known as the chase. When they were finished, sometimes the meadow where it was situated had resembled a small village, with mock buildings, stone walls and small trees that had been felled and brought in to serve as miniature forests.

The Norman revival version was nowhere near as elaborate. It had taken some time for the organizers of the event to convince the older folks in the village to lend their expertise and their help, and by that time, it had been too late to make elaborate plans.

Most of the skill in running the race this year would consist of making sharp turns around posts designated as course markers. There were four jumps, set up with logs, each a little higher than the previous one. The final jump ended in a small pool of water.

This year most of the builders' work had gone into the finale, a crowd-pleasing innovation that hearkened back to the more complex races of years ago. The obstacle was a small model castle, flimsily built of timber and stone, but substantial enough to provide a cunning illusion for the spectators. It was placed on the course in such a way that a rider had to descend a grassy incline, then turn sharply onto the castle's drawbridge. Crossing the bridge triggered the raising of a portcullis gate allowing horse and rider to thunder right through the mock castle and emerge on the other side for a race to the finish line.

Connor had been suspicious about the obstacle since he'd heard from his castle informants that the idea had been proposed by Sebastian, supposedly taken from a jousting tournament he'd attended in Paris.

There had undoubtedly been more dangerous obstacles in some of the races Connor himself had run. The Brand brothers had been fearless horsemen, unafraid of the wildest feats. But he was older and wiser now, and it seemed that there were several problems with the castle stunt. Too sharp a turn could send an unpracticed horse skidding off the narrow drawbridge. It was raised only a few feet from the ground, but the distance was enough to tumble a rider or break a horse's leg.

Then there was the mock portcullis itself. It had been fashioned from pikes such as the one he'd examined in the old armory, fastened together with heavy leather strips. Any problem with the crude mechanism that had been rigged to raise and lower it could send it crashing down on top of the rider trying to pass beneath.

"I can't believe Lord Wakelin has agreed to participate in this," Connor had told Martin the previous evening as the two brothers secretly studied how the course had been designed. "'Tis a young man's game."

"Aye," Father Martin had agreed with a shudder. "This is one of the times I'm glad my holy robes absolve me from worldly activities. But I hear the old lord was goaded into it by a challenge from his nephew."

"The same nephew who proposed the resumption of the event in the first place," Connor had added.

"Aye."

Connor had nodded as if to confirm his suspicions. "You'd best get back to the abbey before they wonder where you are, brother," he'd said.

"Aren't you coming?"

Connor had thought of Ellen, once again getting ready for sleep in the thin chemise that by the light of a single candle showed every detail of her luscious body. "Nay," he'd answered his brother. "I intend to take a closer look at Sebastian Phippen's miniature castle."

By now, as he watched the spectators streaming in to capture the best viewing spots for the upcoming competition, Connor knew every hillock and swale of the course, as did Lord Wakelin's blood bay mount, Firestorm, with whom Connor had spent the better part of the night.

In addition to his knowledge of the course, Firestorm was now also possessed of a few tricks he had not known before his long night with the horse master.

They'd set up a blanket for Agnes on a slope well back from the main part of the meadow where the chase was to be held. The widow had insisted that she and the twins were better off out of the fray. But once she was situated, the four younger people, Sarah, Rolf, John and Ellen, pushed forward, trying to get a better position to see the race.

When people saw that one of the newcomers was the lady Ellen, they stepped respectfully aside, so that little by little the foursome crept closer and closer to the starting line.

Most of the entrants were from her father's guards. Very few of the villagers could ride, and few of those had been confident enough to place their big work-horses against the Normans and their battle-trained mounts.

Ellen saw her father at the far end of the line of entrants, mounted on Firestorm. The big stallion had proved a reliable mount for him these five years past, but it gave Ellen a shiver of apprehension to see her father's gray hair amidst all the rash young men who made up the rest of the field.

"'Tis a foolish trick of my father's to make this attempt,'' she said to John, who stood next to her, trying his best to protect her from the crush of the crowd.

"Mayhap not, your ladyship. In truth, it has boosted his esteem with the lads of the village.''

Ellen shook her head. "Not with the women, I'd guess. They're no doubt thinking *the crazy old coot,* and I'd not blame them.''

John laughed. "Some things are best understood by men,'' he agreed. "While I was being held prisoner, I heard the guards say 'twas your cousin who persuaded Lord Wakelin to race.''

This news increased Ellen's uneasiness. She searched the ranks of the entrants for Sebastian. "Was not my cousin to run as well?"

"Aye, so they said."

"He's not there."

They both looked again, but there was no sign of the slender Norman knight. "Mayhap he's changed his mind, milady," John said finally, with a shrug.

"Aye, and left my father to his foolhardiness," Ellen muttered under her breath.

There was no more time for talking, as the riders had mounted and were bringing their horses up to the line that had been marked off in the grass. Ellen counted fourteen entrants, including her father.

She felt her stomach clench as the starter lifted a banner high in the air, ready to drop it as the signal to begin. Her father sat tensely on Firestorm, his eyes focused on the course ahead. The harsh afternoon sun showed every wrinkle of his weathered face, she noticed with a pang. All at once she wished that she had insisted on taking the time for a reconciliation this morning. She felt sick and guilty that she had not embraced him and offered him Godspeed on his race.

It was too late now. All she could do was watch and pray as the banner came down and the fourteen horses leaped into action all at the same time, like cogs on a giant waterwheel.

Around them the crowd screamed with excitement. The loudest shouts were for the four Saxon riders and for Lord Wakelin himself, no doubt due to both his status and his age.

The horses stayed bunched together through much of the long beginning stretch, but by the time they reached the first jump, they'd begun to string out. Ellen was relieved and secretly proud to see that her father was holding his own. There were only four horses ahead of him, and those belonged to four of the most experienced of his guardsmen.

"Your father rides well, milady," John said with a low whistle. "I see where you inherited the skill."

Ellen stood on tiptoe and craned her neck to scan the crowd. Where *was* Connor, anyway? Family pride made her hope that he was watching the race from somewhere and, like John, taking note of her father's proficiency.

By the end of the third jump, four riders had dropped out of competition after their horses had misstepped, though, fortunately, none had fallen. The fourth jump was the one that ended in water, a hazard that spelled doom for three more of the competitors.

Though seven had now disqualified themselves, Ellen was surprised to see that there were eight, not seven, horses pounding down the final stretch toward the mock castle. Somehow she must have miscounted at the starting line.

Lord Wakelin was seventh in the line. Ellen vowed to say a prayer in chapel on the morrow to St. Theresa if her father finished the competition in one piece. Two prayers, she added hastily, if he didn't finish last.

The first rider had reached the castle, and the crowd let up a roar as his mount's hooves thundered across the drawbridge and the makeshift portcullis shot upward.

Ellen clutched John's arm in excitement, and he screamed above the noise, "'Tis not a marvel, milady?"

"Aye," she shouted back. The points of the pikes gleamed wickedly in the sun as the rider shot through and the gate slammed shut again.

The second rider was fast upon the first, and once again, the gate wheeled up, then came slamming down, just as the horse and rider cleared it.

"It looks dangerous," Ellen shouted to John, cupping her hands to be heard.

"Nay, 'tis just the look of it, milady," he reassured her. "The ropes are strong, and there's a guard at each side to be sure the gate stays open while the rider is underneath."

For the first time Ellen noticed the two men holding thick ropes, one on each end of the gate just inside the mock castle. In the shadows of the interior, she could see that they were dressed in Norman livery, but she could not make out their identities.

She was glad to know that precautions were being taken for the dangerous trick, but nevertheless her knuckles grew white on John's arm as four more riders thundered through, each clearing the gate and emerging from the other side of the castle to a tremendous cheer from the crowd.

Lord Wakelin was still in seventh place, next to pass. Ellen's breath stopped in her throat. Her father spied her in the crowd and flashed her a smile, then leaned over his horse and held tight to the reins in preparation for the sharp turn onto the drawbridge. Firestorm executed the maneuver perfectly, and the crowd roared as, at the other end of the bridge, the gate cranked upward. Traversing the bridge would take only seconds, then he'd be through the little castle and out on the easy home stretch. Ellen let out her breath.

In the distance, the first rider reached the finish line, to the sound of a tremendous cheer. Ellen looked in that direction momentarily, then turned back, expecting to see her father shoot smoothly through the castle as the other riders had before him.

The portcullis gate was up and the way through the castle was clear, but, still on the drawbridge, Firestorm slowed from a canter to a jittery trot. Lord Wakelin had ducked low on the horse's back in preparation for going underneath the spikes. Now he straightened up in confusion, unable to believe Firestorm's sudden skittishness. Ellen frowned, equally puzzled.

Lord Wakelin urged the horse forward. At his back, the eighth and last rider had nearly reached the drawbridge. Firestorm's head was at the castle entrance, when suddenly, above the noise of the crowd, came the sound of a piercing whistle. Her father's horse pulled up and, to Ellen's utter amazement began to prance *backward*. At the exact same instant, the gate full of pikes came crashing down, missing Firestorm and her father by less than a yard. The crowd around her gasped in horror.

Lord Wakelin looked at the deadly gate in astonishment, then down at his horse, which after dancing backward to the far end of the drawbridge, stood quietly, apparently unaware of the tumult going on around him. The eighth rider pulled his mount up next to Lord Wakelin's and stopped.

Ellen slid down the slope into the trench that had been dug around the drawbridge, then heaved herself up onto the bridge itself, disregarding modesty as she sent her skirts flying up. Once on the bridge, she stood up and raced over to her father, who still sat on Firestorm, looking dazed.

She had paid little attention to the eighth rider. From his dress she could see that he was one of the entrants from the village, the only Saxon who had made it to the final stretch. As Ellen approached, the man pushed back his linen hood. revealing unmistakable blond hair. "Connor," she cried.

Lord Wakelin's expression was thunderous. He looked from his daughter up to the Saxon seated on the horse beside him. "What evil prank is this?" he roared.

A guard who had been on the sidelines rushed around the edge of the drawbridge and came to take hold of Lord Wakelin's horse, though Firestorm had not tried to move. "'Tis a Saxon plot, milord," the man said. "Had the horse not shied, you'd have been killed by that gate."

Ellen had come to the same conclusion. She looked up at Connor, her eyes wide with doubt. "Do you know aught of this?" she asked him.

He addressed his answer to Lord Wakelin, not Ellen. "'Tis no Saxon plotted this misdeed, milord," he said. "With your permission." As Ellen and her father watched, he made a clucking sound with his mouth and Thunder bcgan to walk backward, just as Firestorm had done. He backed all the way off the bridge, then Connor wheeled the stallion around, and said to the people who were crowding around trying to see what had happened, "Make way, please."

The horse and rider moved slowly through the

crowd around the drawbridge trench and to the other side of the makeshift castle, then disappeared inside it. In a moment, the treacherous gate creaked open and Connor appeared, now on foot, pushing one of the gate guards ahead of him. The man made an attempt to jump over the edge of the drawbridge, but Connor grabbed him by his shoulders and hauled him back.

Ellen gave a little gasp as she realized that the slender guard now being lifted in Connor's arms like a sack of turnips was none other than her cousin, Sebastian.

"Methinks this gentleman is your culprit, Lord Wakelin," Connor hollered, holding the struggling man firmly.

"What is this chicanery?" Lord Wakelin asked, turning a glowering gaze on his daughter.

But to Ellen, the meaning of the quick succession of events was finally becoming clear. She had no idea how Connor had known of the danger, nor how he had made her father's horse back away from the potentially fatal gate, but she knew that somehow it had been his doing.

She met her father's wrath with a steady voice. "I've tried to warn you about Sebastian, Father. Now perhaps you'll be ready to listen. 'Twas not a Saxon pulling those ropes to let the gate fall on you. 'Twas your own nephew."

Her father looked to the end of the bridge, where Connor had thrown Sebastian to the ground and was holding him pinned there with a foot in the middle of his back. "We'll see to this thing," he said gruffly, swinging down from his saddle.

He walked across the bridge with long, angry strides, and Ellen scurried to keep up. When they reached Connor and Sebastian, her cousin twisted his body to look up at his uncle and sputter, "'Tis a foul lie, Uncle. I can explain—"

His words ended in an "oof" as Connor pressed his foot more tightly into his captive's back.

"I think this man shall do the explaining," Lord Wakelin said, looking sternly at Connor. "And you can begin by telling me what devil's spell you worked on my horse."

Ellen stepped forward to protest. "Devil's spell or no, you'd best thank heaven for it, Father. For in another instant you'd have been cloven in two by that gate."

Connor smiled at her before turning to her father. "When I learned from some of your guards that Sebastian would be manning the castle today, I decided it would be best to ensure that this fine mount of yours chose another route."

"By going *backwards?*" Lord Wakelin roared.

"Aye, milord."

Her father's chest was heaving from anger, and he still looked confused. "It saved your life, Father," Ellen pointed out. "If you don't believe it, why don't you ask my cousin what he was doing manning the gate mechanism, disguised as a guard, when he'd told you that he was going to ride in the chase himself?"

Lord Wakelin looked down at his nephew, who finally lay still under Connor's foot. Suddenly the anger went out of the old lord, and he looked sad, as if coming to terms with some things that he had long known, but had not wanted to admit.

He nodded to a quartet of guardsmen who had followed him across the bridge, but had remained a respectful distance behind. "Take Sir Sebastian to his quarters and see that he's kept there under guard until I can deal with him," he told the men.

Connor removed his foot at once, but Sebastian didn't move. The guards finally had to pull him up to his feet. His eyes were glazed when they looked at his uncle, and this time there was no doubt that they held a glint of madness.

Lord Wakelin watched with a troubled expression as the guardsmen dragged his nephew through the raised gate and disappeared into the shadows of the mock castle. Then he turned to Connor. "As my daughter keeps trying to point out," he said, sounding weary, "it appears that I owe you my life, young man."

"I was happy to be of service, milord," Connor said with a bow.

Ellen held her breath as the two men she loved most in the world stood face-to-face, sizing up one another. After a long moment, her father gave a little nod of approval. With a half a smile, he asked, "So how *did* you get my horse to perform such a stunt?"

Connor grinned and winked at Ellen before answering, "One could say that I talked him into it, milord."

Lord Wakelin looked at his daughter, then gave a harrumph. "I'll know more of this, but not at the moment. I don't want this to spoil the festivities. We've a race champion to crown."

In fact, some of the crowd had left the area around the castle and had moved up to the finish line, where the top three finalists were waiting to claim their prizes.

"Wait a moment, Father," Ellen said. "This morning you declared that Connor was still an outlaw in the eyes of the realm. Surely now that he's saved your life, you'll have to rescind that edict?"

"Ah, females, they are ever slaves to detail, are they not?" Lord Wakelin flashed his daughter an exasperated smile, then said to Connor, "It would appear that I am in your debt, sir. The edict of outlawry will be canceled. But in truth, I did not intend to hold it valid in any case, as the Cooper lad was innocent of the crime. So tell me, what boon would you have of me in return for my life?"

Ellen sucked in a breath and felt a pounding behind her ears as she waited for Connor's answer. But when he spoke, she stiffened with disappointment.

"The only boon I would ask, milord, is for your cooperation in working to see that the Normans and Saxons who now share this land will live and prosper in peace."

Lord Wakelin looked sharply at Ellen, and she could tell that he was aware of her reaction to Connor's request. But he turned back to the tall Saxon, put out his hand and said firmly, "You have my hand and my word on it, sir."

Connor took the offered handshake, then backed away. "By your leave, sir, I'll take Firestorm and my own horse back to the stables and be sure they are none the worse for their efforts here today."

Lord Wakelin nodded his permission, and Connor reached for Firestorm's reins. As he turned to leave with the horse, he gave Ellen a smile and a wink. She mustered an answering smile, but as she watched him lead Firestorm off the bridge, she felt as if her heart had just been split in two.

"My child," Agnes began, then she reached over from her chair to touch Ellen's hand, which rested beside her on the trestle bench. "I trow you'll not think me disrespectful to call you thus, since you've become as dear to me as one of my own."

Ellen bit her lip and nodded. She looked around the little cottage. Karyn and Abel were sitting in front of the hearth, playing with the two little wooden dragons Ellen had brought them as farewell gifts. The tiny house was louder these days, with two children's voices chattering instead of just one. "As you all have become dear to me," she said.

"Then I'll speak to you as I would to my own daughter. When love comes, 'tis a precious thing, not to be discarded lightly. Are you *sure* you want to give up and return to that foreign land, when you know very well you'll be leaving your heart behind?"

"Ah, Agnes, 'tis not I who has given up. Connor had a chance to ask any favor he wished of my father. He asked not for himself, but for his people. That is where *his* heart lies. He has no room in his life for anything else."

"If 'tis so, then he is even more sadly mistaken than you. Connor has been a good leader to the Saxons. He's brought us through a difficult time. But now 'tis time for him to plan for a life of his own." The widow looked over at her youngest children. "Mayhap 'tis his destiny, and yours as well, to bring the most permanent kind of alliance to the Normans and Saxons of this land.''

Ellen followed the direction of her gaze, colored and said tartly, ''I know little on the subject of producing children, but I believe it requires the active participation of both parties. I've hardly seen Connor these two days since the race. My father has occupied every minute of his time making him show off those infernal horse tricks.''

At Ellen's response, Agnes sat back in her chair, a smile of satisfaction on her face. ''A fact that appears to bother you no little bit,'' she said.

''Nay. I'd merely hoped to be able to say goodbye before I left for Normandy.''

''I think you'll have the chance,'' the widow said as a light knock sounded on the door.

Abel ran to open it, and when he saw the identity of the visitor, he proudly held up his dragon. ''See, Connor, 'tis a fierce one, is it not? Karyn's is gentle, but mine's fierce and 'tis called Gorgon.''

Connor smiled down at the boy. ''How d'ye do, Gorgon?'' he said. ''Please don't take a bite out of me.''

Abel grinned. ''Nay, I'll tell him you're our friend.''

Connor nodded, but had already turned his attention to the ladies seated across the room. He gave a little salute with his hand to the widow, then said to Ellen, ''I've been looking for you.''

Ellen's fingers fumbled nervously with the braided rope bag in which she'd brought the farewell gifts, and which now lay empty in her lap. ''I've not been hiding,'' she answered.

Connor's eyebrows raised at her chilly tone. "Widow Cooper," he said firmly, "I don't mean to cut short your visit, but I'm going to escort Lady Ellen back to the castle."

"Mayhap I'm not ready to leave," she said stiffly.

"Run along, child," Agnes said. "I'll see you again before, ah—" she looked over at Connor "—before you leave for Normandy."

Without the widow's support, Ellen could see no way to avoid the meeting. She might as well get it over with, she thought angrily. She'd ride out with him and let him tell her all about his great new friendship with her father and how much it would mean for his precious Saxons. Then she'd say goodbye and be done with it.

Connor was unusually quiet as she made her farewells and they started out on the road back to the castle. But when they reached the high meadow, he turned in his saddle and said, "Would you favor a race across the lea?"

She looked at Thunder, who was prancing nervously, sensing that he was about to be told to run. "'Tis Jocelyn's last chance for revenge, I warrant," she agreed without enthusiasm.

Connor smiled, then nodded. "Give the word."

She wheeled Jocelyn around and headed out over the smooth meadow, with Connor close beside her.

At the midway point, when she saw him rest his hand on his horse's neck, she did likewise with hers. The two mounts matched each other stride for stride, cutting a path through the long grass, their manes streaming in the wind. As the end approached, Connor leaned down and spoke to Thunder, who leaped forward, but at the same instant, Ellen whispered to Jocelyn, "Let it fly, girl." Connor threw back his head and laughed as the two animals stayed neck and neck all the way to the edge of the woods.

"A draw," he shouted, when the trees forced them to stop.

Ellen's mouth turned down in a pout. "Thunderation," she said. "I'd wanted to beat you."

Connor laughed again. "Follow me," he told her, urging Thunder into the trees. The narrow passage forced Ellen to move behind him. She followed reluctantly. She had a feeling that she knew where he was heading, and she wasn't sure she ever wanted to see the place again.

She recognized the clearing immediately. Connor pulled up and jumped lightly to the ground, then turned to hold out his arms to her. "I realize that you can tend to yourself, princess, but allow me the pleasure of assisting you."

She slid into his arms, half expecting that he would take advantage of the opportunity to kiss her, but he merely set her on the ground and stepped back. She fought back a sense of disappointment and said breezily, "I'd hoped to be able to best you before I returned to my country, horse master, but it appears I'll have to be content with calling myself your equal."

There was amusement in his eyes and a deeper intensity that was making it difficult for her to concentrate on her words. "You rode as well as any man in the shire. Nay, better," he amended.

"Not better than you."

"Ah, well, I'm the horse master, remember? 'Tis my lot in life." He tied the reins of both horses to a branch, then turned and reached for her hand. "Shall we see if there are wood faeries about today?"

They walked into the center of the clearing. Once again Ellen marveled at the magical feeling of the place. The mossy grass made a velvet carpet underneath their feet, and sunbeams seemed to dance in and out of the shadowy trees. "I could almost believe that they are really here," she said wistfully.

Connor's smile faded. "Aye, believe it, princess," he said huskily. "They're up to their tricks again, and they're about to make me kiss you."

She was surprised to see the sudden tension in his face, as if he was waiting for her to refuse him. In the past he'd kissed her without asking, without apology. Suddenly he seemed tentative. Surely he knew by now her feelings for him?

She ventured a small smile. "Do you need faeries to force you to such action? I thought my horse master was bolder than that."

"Mayhap your horse master has heard that the lady Ellen is determined beyond all reason to return to her court dances and her royal suitors and her fine gowns. Mayhap he thinks the wood faeries are foolish to believe that she would exchange all that for a simple life in the forests of England."

For perhaps the first time since she'd known him, Connor Brand appeared to be uncertain. The knowledge filled her with tenderness, and, strangely, suddenly freed her of her own doubts. *A simple life in the forests of England,* he'd said.

Her smile became teasing. "Mayhap the lady Ellen thinks the faeries of England much more entertaining than all the courts of Europe."

He turned her to face him and put his hands on her shoulders. "Truly, sweetheart?" he said, his voice low.

She moved closer so that his arms slipped around her, then she wound hers around his neck. "Truly, my love."

She offered him her mouth for a long, fusing kiss, before pulling away to look up at him. His eyes were shining. She gave him an impish grin. "I'll tell thee true, horse master, I do indeed like this English forest, but 'tis not the faeries I find entertaining."

He grinned back at her. "'Tis only their magic," he agreed. Then his expression sobered. "'Twill not be easy, Ellen, this thing between us. I'll be your servant in love and in body, but not in station, which means I'll have to start afresh to find a place for myself in this new order."

"You could have already had your place if you'd but requested it of my father. I waited the day of the race for you to ask for a match between us."

"I'd not win you that way," he said, shaking his head.

"I thought 'twas that you didn't want me." She looked down at the ground.

He looked at her in amazement, then laughed and picked her up and carried her to the same small hillock where they'd lain long ago. "Ah, my foolish Norman beauty. Don't you know by now that any man would want you, and I most particularly? If I hadn't sworn to become a peaceful man, I'd spend my life fighting duels to ward off all my rivals."

Ellen giggled as he laid her back against the grass and nuzzled her neck, but before she would give herself up to their lovemaking, she wanted to make her point. "My father will be returning to Normandy, and with Sebastian gone, Lyonsbridge has no castellan. I'm sure my father could be convinced to appoint you to the post." When Connor began to protest, she put her hand on his lips and continued, "Not because of me. The tenants here look to you as their leader. You were Lord of Lyonsbridge before my people even knew of this place. What better choice could he find?"

Connor pulled back a little as he considered her words. After a moment he said, "Think you that your father would deem a Saxon worthy of such a post?"

"Not only worthy, but entirely the best-suited candidate. As I've tried to tell you, my father's a broad-minded man."

Connor smiled down at her. "Will he be as broad-minded when he discovers that that same Saxon intends to marry his daughter?"

Ellen forced herself to refrain from giving the whoop of joy his words inspired. Instead she said casually, "He will, if the daughter is in favor of the idea."

His full lips quirked in the sensual way that always seemed to make her insides begin to melt. "And is the daughter in favor of the idea?" he asked.

"Mayhap," she replied, letting her eyelashes flutter teasingly. "Though she might take some time to consider the offer."

With a low growl, Connor lifted her in his arms and rolled over on the grass so that she rested on top of him, their bodies intimately pressed together. "Princess," he said in a low voice. "You'd better start considering, because I intend to make love to you until you agree.''

Ellen's eyes closed as his hands began a slow exploration of her backside. ''It might take me awhile,'' she said, the words coming between breaths.

''Take your time, milady. The wood faeries have promised to keep you here as long as necessary.''

She opened her eyes and looked into his intense blue gaze before offering him her lips. The wind sighed through the trees around them, and in the rustle of leaves she was quite sure she could hear the wood faeries' silvery laughs.

* * * * *

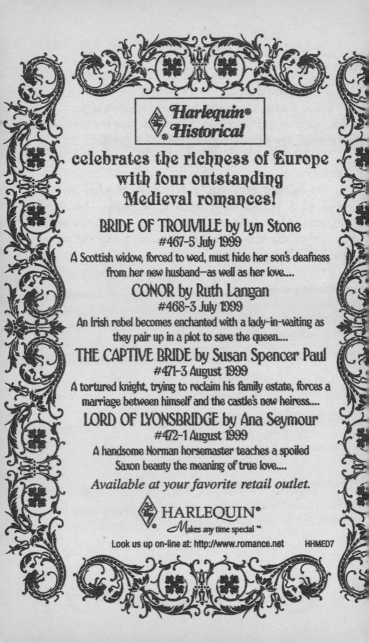

HARLEQUIN®
Makes any time special ™

In celebration of Harlequin®'s golden anniversary

Enter to win a *dream!* You could win:

- A luxurious trip for two to *The Renaissance Cottonwoods Resort* in Scottsdale, Arizona, or

- A bouquet of flowers once a week for a year from **FTD**, or

- A $500 shopping spree, or

- A fabulous bath & body gift basket, including **K-tel**'s *Candlelight and Romance* 5-CD set.

Look for **WIN A DREAM** flash on specially marked Harlequin® titles by Penny Jordan, Dallas Schulze, Anne Stuart and Kristine Rolofson in October 1999*.

RENAISSANCE. **COTTONWOODS RESORT** SCOTTSDALE, ARIZONA

 K-TEL

*No purchase necessary—for contest details send a self-addressed envelope to Harlequin Makes Any Time Special Contest, P.O. Box 9069, Buffalo, NY, 14269-9069 (include contest name on self-addressed envelope). Contest ends December 31, 1999. Open to U.S. and Canadian residents who are 18 or over. Void where prohibited.

PHMATS-GR

COMING NEXT MONTH FROM

HARLEQUIN HISTORICALS